OTHER BOOKS BY JOEL B REED

The Jazz Phillips Mystery Series

Murder in the Choir*
Murder by the Board*
Murder in the Kirk*
Murder was a Blast*
Murder on the Run*
Jazz in the Twilight Zone*

The McKee Clan Intrigue Series

Angels Fight Dirty*
The Red Lion*
(Original title - *The Black Seraph*)
Children of Dust*
A Devil on DOS*
Even Angels Cry*

Other Novels

Paul Radford's Private War*
Paul Radford's Alaskan Exile*
Lakota Spring*
Raven Wolf*
(Original title - *The Journal of Martin Quinn*)

*Currently available in print

MURDER BY THE QUEEN

A Jazz Phillips Mystery

by

Joel B. Reed

White Turtle Books

❦❧

Canby, Minnesota

This is a work of fiction. It is a product of my imagination. While geographic places and governmental offices are more or less accurately placed, any resemblance to any person living or dead is purely coincidental. To my knowledge, there is no such entity as McKee's semi-official Agency. Nor am I aware of any organization which calls itself the Cadre and deals in illegal drugs and corporate crime.

The hymn verse quotation on page 66 is from Softly and Tenderly by Will L. Thompson, 1880, common domain. The prayer quoted on page 240 is from *The Book of Common Prayer, 1979,* page 134, common domain.

ISBN 978-1-933482-47-7
Library of Congress Control Number: 2008943596
Cover and interior design by Joel B. Reed

White Turtle Books LLC
PO Box 2113
North Mankato MN 56002
WhiteTurtleBooks.com

Dedication

This one is for Patricia Jo.

CHAPTER ONE

Coming Home

I was a long time coming out of the coma. The amnesia took much longer. When the body is injured the natural healing process starts right away. When the soul is battered it can take years finding its way home. I tell myself that every day.

The way it happened was odd. Jeanne and I were standing at the desk of our hotel in Tulsa and Jeanne was checking us in. I'm told she normally did that in those days. I was looking around the lobby, thinking what a pleasant place it was. The only fly in the ointment was the television set in one corner. It was tuned to a local station and the sound was turned down so far I couldn't hear most of what was being said. Yet I found it annoying, the way a fly can be, buzzing around your head and never lighting.

Then I saw someone I recognized. The mobile crew was at a local crime scene and the reporter was interviewing a middle aged police officer. I was intrigued by the circle of five stars on her collar and the gold braid on her hat. Then something clicked and I knew her name.

I also knew exactly where I met her. It was at a seminar I gave for police investigators several years before. It was a regional seminar and this hotel was where I stayed. The subject of the seminar was investigating financial crime and it wasn't that well attended. I'm better known for catching multiple killers, and if I'd been talking about that, there would have been standing room only. Yet, corporate crime has always been my passion. I'll take a dusty set of ledgers over a bloody crime scene any day. Unfortunately, I don't get to make that choice very often.

It startled Jeanne when I crossed the lobby and turned up the volume of the TV so I could hear. One of the things I seem to have lost in the explosion that put me in the coma was a large part of my hearing. Yet I was lucky to survive the blast, and if being half deaf is the price I had to pay for these extra years of life with Jeanne, it was well worth it. I could still hear well enough to enjoy the music I love most, which is the sound of Jeanne's voice.

I listened to the rest of the interview with the officer and then to the synopsis given at the end of the story. Then I took out my cell phone and dialed information. When the system gave me number I was after, I paid the extra dollar or two and had it dialed automatically.

Tulsa is still small enough a city that I was put through to the Chief of Police fairly quickly. Or maybe I was still well enough known that my name rang a bell, even after two years of involuntary sabbatical. At least my sabbatical was for amnesia and not as a guest of the state or federal government.

As a matter of fact, the Chief remembered me well. Her voice was warm when she came on the line. "Jazz Phillips! Of all the people I never expected to hear from today."

"The pleasure's all mine, Mendoza," I told her. One of the things I remembered was her dislike of being called by her given name or even by her initials. She was not Hispanic but her husband had been, and like many women who divorce, the Chief had elected to keep her husband's name. It made things simpler with schools and doctors and the PTA to have the same surname as her children.

"You know, I was just thinking about you today," the Chief replied. "The last I heard, you were…retired."

I heard the slight hesitation before the last word. "Rumors of my death have been greatly exaggerated," I replied, quoting the famous telegram from Mark Twain. "I have apparently been quite ill." The truth is I couldn't quite believe the date I saw on the television screen during the story. I knew I had been injured, and I even remembered some specific things about the explosion, but how had I lost two years?

"Are you calling about the case?" the Chief asked. Her voice lost some of its warmth.

"Not really," I said, wondering why I *had* called. "I just saw your face on the tube and remembered you from the seminar. You asked good questions." There was silence on the other end and I knew Mendoza didn't buy it. "Look," I said. "I don't have any idea why I called. I just recognized you as a friendly face. I'm sorry to have bothered you. Congratulations on the promotion. They couldn't have made a better choice."

I hung up and Jeanne was standing there, looking at me in the strangest way. "You're back," she said, giving me a hug that almost dislocated my neck. Then she looked at me again and I saw her joy was tempered by a world of grief. "You're really back, aren't you? All of you?" Tears were streaming down her face.

"I seem to have lost two years, sweetheart," I told her. "Did we get married yet?"

"No," she said, grabbing me again and holding tight. She was trembling and crying so hard it almost broke my heart. "Oh, Jazz, don't ever leave me again."

"I apparently couldn't help it," I replied and she snorted. Any reply she might have made was interrupted by my cell phone ringing. Out of habit I dug it out and looked at the caller screen. This told me the caller's identity was blocked but I decided to answer, anyway. Somehow I managed to push the right buttons. "This is Jazz Phillips," I told whoever was on the line.

"I guess I've been in this business too long, Jazz," the Chief told me. "You wouldn't believe the shit I've had to put up with getting where I am. Or, maybe you would. Anyway, I'm glad I caught you."

"No problem, Chief," I said. "You know, that sounds a lot better than Mendoza."

"Yeah," she laughed. "How in the world did an Irish girl like me end up with the name Mendoza?"

"Well, I owe you a favor," I replied. "Seeing you apparently jogged my memory. I seem to have been gone a long time."

"That's what I heard," Mendoza told me. "And if you want the truth, I was wishing I could talk to you about the case when I thought of you."

I looked at Jeanne. "Could it wait a day or two?" I asked. "I need to get married."

The chief laughed. "That's the first time I've ever heard a *man* put it quite that way. Congratulations!"

"I may need a couple of officers for witnesses," I said and Mendoza laughed again. "Just let me know when," she told me. "We're here 24/7."

"I *will* get back to you about the case," I promised. "I just need to catch up at home first."

"Don't worry about it," the Chief assured me. "It's not going anywhere. For once, time isn't an issue and there's not a lot of pressure to clear the case."

My silence must have been eloquent because the Chief added, "We're really in the dark on this one, Jazz. It looks like we *may* have a serial but it's not for sure. There are some inconsistencies. The public is not aware of anything yet and we've been very careful to keep them as much in the dark as we are. On the other hand, I don't think there would be much sympathy for the victim." Mendoza paused. "I don't want to get into the details over the phone, but this one is right up your alley. You'll see when I brief you."

As I learned later, Mendoza was right. It was right up my alley but maybe I should fill you in a bit. My name is Phillips, John S. Phillips, PhD, and former chief of the Arkansas Criminal Investigation Division. I go by Jazz most of the time and I always have. Dr. Phillips sounds too much like foot powder and I love jazz. My favorite movie is The Cotton Club and up until recently my favorite artist was Smiley Jones. Then I was called in as consultant on his assassination and I learned too much about the man. Clay feet is one thing, but Smiley turned out to be a real scumbag and I can't listen to his music without feeling very sad.

Anyway, I picked the nickname up from a high school football coach. He had a voice as loud as a foghorn and an Arkansas rasp that could peel paint off an outhouse. It was his way of saying "J.S." that became "Jazz," and the name stuck.

I didn't mind the change at all. Up to then I went by J.S. because I knew what my cohorts would do with my real name. When I became Jazz, the girls seemed to like the nickname and nobody found out my real name until it was published in the bulletin at graduation. That might have been bad enough, but there were lots of other people saddled with strange names I'd never heard before. Somehow we reached an unspoken agreement not to make it an issue. We all had too much to lose. Or so it seemed then.

Don't get me wrong. My real name is not that bad but it is unusual. Both my parents were band musicians who cut their teeth on military marches. Both my grandfathers were named John, so what they came up with, given my dad's last name, was John Sousa Phillips.

John Sousa is sort of a clumsy thing to say, and my parents understood I might have to defend the name Sousa with my fists if they called me that. Fertile young minds could easily turn it into Suzy or Sissy or even Johnny Sue. So they went along when Grandpa Jack shortened it to J.S. while I was still in diapers and that's what my cousins call me to this day. As a child, I loved the nickname. J.S. sounded sort of tough, like Humphrey Bogart with a dead cigarette butt hanging out of his mouth. Then the coach called me what sounded like "Jazz" and it was even better.

So that's how I got my name. How I earned the coma was going after a serial bomber. Those are rare and it's even more unusual that the bomber was a woman. Not that she was any less competent than the specialist who trained her. Yet, detonation is mainly a guy thing, and it's even more so in the South. We grew up setting off strings of lady-fingers and using cherry bombs to launch tin cans. When we were older, some of us graduated to more serious stuff.

Those of us who were lucky got through this phase with our sight intact and all our fingers still attached, but the fascination with demolition lasts a lifetime. Sad as it may be, there's something fascinating about watching a building fall in on itself after a planned demolition.

Or maybe it's our way of recognizing the truth of *sic transit gloria mundi*. Say that in Arkansas and a lot of folk will think you're a surveyor talking about beginning the week with faulty equipment. Either that, or they'll think you're speaking in tongues. Yet, I'm told it's something every new Pope is reminded of by a monk three times during his coronation parade. *"Pater sancte, sic transit gloria mundi!"* Holy father, thus passes the glory of this world.

Anyway, I happened to be way too close to ground zero for the lady bomber's swan song. I've read what Dee had to say about it when he finished my last report and I'm amazed I survived. Nor do I wonder why it took so long for me to come back. I am definitely an old fire horse, just like Dee said. When the call comes it's hard for me to turn down a case. This is particularly true when it comes to serial murder and I always suit up and show up. This has nearly got me killed four times and I think Dee was right on in saying my subconscious mind decided it was time to take a time-out and it shut the old fire horse down.

So it doesn't surprise me it took so long before I could remember who I am and the details of my life. Even with Patrick, who helped me most, it still took me a long time, just like it did for him. The odd coincidence, if there is such a thing, is that he went through this exact thing himself after an earlier blast by the same bomber. Pat was there when the bomb that took me out exploded. He was the agent who shot the bomber before she set off a second device that would have killed a dozen police officers, including me. Jeanne tells me there has not been a week since it happened that Pat has not been in touch with me or her. I wish I could remember his visits, but the truth is I cannot.

I'm also told that Patrick's boss, Sam McKee, has been good to us, too. I've done a lot of work for Sam as a consultant to the Agency over the years. At least, I did before the coma, and I was actually working on a case for McKee when I was blown from here to amnesia. When I was given the case, we weren't really looking for a multiple killer. Sam was having me check out a suspicious bombing. My cover was looking over a couple of corporations with possible connections to an international crime network called the Cadre. Yet the Cadre had nothing to do with the bomber and the cover wasn't to fool them. The cover was to shield me from the wrath of a couple of FBI agents who have crossed swords with me over the years and who have always stabbed themselves in the foot doing so.

The fact is, cover isn't possible when it comes to me and the Cadre. I have done them a lot of damage working for McKee and all I have to do to alert them is to show up anywhere nearby. Even though I'm best known for taking down serial and multiple killers, financial crime truly is my passion. I am very good at tracking it down. There are a lot of corporate boards around that are very dirty, and the crimes they commit are far more damaging than anything a multiple killer can do. Serial killers destroy families and even communities. Dirty multinational corporations can destroy entire nations.

The Cadre is a cartel of the worst of the worst dirty multinationals, and they play rough. One of the questions I was trying to answer is if they were behind the bombing, and I know for a fact there's a bounty out on Sam McKee. The last I heard, the ante was up to five million dollars, and I wonder if they've put a price on my head yet. I've cost them at least forty million tracking down their dirty cash reserves, and I'm sure they were happy when I was blown out of the game.

Anyway, that's who I am, John S. Phillips, PhD. Have reading glass, will travel and I'm damned glad to be back. Even if there *is* a price on my head.

When we got to our room in Tulsa, Jeanne headed for the shower and I did some basic research. The hotel had a wireless network and Jeanne had brought her laptop along. So I was connected to the Internet within a couple of minutes. Apparently I had not used a computer that much over the last two years because my fingers felt clumsy on the keyboard and I had a hard time remembering how to do certain things.

Even so, I found what I wanted to know very quickly and by the time Jeanne came out of the bathroom, wrapped in a towel and drying her hair with another, I had a plan. Evidently, she did, too. Before I could say a word, she tossed the towels and we spent a long while showing one another exactly how happy we each were to have me back.

However, I was not about to be put off. During a brief intermission I looked at her and said, "You know, sweetheart, Oklahoma does not have a waiting period."

"Well, goodness, Jazz," she answered in the Southern belle voice she knows fogs my glasses. "I hadn't noticed us waiting at all."

I ignored her diversion. "We could go to the courthouse in the morning and be married by noon."

"Gracious!" she declared in the same voice. "Are you proposing to me Dr. Phillips?"

"No, woman, I am not. I have already proposed to you on fourteen occasions and you have accepted every time. The issue is not if, but when."

"Oh, I just love it when you're so assertive," Jeanne cooed. "Yet I had hoped to have our children present. Can't you wait until we get back to Ft. Smith?"

"We should have been married two years ago," I told her. "I will wait if you think it best, but I would prefer not. We can always do the civil part now and have a huge celebration in Ft. Smith later."

Suddenly Jeanne fell apart, bursting into tears and violent sobs. I was startled but it came as no surprise. After living through terminal cancer with Nellie, I had a pretty good idea what was going on with Jeanne. Even the strongest of us have our limits, and in a very real sense, she had lost me. Having me back had to be quite a shock.

So I simply held her until the storm was past. We lay quietly then but after a while she raised her head and looked me in the eye. Then she smiled and kissed me lightly on the lips. "We have waited a long time, haven't we? You don't suppose there's a county office open this late, is there?"

"No, but I'm sure we can find a way to get through the next twelve hours. Why don't we start with dinner?"

"Yes, we better. We need to keep your strength up. I have plans for you, you know." The look she gave me led to other things, but we did make it to the restaurant before closing.

True to her word, the chief gave us the royal treatment. She not only took time to be one of our witnesses, but she insisted on treating us to lunch and gave us a motorcycle escort back from the courthouse. "Don't get me wrong," she told Jeanne over lunch. "There's nothing altruistic about this at all. When you're done with him I plan to see what Jazz thinks about this case." Then, seeing the look in Jeanne's eyes, Mendoza knew precisely what she was thinking. "No, don't worry, Jeanne. I have no intention of putting Jazz in harm's way. This is strictly consulting."

"It's not you I'm worried about," Jeanne told her, giving me a stern look. "It's Jazz. He can't seem to help getting in the line of fire."

Looking at the two women, I knew Mendoza meant exactly what she said. Yet I also know the realities of police work, and Jeanne was right. Those of us who go after killers are always in harm's way and with multiple killers things can go to hell in a hand-basket in split seconds. There are simply too many factors to control. As things turned out, the chief was not able to keep her word.

CHAPTER TWO

Criminal Intent

Less than a week later I was able to get back to Chief Mendoza. Jeanne had come to Tulsa for a week-long gardening show that I insisted she attend. She was scheduled as a speaker at two of the workshops and I knew there were other sessions she wanted to take in. Raising flowers is a passion with her and I knew how much it would mean to her to tour some of the local masters' formal gardens. These ranged from simple elegance to grandiose productions that would have been downright tacky if they had not been done so well.

I enjoy these things, too, but just then there were a number of items I needed to take care of right away. One of these was a long list of personal calls to people like Dee, Sam McKee, Patrick, and some others to let them know I was back. I knew each of these calls would take a good while and by the time I was half way through the list I hit tilt and had to stop for a nap. While I was anxious to be back in the loop, the last thing I wanted to do was push myself so hard I had a relapse.

Another item on my personal agenda was catching up with what had happened in the world in the two years I was cruising Cloud Amnesia Land. This was not so urgent but I did spend an afternoon reading headlines from weekly news magazines. This was easier said than done. Quite often a headline pulled me into the story and I was only able to get through the past year before I had to meet Jeanne for dinner.

Over dinner Jeanne brought me up to date on some

of the other happenings while I was away. These were mostly family news and I had a vague memory of a lot of these things when she told me about them. Yet the sense of unreality was so overwhelming I had to stop her half-way through dinner and be quiet for a while.

I could see this worried her and I tried to calm her fears. "This is like one of those year in review in sixty seconds things they do on television at New Year's," I told her. "I'm just having trouble taking it all in at once. I need time to let it settle."

I could see she didn't really believe me but she nodded. "Look," I said. "I've only been back a matter of hours and I'm still getting my feet on the ground. Let's take it a little bit at a time. I really don't remember what happened during the amnesia all that well. The feeling's sort of like deja vu, but the disorientation is stronger. I'm sure the connections will happen, but they need to happen at their own pace. I don't think we can force it. What I really want to know is how my sweetheart is doing."

This got a smile and then a sly grin. "You have to ask?" she said, raising an eyebrow. "I thought I demonstrated that quite well."

"Yeah, and I have a sore back to prove it!" I chuckled. "Seriously, Jeanne, how have you been? I know it can't have been easy."

"It wasn't but I had a lot of support," she answered simply. "My children—our children were great and Zilpha and the kids kept me going. You know, she moved into the house for a while until you were able to do things for yourself." She looked at me directly. "How much do you want to know, Jazz?"

"Please don't hold back," I asked her. "I need to know everything."

"Well, for one thing, we had to teach you how tie your shoes all over again. The kids had a lot of fun with that. On the other hand, there was a lot of stuff you remembered.

You were still able to use your cell phone, for example. You couldn't remember who the people were, even after we told you, but you knew how to dial the phone and look up numbers. So we wrote down all the numbers you didn't need and only kept the ones you did." Seeing my look of alarm, she was quick to add, "Don't worry about having to reprogram the phone. Jack McKee set it up so you won't have to do that. All you have to do is hook the phone up to your computer and restore the memory."

I laughed. "I bet he told you it's foolproof."

"Yes, he even wrote down how to do it and he made backup disks."

"Good!" I told her. "That improves the odds. It means I have at least a 50-50 chance of actually getting it done without screwing up the whole system." Like Sam McKee, I was born with a technological bypass. Anything more complicated than pencil and paper or a standard police revolver was a challenge to us both. His brother Jack once told me I have a positive genius for finding the weakness in any high tech system. Foolproof means I can't mess it up within the first three hours. Sam is no better, or no worse, depending how you see things.

The more we talked, the lighter the conversation became, and by the time we left the restaurant, Jeanne had me in stitches telling me about some of the strange things that had happened over the last two years. Then I had an odd thought and I shared it with her. "Does this mean you've been sleeping with a stranger all these years?"

"Now that would be telling!" she declared. Then she turned serious again. "No, Jazz, the physical part was the one thing that changed the least. As a matter of fact, your libido was much more pronounced." She eyed me solemnly, then giggled and added. "Of course, sometimes when we were in public...."

"Surely not!" I said. I could feel myself flushing and

Jeanne laughed. "Woman, you're leading me on!"

"I hope so," she giggled and shortly after that we paid the check and walked back to the hotel.

The next day I did more catching up at the library but by late morning I'd had enough. I called the chief to set up a time to get together and she suggested lunch. When I asked directions, she told me she was sending someone to pick me up and apologized for not being free to pick me up herself. Who she was sending was the detective in charge of the investigation. "I think you'll like working with Hoagie," she told me. "He's the best we have and very down to earth. As a matter of fact, he reminds me of you in a lot of ways."

"You mean short, stocky and challenged by gravity?" I asked.

Mendoza laughed again. "Actually, I was thinking of his approach to police work. I'm glad he was willing to come out of retirement for this case." My silence must have been eloquent because she added. "You know how it is, Jazz. A lot of our resources are tied up with Home-land Security and the budget is tight. Our investigators carry an unreal case load and I wanted someone who could devote full time to the case. I think you'll find Hoa-gie very competent."

"I don't suppose his last name is Carmichael," I laughed. With a name like mine, the first thing that came to mind was the famous jazzman. I was surprised when I had to explain the reference to the chief .

"That was before my time," she told me. "My taste runs to classical more than jazz."

"I have a question I need to ask, just between us."

"You want to know why I even bothered to pull in someone from retirement on such a low priority case?" she asked.

"That's one thing," I agreed.

"Well, it's not that complicated," the chief answered. "Whether the victim deserves it or not, he is entitled to a thorough investigation. There's another element involved, as well. We'll tell you about it at lunch. The victim isn't someone who counts. Nobody gives a rat's ass what happened to him and whoever killed him knows this. The killer also knows the budget constraints we're under and is taking advantage of the situation."

"And none of this sits well with you?"

"Actually, it pisses me off royally. I grew up in a neighborhood of people that nobody else thought counted. I watched my parents and my friends getting run over all the time." There was a raw edge of bitterness behind the words.

I knew what she meant but said nothing. After a moment the chief spoke again. "So it's personal, Jazz. What else did you want to know?" She sounded defensive and she knew it. I decided to grab the bull by the horns.

"Shit, Mendoza, it's all personal," I told her, speaking lightly to take any offence out of my words. "I've had four of the assholes come after me. There's nothing more personal than a professional assassin on your ass." Mendoza said nothing. "What I can tell you, Chief, is it gave me plenty of motivation to catch the bastards."

"There is that," she replied and I could almost see her smile. Mendoza was her competent professional self again. "What else do you need to know?"

"I want to clarify my role," I answered. "I'm certainly willing to share my thoughts pro bono as much as you need, or as much as Hoagie can stand. I'm also aware I may not be firing on all cylinders yet. I seem to be, but who knows?"

"What are you telling me, Jazz?"

"Well, if there comes a point I seem to be totally off the wall, you need to be very direct about it. I need to count on you for that."

Mendoza chuckled. "I think any of my officers would assure you on that point. Certain city council 'persons' could vouch for it, too." I had no doubt they could.

కఞౕ

She awoke early, coming awake slowly, still caught in the grip of disturbing dreams. Yet she had no idea what the dreams had been. The memory of them faded quickly, leaving her with only a vague sense of danger. Something was not right and she had no idea what this might be. Even so, she had learned to trust this sense of danger. It was what first saved her when the killer attacked out of nowhere ten years back, and it had saved her since. She could think of at least three occasions when it made her pause just before reaching a point of no return. Each time it had saved her from disaster. Without it she would be dead, or worse, in prison.

She lay there for a long time, keeping still while her hand gripped the butt of her automatic pistol. As she came awake she realized the danger was not immediate. Her dog, Homer, was curled up peacefully on the rug, his tail over its nose, but his eyes were open, watching her. When their eyes met, the end of his tail flickered, telling her good morning. Then, when she lowered her free hand over the edge of the bed, he got up and stretched before coming to be petted. When he came, he licked her fingers.

"Silly beast," she said softly. "I suppose you want to be fed." At this the small brown body became animated, the tail wagging wildly while the toenails drummed cadence on the wooden floor. Two quiet barks told her to get up and attend his needs.

Having fed the dog, she started coffee and out of habit turned on the computer stationed at her desk. Typing in the appropriate passwords, she left it to boot itself and poured herself the first half cup of coffee. Crossing to her front door, she stuck her head out to check the weather and then went out to sit on the rocker while watching the day being born.

The morning was incredible, as they tended to be where she lived. The play of light and shadows dancing through the high pines was almost enough to allay her sense of danger. Yet the feeling remained, like a guest who has overstayed her welcome, and after a while she rose and returned to the computer.

Signing onto RISS, the Regional Information Sharing Systems network used by law enforcement agencies, she quickly browsed the latest postings. There was nothing from Tulsa, no mention about the operation there four days ago. *Or maybe it should be called a sanction,* she thought. It had certainly carried out with extreme prejudice. She chuckled at the play on words.

After RISS, she tried CODIS, the national DNA database, and she saw the query the Tulsa PD had sent. Taking a leather notebook out of her bag she looked up the identity and password for Tulsa and was able to call up the response. Reading this, she was gratified. The investigators had made the connection. Now if they followed through with another query and asked the right questions, at least three cases could be cleared. She thought about how she might get them his victims' names so they could clear more, but it was too risky. Let them dig for the information just as she had.

Logging off CODIS, she turned to another rich source of information, web logs she often found helpful. These blogs focused on discussion of serial homicide, and while any information found there was speculative and had to be verified, it did reflect what was floating through cyber space about specific people and specific cases. She suspected that even the police used blogs anonymously to glean information, and perhaps to plant misinformation. They did this with the media, and it was much easier to do with blogs.

There was no word about murder in Tulsa or any of the related cases on the blog she used most. Just to be thorough, she checked three others. There was nothing on any of them, either. This meant the police were either not aware of what was going on or else were keeping a tight lid on things. For a moment she considered sending an anonymous tip to the Tulsa paper but decided against it. There was simply too much risk and she was pushing the edge of the envelope as it was. The last thing she wanted was to be caught.

She was about to sign off when something on the last blog caught her attention. It was a query from someone who called himself Dogmeat. She wondered once again where these people came up with their names. Most of them didn't seem to have much of a life offline, either, but maybe they did. For all she knew, they were painters or sculptors or stockbrokers who simply made the time.

The query she noticed wanted to know if anyone else had picked up on a rumor that the grand old man of serial investigation had come out of retirement. There had been a lot of discussion two years back when Dr. Jazz, as he was called among those on the site, was almost killed in an explosion and dropped out of sight. He was a favorite of the bloggers on this site and many of them had read his books on serial killers. Some of them even claimed to have been in touch with him.

There were a half dozen responses to Dogmeat's query. As she read them, her sense of danger returned, even stronger. From the postings it sounded like the good doctor *was* back in the game and this could spell trouble. Though it was unlikely that Phillips would be involved in the Tulsa case, if the police discovered everything she had pointed them toward, he might be called in. If he was, things could get dicey. Dr. John S. Phillips was someone to fear. She knew because she'd seen him work.

CHAPTER THREE

Making the Team

Hoagie Zadovski turned out to be a tall, lanky soul with a craggy face and a steel gray flattop. He was dressed casually; tan chinos and a knit green polo that hung from his broad shoulders like a cape. He favored white walking shoes, with socks to match his shirt, and round granny glasses, and the unevenly trimmed moustache that graced his upper lip made him look more like a distracted college professor than a cop. Yet, I also had the impression that the apparent distraction was a guise. I was sure his dark brown eyes missed nothing.

When Zadovski introduced himself at the hotel, his distinct accent answered my question about where he got his name. "Pennsylvania or New Jersey?" I asked him.

Zadovski grinned. "New Jersey, where else?" he answered. "Home of the true blue Hoagie. How did you end up Jazz?" He thought the story was funny when I told him. "Sure beats Oliver," he remarked. It took me a moment to realize he was talking about his own first name.

We rode in comfortable silence the rest of the way to the restaurant. The chief was running late but the waiter showed us to our table and we swapped tales about growing up in urban New Jersey and rural Arkansas. "I tell you, it took some convincing to get me to move here to Tulsa," Hoagie said. "Up until then all I thought Oklahoma had was oil wells, Indians, and hillbillies. You can't imagine how shocked I was to find out Tulsa actually had a symphony. I thought culture meant football and drag racing down here."

"A lot of people have that idea about Arkansas, too," I replied. "On the other hand, some of our rural counties make strong arguments for rural gene pool depletion. It's real *Deliverance* turf."

"That seems to be true just about anywhere in the country," Zadovski observed. "The brightest and the best move to the city and the culls marry the culls and have more little culls." He frowned. "I guess I shouldn't call them culls. Who I'm talking about are sweet people with not as much ambition or drive as those who move away. It's just as hard to break out of a Polish neighborhood."

The chief arrived about then and our conversation shifted to other things. I was surprised how much I found myself enjoying the company of other professionals again, but I was also aware I was being evaluated. It was a little uncomfortable, but I certainly couldn't blame Hoagie and the chief. I'd be doing exactly the same thing in their place.

The talk hit a lull after a while and I decided to take the initiative. The answers I got would let me know the preliminary verdict right away and I started with Zadovski. "So what's your take on the case in a nutshell?" I asked.

"I'm pretty sure we're not dealing with a typical serial killer," he told me. "It's too well organized, if that's possible."

"So you think it's a one-time killer masquerading as a serial?" I asked and he nodded. "What makes you think so?"

"It's not that clear cut, but that's my gut feeling. For one thing, it's the time factor. The killing coincided with the full of the moon. It's pretty well accepted that's when crazies come out of the woodwork." Zadovski stopped and waited for me to prompt him and I realized the chief had instructed him to do so.

"The jury's still out on that one," I observed. "There's

no compelling research I'm aware of either way. Of course, I've been out of the loop. I personally think the full of the moon theory is either an urban myth or a self-fulfilling prophecy. What about methodology?"

"That's what's strange," Hoagie answered. "Death was actually from a gunshot wound to the back of the head. There are eleven deep knife wounds, eight of which could have been fatal. Yet these were post mortem. What bothers me is the precise way the wounds were inflicted. It's almost like the killer used a tape measure and did as little damage as possible. There's a stab wound two inches below the left nipple, a three-inch slash an inch below the right nipple, and another stab wound an inch below the belly button. All the other wounds are just as precisely placed." Zadovski stopped again.

"What about the weapons?" I asked.

"Forensics tells us the gun is a .22 subsonic long rifle and the marks seem to indicate a silencer. There was no powder burn and two bullets have been recovered from the skulls."

"Two bullets?" I asked and Zadovski nodded. "Was there a second entry wound?"

"That's a real puzzler," he answered me. "The coroner couldn't find a second entry wound."

"What's the placement of the entry wound?" Zadovski gave me an odd look and I clarified, "*Where* in the back of the head?"

"Almost precisely where the neck attaches to the skull. Right where they stab to put the bull out of its misery in bull fights."

"The angle?" I added.

"Pretty much level and perpendicular, but the coroner wasn't sure. The victim could have been looking down."

"Any idea of how far away the killer was?"

"None. The coroner tells us the victim was killed somewhere else."

I nodded. "So the body was dumped where it was found. Were there any drag marks or was it carried?"

"It was carried, but it wasn't dumped." I must have raised my eyebrows because Zadovski added, "The killer arranged the scene to look like the victim was killed there."

"Oh, shit!" I answered and the other two nodded. "Any idea what the message might be?" Quite often serial killers will carefully arrange the bodies of their victims to send a message to the police. It's part of the sick game they play. This was bad news since it meant we *were* dealing with a serial killer. The only good news was that these sick games were often the way police broke the case. A case in point was the BTK killer. He was caught when the church computer he was using to play cat and mouse was identified.

"That's just it," Hoagie answered. "There doesn't seem to be any message in the arrangement. It looks like the killer set things up to make it look like the killing took place at the crime scene. The coroner says the knife wounds were probably done there."

"Did you find the knife?" I asked and Zadovski shook his head. "How about the bullet wounds, what's your take on those?"

"The killer had to be standing at least a dozen feet away," Hoagie told me. "Even then, there could have been residue so I think the first shot was probably from twenty feet or more."

"Was it a rifle or a pistol?" I asked.

"We don't know," Zadovski said. He started to say something more but stopped.

"Ballistics didn't tell you?" This wasn't making sense to me.

"There weren't any rifling marks," he explained. "There was evidence of Teflon but not enough. The only marks on the slugs were flat spots that could have been from brushing the side of a silencer or something else. Both bullets had the same rub spots."

"What's your gut feeling? A custom weapon?"

Zadovski nodded. "Could be something like a Contender with an integral silencer. The slugs are definitely center fire and probably hand loaded."

I thought about this. "That helps explain the precision," I observed. "It's also damned good shooting. I can think of only two multiple shooters I've known capable of that much accuracy." When both Hoagie and the chief stared at me I added that both were dead. "I shot one of them and my late wife, Nellie, shot the other while he was trying to shoot me. He died in prison but I went to see the body to make sure."

Zadovski and Mendoza shared a look and I knew a decision had been made. "How about the knife?" I asked, ignoring the look and plunging on. "What kind and how long a blade?"

"Have you ever seen a genuine Italian stiletto?" Hoagie asked. "You know, the ones with a seven or eight inch blade that tapers from maybe a half inch to a needle point?" I nodded. "The deepest stab wound was seven inches and the shallowest, five."

"Where was the deepest wound? Under the belly button?" It was the chief who nodded this time. "What about sexual ritual?" I added.

"That's where it looks more like a single or a multiple than a serial killer to me," Zadovski answered. "The killer left a calling card, the queen of spades, as a matter of fact, but other than the precise placement of the wounds, there didn't seem to be much ritual. I didn't get the sense it was sexual at all. There wasn't any ejaculate or any other evidence of that, and there wasn't sexual violation. It was like a butcher cutting up a side of pork."

"Well, it sounds professional to me," I said. "I have an eighty-seven percent confidence about that. It sounds like a butcher going about his work in the most efficient way possible, maybe someone doing custom cutting requested by the client. Maybe that included leaving a specific calling card, too. Of course, that's based on what you've told me and not on looking at the files. I might see something there that could change my mind. Excuse me for a moment."

I really didn't need to make a trip to the rest room, but I wanted to give Mendoza and Zadovski a couple of minutes to talk. I have also followed the advice given by Napoleon to his generals and have rarely passed up an opportunity to visit the loo. So I took my time going about my business.

When I got back to the table, I decided to do some gentle prodding. "So, Mendoza," I said, taking my seat at the table again. "Is the old fart off the wall? Or maybe I should ask how far off the wall is he?"

The chief laughed. "You haven't missed a trick yet, Jazz. Were we that obvious?"

"No, but I knew what you had to be concerned about. All I've had is a week back and I'm still getting used to the notion I was gone. I feel just as ornery as ever." I paused for a moment. "Are you going to show me the case file?"

Mendoza paused and once again I sensed what was going on in her mind. I responded without waiting for her to answer. "What I'd be wondering right now, if I were in your shoes, is whether old Jazz can handle looking at the crime scene photos."

"Well, can you?" she challenged.

"I don't know," I answered. "I think so but it would be a good test. I do remember some rather bad ones. How about I take a look and tell you if I can or can't handle it? I suspect Zadovski reads people pretty well and I trust his opinion. Then, too, I might actually spot something. Even a blind hog sometimes finds an acorn."

Mendoza agreed and fifteen minutes later, Zadovski and I were on the way to the main police station. When we got there he set me up at a table in a conference room and handed me the file. "I'll be at my desk around the corner when you're done," he said. "Coffee's all the way down the hall to your right and the john is all the way down to the left." He gave me a broad grin. "That's the only way some of the pencil pushers around here get any exercise."

I walked down the hall to the coffee room for a foam cup and found a water fountain. Then I settled in to look over the file. Over the years I have learned to scan files quickly first to get a feel for a case. Then I go over them in detail.

I had finished my first run through the file and was about to pick it up again when I realized I had spotted a critical detail in the last section without realizing it. So I flipped through the file until I spotted what I was looking for. It was a lab report with a handwritten note attached. When I looked the note over carefully, deciphering the messy scrawl, I got up and headed down the hall.

I found Zadovski in the coffee room swapping tales with a couple of other investigators. When I came in he introduced me to the others and asked what I needed. I told him there was something in the file I needed to ask him about, and he excused himself and followed me back to the conference room. When we got there I made sure the door was shut.

I showed him the lab report and the note. "Is this for real?" I asked.

Zadovski nodded. "I had the same reaction when I saw it," he told me. "I called the other investigator and he was just as surprised as I was when he first saw it. It's the damnedest thing."

"What does it tell you?"

"I don't believe in coincidence," he replied. "I guess it

could be that but what are the odds?"

"Have you seen the other case file yet?" I asked. "The complete file?"

"No, the other investigator is sending me copies of what he has and his case notes, but he said they're a little short handed. Not much of what they have has been converted to electronic files. They're a smaller department than we are and still use mostly paper."

I thought about all this for a moment. Assuming the lab report was correct, the Tulsa victim had been identified by DNA as the perpetrator in a series of murders on the West Coast. "I don't think it's coincidence, either," I told Zadovski. "On the other hand, how could it be anything else? What does the chief think?"

"She's in the same boat with us," he assured me. "She doesn't know what to think."

I shook my head. "Assuming our perpetrator went after a serial killer, how in the world did he—or she—identify the victim? Was the victim even a suspect in the other case?"

"Not at all. The only reason there was a match was because we sent our victim's DNA in to identify him. There weren't any hits on his fingerprints at all. Our John Doe wasn't in the sexual predator database or any other database we tried. We still don't know who he is."

"So how in the world did our killer identify the victim?"

"Exactly! That's the strongest argument we have for coincidence and neither of us goes to that church." Zadovski shook his head. "The other issue is motive. Whoever is doing this must have a pretty strong motive to risk going after this guy."

"Let me go through the file again," I said. "Then we can brainstorm. I don't suppose the chief has time to join us, does she?"

Hoagie grinned. "The chief will *make* time for this one,

Jazz. She doesn't have much opportunity to get her teeth in much real police work these days."

"That's the price of being promoted," I told him. "Retirement allowed me to get back to sticks and stones investigation, but maybe I'm preaching to the choir."

"Not with me," Hoagie grinned. "I never left. I'll call the chief."

∻

There was nothing on the RISS network this morning, or on CODIS, and the blogs had nothing new. The thread of a discussion blossomed like a morning glory and lasted about as long without new information or gossip to feed it. The thread about Jazz Phillips' return from retirement was still limping along but showed signs of running out of steam. The last posting had been fourteen hours before she checked.

The lack of information didn't worry her much. All of the law enforcement networks were slow, not because of limits of the system but by attitudes toward it. It never ceased to amaze her how dumbfounded street-smart cops got when it came to anything beyond computer basics.

Even the young ones who had grown up with computers as a part of their world seemed to share this basic mistrust in electronics. They knew how to turn the machine on, how to get most of the information they needed, and how to turn it off when they were done. This is what they learned when the department sent them to orientation workshops. They might even pick up enough computer-speak along the way to make it through a cocktail party, though not many of them went to these.

Yet even the smallest malfunction intimidated them. When these happened their first instinct was to pull their weapon, a machine they understood well, and put a round or two through the display. Granted that it would be far more effective to put a round through the CPU, this wasn't an obvious target and few officers would know where to aim.

However, their supervisors discouraged their discharging guns in the office, even though they were severely provoked. Not being able to blaze away, their next instinct was to call in a cyber wizard to lay hands on the beast and soothe it with code. Nor did they care to ask questions so they didn't repeat the same mistake the next day. Cop culture is far too macho to do something stupid like admitting ignorance to what any child ten years old knows.

She smiled as she thought about how nervous these seasoned veterans of the crime wars got when confronted with a glitch they themselves created. The problem was not with RISS or CIDS or even the older NCIC. The problem was not in the machinery or in the programming or obsolescence. Hardware and programs had been tested and de-bugged for years. Now they were almost foolproof and even the oldest machine could do the job if one took time to help it along.

No, the problem lay on the other side of the keyboard. The problem lay in the expectation that technology should work perfectly all the time. The problem lay with action-oriented people whose lives depended on fast reflexes in chaotic situations, and on the reliability of their weapons. Great care was taken making sure weapons were always in good order and that the people who used them knew how to do this safely and effectively. Officers took a great deal of pride in this and had no problem maintaining the fairly complex mechanism they kept at their side. They knew how to make simple field repairs, and when a pistol malfunctioned, the first assumption was that it was not properly cared for or properly used. The burden of proof lay on the officer.

This was not so when it came to computers and other electronic equipment. After trying to fix an operator error by spitting in the box and giving it a hard knock or two, a call was made to someone like her. Sometimes it was someone in the department who was called in, but quite often it was not. Smaller departments found it cheaper to call in an outside consultant, and she made it easy by being on call 24/7.

This was how she made a living. Nor did she harbor any illusions about ever bringing Bubba-cop out of the Iron Age, even if she wanted. Long ago she'd discovered the best way to build her business was to correct the mistake without making it look too easy, and then to leave Bubba with the feeling it was not really his fault. The first was sometimes difficult to do, but the second was always easy. This is what he wanted to believe, anyway.

CHAPTER FOUR

Brainstorm

After talking with Zadovski, I spent the next hour going over the file again carefully. I made notes, but I didn't notice anything new that seemed important. There were some odd things I did come across, like the presence of small amounts of illegal substances in the victim's blood, but these peculiarities didn't seem that significant. Guessing from the state of his dental health and the scars he carried on his body, the victim was marginal to the mainstream of American life. So the possession of street drugs would not be unusual. As a matter of fact, the presence of these substances in the victim would suggest that drugs could be the bait our killer used to lure his prey into a trap.

By the time I'd gone through the file the second time, I was fairly sure the chief and Zadovski were right. The crime was too organized for a serial killer. This suggested we were dealing with either a professional killer masking himself as a serial, or with a vigilante or someone seeking revenge.

This was good news and a bad news. The good news was that a professional killer doesn't play mind games the way a typical serial does. For a professional, the object is to get the job done efficiently and get out without a fuss. There is no payoff in generating publicity the way serials often do to gain notoriety. This meant there would be less pressure on the police to clear the case. This was especially true if this was a one-time killing.

This could also work for us if this was a vengeance killer with several scores. There was a good chance we might get a line on the identity of our killer by looking at these victims. Somehow I didn't think we were dealing with a one-time perpetrator, but I could easily be wrong.

The bad news was that professionals have to be well organized to keep from making a mistake and being caught. Nothing can be left to chance, and without some incredibly good luck, we could not count on a professional assassin making a fatal mistake the way serial killers almost always do. Even if we lucked out and discovered the identity of a professional hit man, it would probably be very difficult to make a case.

I sat and thought about all this for a few minutes before I talked to my partner and the chief. The whole thing had an odd smell I couldn't quite identify and it took me a while before I realized exactly what it was. It was something Hoagie had said earlier about motive that finally made the connection.

The question this line of thought raised for me was why our killer even bothered trying to appear to be a serial. Nothing professionals do is without a reason, whether it's airline pilots, accountants or assassins. So the first question was what our killer was trying to accomplish. As Zadovski had pointed out, it would take a pretty strong motive to explain the trouble our killer had taken. *Or the planning this involved,* I thought and made myself another note.

I write these things down out of habit. Sometimes these notes are on index cards, and sometimes on paper napkins or the back of envelopes. Yet I religiously transcribe them into the spiral steno books I always carry on a case. There have been than a few times when these notes have broken loose a stalled investigation when I reviewed them later, and even more times that they have reminded me of a line I wanted to follow up later. Since I was trying to make a comeback as a consultant, I thought it very important to follow the procedures I had outlined in my own textbook. I knew the chief had read it and I suspected Zadovski had, too, and it was a safe assumption that my alleged investigator's bible would be the standard by which I was judged.

Once we were together again in the conference room, I took out my notes and began to outline my thinking. Yet the chief held up a hand and stopped me. "I agree we need to go over this, Jazz, but there's something else I need to know first. How did you do with the crime scene photos?"

I shrugged. "I've seen a lot of crime scenes, Chief, but I've never, ever become comfortable with them. These were no exception even though there's not much blood at the scene."

Zadovski nodded. "I haven't, either. I hope to God I never do."

"You'd never know it from looking at you at a crime scene," Mendoza told the investigator.

"You'd never know it watching Jazz, either," he replied. "You don't have anything to worry about with him, Chief."

"Except keeping him out of the line of fire!" she snorted. "Jeanne filled me in, Jazz. It's been four times *since she's known you*. On one of those occasions the thief you were chasing saved your life."

There was nothing I could say that wouldn't make it worse. So I put up a flip chart and wrote some things I'd thought about on it. When I turned back the chief was shaking her head but didn't say anything. It was probably good she couldn't see Hoagie, who was grinning.

"Well, here's what I've come up with so far," I said, pointing at the board. "Why don't we go through these and I'll note anything else we come up with so we can come back to it later?"

> Basic question: A one-time thing or part of a series?
>> A professional? (one-time or series?)
> Possible motives: Monetary gain –
>> Professional someone is paying?
>> Personal mission – professional or trained amateur
>> Revenge – amateur or professional
>> Vigilante
>> ???

"I have a hunch we are not dealing with a one time killer," the chief said. "What bothers me is how the perpetrator finds victims if this is a professional or a vigilante," the chief said. "Make a note of it and we can get back to it later."

I wrote that on the board. "We can start with that, if you like. That could give us motive. Any ideas?"

"You never had any parallel cases?" the chief asked me. "Anything close?"

"The only one I can think of was a case in Ft. Worth. The perpetrator was killing off clergy who were involved in domestic and sexual abuse. As it turned out, he was violently abused by a priest growing up."

"Didn't I hear he was a professional?" Zadovski asked.

I nodded. "He was trained as a military sniper but never worked as a professional killer as far as I know. He also trained several protégés. This might be one of them, but I don't think it is. They were aimed at known sexual abusers. That might be something we can follow up if nothing else works out." I made another note in my steno book.

"Maybe the first place to start is treating it like a common homicide and getting background on the victims," the chief suggested.

"That's already in the works," Zadovski told her. At her look of surprise, he added, "Sorry, Chief. That was on my list to do today, bringing you up to date. I got sidetracked."

The chief smiled at me. "What he's really saying is that I sidetracked him this morning by asking him to pick you up." Then she became serious. "That does raise an issue, though. Someone needs to brief me first thing in the morning and again in the afternoon—late in the afternoon. I don't want to cramp your style but I need to know. You're it, Zadovski." She turned to me. "You keep one of us informed of anything that comes up, Jazz. Even if nothing does, be in touch. Now, which one of these do you think we need to start with?"

"Revenge," I told her without hesitation. "I had a case where a professional sniper freelanced and came back for a personal hit." I outlined the Smiley Jones case briefly. "Don't ask me why, but this feels like revenge to me. That goes back to what Hoagie said about a strong motive to explain the planning. Assuming we're not dealing with insanity."

"It's a pretty distinct *modus operandi*," the chief said. Seeing the way we looked at her, she added, "Well, if we're going to use Latin, we need to use it right."

"*Abusus non tollit usum*," Zadovski nodded.

"*Ab ovo usque ad mala*," I added. Hoagie looked at me in surprise.

"*Braccae tuae aperiuntur*," I added.

"Hold it!" the chief demanded.

"I was just agreeing with you," Hoagie said, somehow keeping a straight face. "All I said was that wrong use does not rule out proper use."

"From the egg to the apple," I told her. "You know, from beginning to the end."

"I got the idea," Mendoza told me. "What else did you say to him?"

"That his fly is open," I answered.

The chief rolled her eyes toward the heavens. "Two jokers! What did I do to deserve this?"

"Well, it wasn't!" Zadovski told me.

"Made you look," I replied and he laughed.

"Could we please get back to serial murder, gentlemen? This junior high shit is killing me." Mendoza sounded stern but I could see she was trying hard not to smile. She shook her head, "I swear, you can take the boy out of junior high, but you can't take junior high out of the boy!"

We kicked it around for another half hour without coming up with much but potential lines of investigation. Then we put these in order, and when we finished we had a priority list. At the top was sending out a confidential query to other departments in the region, listing the most salient details of our case and asking if anyone out there had similar cases. The chief was inclined to hold back some of the details, which is normal when the press is involved, but I persuaded her that the more information we sent to our colleagues, the more likely we were to get a helpful response.

One of the lines of investigation on our list was the distinct calling card the killer left. We had just started our discussion of this when the chief almost jumped out of her chair. Looking at the text message on her cell phone, she growled, "Damn, just when it's getting fun. I have to go. I've got a major fire on the north side, maybe arson. Keep me posted."

"Does the chief make every major fire?" I asked Zadovski after she left. With cities the size of Tulsa, it's the fire department that usually investigates arson. Police involvement is normally lower level liaison.

He nodded. "It's a long story, but larger cities kept stealing our arson investigators. Yet, I can't blame the guys for leaving. We don't have the caseload to keep them busy and we even lost the fire chief. So our chief had to cover both departments, After she lost two investigators, she went to arson school herself. We've got a new fire chief now, but he doesn't know much about fire bugs." He grinned. "Besides, it gives her a good excuse to get out of dull meetings."

I smiled. "So what do you think about the calling card?"

"It's hard to say. The possibilities are, first, that it's a distraction the killer left to put us off track. Related to that, it could be window dressing to help us believe we're after a serial killer. Or, third, there may be some obscure symbolism that means something special to the killer. How about you?"

"I think you're probably right," I replied. "However, it occurs to me we may be reading too much into it. We have to take it seriously, but maybe we're being too creative."

"What do you mean?"

"Didn't you ever play Hearts when you were a kid?"

"I still do," Hoagie answered. "The queen of spades is the bad news card, the one you don't want to catch unless you take them all."

"Well, being very simple minded, maybe it was the killer's sense of humor. Sooner or later everyone catches the queen, even the best players. Maybe the killer was simply telling us it was the victim's turn."

"That would fit with the knife wounds," he said. "On the other hand, it's too poetic for your normal serial, isn't it?"

I nodded. "Most of them don't have much sense of humor, or if they do, it's pretty grim. This seems like a lighter touch, *ad absurdum*."

"Isn't there something about the queen of spades in Tarot reading? I seem to remember it's a bad news card."

"I have the same impression, but I think even that's being a little too highbrow. I know it sounds pretty simple minded, but maybe the killer chose the queen of spades because she's a black woman."

Hoagie smiled. "Either that, or he's telling us he's gay. Personally, I'd vote for the red herring theory. Which means that right now we're doing exactly what the killer wanted, spinning our wheels."

I nodded. "You're probably right." I glanced at my watch. "I better quit. I'm supposed to be meeting Jeanne for supper in about an hour. We can hit it again tomorrow."

Zadovski shook his head. "I can't tomorrow. It's my granddaughter's birthday and I promised to take her fishing." He grinned. "That's been a standing date ever since she was four. Tomorrow's our twentieth anniversary."

CHAPTER FIVE

Queen of Spades

Jeanne was presenting a workshop the next morning, so I was on my own. I'd really like to attend one of her workshops sometime. Jeanne is a master gardener and I find listening to her explain what she's doing in our yard and garden in Ft. Smith fascinating. Yet she doesn't like me to attend when she's presenting a public session. On the single occasion I asked why, she looked at me like I was a dolt. "I need to keep my mind on gardening, silly man," she told me. "When you're there I get distracted."

"You don't get distracted when you're explaining things to me at home," I answered.

"At home I don't have to keep my hands off you," she replied. "I can fling you down behind the nearest rosebush and have my way with you. Why did you think I had that high fence built around the yard?"

"To keep the deer out of the petunias?" I suggested and ducked just in time when she threw a pillow at me.

So that morning I was on my own. I decided to spend it in the library, catching up, but when I got there I decided to do a little research first. There was a vacant computer station, so I sat down and was quickly online. I checked my e-mail out of habit, but there was nothing that required immediate attention, so I typed "queen of spades" into the search engine and hit the return.

The results were interesting. I learned that *The Queen of Spades* was a short story written in 1833 by Alexander Pushkin, an opera by Pyotr Tchaikovsky based on the short story, and the title of no less than four motion pictures between 1916 and 1982. It was also the title of a musical score and a popular song by Styx.

Thinking about what Zadovski said about Tarot, I typed in "queen of spades tarot" and got over 11,000 hits. Looking at some of the sites at the top of the first page, I learned that the queen of spades represented feminine power traditionally associated with a widow, divorcee, or crone. Following a link to playing cards, I learned that while English playing cards did not represent real people, French cards did. The queen of spades in a French deck was named for Athena, the Greek goddess.

I couldn't remember much about Athena. It was too long since I had read about her in the mythology book Nellie had given me when we were first married, so I typed "Athena" into the search engine and was fascinated by what I found.

Athena is a warrior goddess associated with the more subtle arts of war, though her weapons are thunder bolts and the Aegis. There's nothing subtle about thunder bolts and the Aegis is a goat hide shield decorated with a gorgon that was horrible to behold. The subtle part was so understated I couldn't get it unless it involved scaring enemies to death.

The other interesting thing about Athena was her choice of companions. She is frequently portrayed with an owl in classical art and a snake is often at her feet or wrapped around her staff. While both snake and owl are symbols of wisdom, both are also invisible predators. The snake strikes from concealment and the owl kills by night. An owl's feathers are shaped so that they make no noise when it flies, and it strikes without warning.

This was all very literary, but it made me wonder. Was our killer telling us she or he was educated? Were we dealing with someone with a classical education, and if so, what turned such a person into a ruthless killer? Even if the killer wasn't playing mind games and leaving us a conscious message, this was worth looking at. It was possible we were dealing with a very subtle serial, though I really didn't think so. There wasn't the sense of distortion I get with serials. Our slayer had a good reason for killing, or so it seemed. Learning exactly what this might be was the challenge.

Thinking about all this, I remembered something I'd come across earlier and typed in "face recognition software." Technology tends to develop very quickly and I was curious about the state of the art. I remembered reading an article about this not long before I was blown into a coma and the technology was promising. There were some major challenges to overcome back then and I wondered what progress had been made. It was possible this might help identify our Tulsa killer-victim. Doing so would increase our chances of finding who killed him.

The search engine hit pay dirt immediately. There was an article on something called the Face Recognition Vendor Test run by the National Institute of Standards and Technology. I was aware of the first NIST challenge in 2002, but another test had been run in 2006, and the results were just out. I discovered that the technology had developed more quickly than expected. The software available in 2006 was judged to be ten times more effective than the 2002 software, and a hundred times more effective than anything that was available in 1995.

This raised some interesting possibilities. Not only did we have a very strong chance of identifying our victim, but if the Tulsa killer's image was caught on a surveillance camera, we might get the killer, too. This is not as easy as it's made out to be on television, but it was a real possibility. Even if we could only identify the gender of our Queen of Spades, it could be helpful breaking the case.

I was so absorbed in thought I jumped like a frog when Jeanne slipped up behind and kissed me on the cheek. I must have looked ridiculous because she almost choked trying to stifle her laugh. One of the library staff pushing a cart of books glared at us, but Jeanne smiled and said, "It's all right. We're newlyweds." To my surprise, the librarian nodded and smiled back.

"What are you so involved with?" Jeanne asked as we left the library.

"Athena," I said, not realizing how cryptic I was being.

"The goddess?" Jeanne asked. "Was this thinking or fantasy?" she added with a smirk. Yet there was an odd look in her eyes.

There was only one safe answer. I grabbed Jeanne and gave her a soul kiss, right there in the reference room. "Who fantasizes about the moon when the sun is in his arms?"

"Goodness," Jeanne answered, gasping. "We better quit or we're going to make a public spectacle." I noticed, however, that she did not try to pull away.

"You're just lucky I'm starving," I said, releasing her. "Where are we having lunch?"

"Maybe we ought to try room service."

That afternoon we spent looking at wonderful gardens. Rather than being arranged in guided tours, there was a list of gardens we could visit and a street map showing where these were. To avoid renting a car, I hired a driver for the afternoon and we really lucked out. Our driver was about my age and an avid gardener himself. His son ran a landscaping service and he was glad to show us a number of delightful spots that were not on our list. To top it off, he took us by what he said was the best source of barbecue ribs in Oklahoma, and at Jeanne's insistence, joined us for supper.

When we got back to the hotel, there was a message from Hoagie Zadovski suggesting he pick me up at nine the next morning unless I had other plans. There was also a number that turned out to be his home phone, but when I called, it was answered by what sounded like a young woman.

"Oh," she said when I identified myself. "You're the Jazz-man from Arkansas. Gramps told me all about you."

"How was fishing?" I asked.

She laughed. "Don't believe a thing Gramps tells you about fishing. He only caught a small one."

"I can't get away with a thing with her around," Hoagie told me when he came on the line. "That's my grand daughter in case you didn't figure that out."

I told Hoagie how I spent the morning and asked him if the Tulsa PD had face recognition software. "Are you kidding?" he said. "Do you have any idea what that shit costs?"

I confessed I didn't and after a couple more minutes, we ended the call. Glancing at my watch I decided it was not too late to call Jack McKee and punched the quick-dial on my cellular. I was surprised when the call was answered on the first ring and said as much.

"I'm waiting for a call," he told me. I suggested he call me back when it was convenient, but he said he had call waiting.

"Well, I'll keep it short then. Does the Agency have face recognition software yet?"

"Does a hog have hams?" he laughed. "We've had that for almost five years now. State of the art."

I told Jack about the NIST article I'd read. "Is it really that effective?"

Jack laughed. "I know the article you're talking about. What it didn't tell you was that there was another compet-itor that beat the ass off the commercial applications."

"Why do I suspect you developed it?" I asked him. "Why didn't the article mention it?" Yet I knew the answer before I asked. One of the ways the Agency funds itself is by doling out the results of its Research and Development operations. This was the brainchild of Michael Angelino, and Jack and Michael were as thick as arctic oil.

"Oh, I just helped," Jack told me. "Michael pirated the code and jazzed it up. He took it from the level of your basic Mercedes and made it into a Formula One racer. It's spooky what that stuff can do."

"Spooky sounds about right for Michael and the Agency," I told him and he laughed. "How would I go about getting the software?" I asked. "I have a strange case and need to identify the victim." I told him about the serial killer for a victim and what we needed to do.

"You catch the easy ones, don't you?" There was a pause. "You know, Sam told me you were out of the coma, Jazz. You were out what, three or four years?" I told him three. "Do you remember a book called *Darkly Dreaming Dexter*?"

I confessed I had not and Jack continued. "It sounds like exactly the same thing. They made it into a TV series and the basic thing is that Dexter is a serial killer who goes after serial killers the law can't touch."

"I think *Dexter* is something I better read," I told him. "It could be that our killer used the book for a model. It wouldn't be the first time that's happened. What about the software?"

"Michael's kind of possessive with it," Jack told me. "He won't even let the FBI have it. The only reason he gave me a beta version is so I could tweak it. You might do better asking him to run your face for you. Can you send him a stereo image?"

We talked about this a bit, but were interrupted by an odd series of beeps. Jack said it was the call he was waiting for and signed off. I gave this some thought and decided to go to the source and call Sam. It would be easier to get the answer I wanted from him than from Michael. Yet when I called, Sam was out and Megan wasn't sure when he might be home. I told her it wasn't that urgent and that I'd call him in the next couple of days.

When I put the phone down I was torqued. I realize there is a need for secrecy, but I couldn't understand why Michael was being more retentive than normal. Put in the proper hands, such effective facial recognition software could be a real boon in police investigation and even in situations where security was vital. Nor could I understand why Homeland Security had not stepped in and demanded it. Even though the Agency was not under their authority, HS surely had the clout to make it happen.

I was still mulling this over when Sam McKee called me back. I glanced at my watch. Only four or five minutes had elapsed since I hung up. "That was fast," I said. "I must have just missed you at home."

"As a matter of fact, I was with Jack when you called him," McKee told me. "I still am. Megan called to say you'd tried to reach me at the house. Are you all right?"

"Sure. I seem to be firing on all cylinders," I told him. "All seven." He laughed even though he'd heard me use the same expression before. "It wasn't that urgent, Sam."

"We needed a break, anyway. Listen, what Jack told you was true about Michael being hinky about the software. However, it's because I told him to be."

"All right," I answered. If it was Sam, he would have his reasons. Yet I wondered what these might be.

"The reason is very simple, Jazz. The software Michael and Jack have developed is phenomenal and we have a lot of people undercover. I'd hate to see them burned by our own R&D."

"That makes sense," I told him. "I was approaching it as a policeman."

"I know you were. There *is* a world of good it can do, but I'm afraid that if I let it out of our control, it will inevitably fall into the wrong hands. Suppose the Cadre had it."

"That's frightening," I told him. "Just how good is this stuff?"

"We can almost do what forensic reconstruction from a skull can do. That's from a flat picture. With the actual skull, we can do things in a few minutes that takes them days."

"Wow!" I was impressed.

"Oh, it gets better. Even with low quality video data, the system has never been fooled if it has seven seconds of recording. With the high definition systems banks are using now, it only takes three seconds."

"Which means you can pick out a bank robber while he's still waiting in line. That's assuming he's been recorded before."

"Exactly. Or think of it in an airport with known terrorists coming through the doors. Within ten seconds they can be identified, even with sunglasses and different hair. Like I said, it's phenomenal. I just don't want it used against our own people."

"As one of 'our own people' I can appreciate that," I answered. "I don't guess there's any way you can keep it from being hijacked."

"Michael claims he can," McKee told me. "He and Jack built some kind of virus into the system that goes wild if someone tries to hack it. It happened when one of our sister agencies was given a beta version and tried to hack it. We told them not to try but that was like throwing gas on the fire for a bunch of spooks and nerds. Fortunately, they tried it on an isolated computer. It froze tight. Not even Jack's crew could get it up and going again." He chuckled. "They were really pissed when I wouldn't give them another copy to hack."

"That's not so much, Sam," I told him. "As you know, I can lock up a computer without trying. I see your point. I thought it might help us with a case but I'm sure we can find some commercial stuff and use that."

"You'll pay an arm and a leg doing it, too. No, just send us the images and we'll run it for you. Just like we do for Homeland Security."

"I wondered about them," I answered. "They must think you're the goose with the golden eggs."

"They *know* we are and they know the eggs will stop coming if they try to take us over. We try to be too valuable to them to mess with."

I thanked him for the favor and we chatted for a few more minutes. He and I are friends, but he's also the head of an agency that uses me as a consultant. So I knew he was also still checking me out to make sure I was really back. I knew because that's exactly what I'd do in his place.

When I hung up, I turned my phone off and looked for my bride. She was in the other room talking to her sister, so I turned on her computer to do a little more research. When I signed in a white screen popped up with a huge puffy red heart and large pink letters that said, "Welcome home, Jazzman! We sure missed you."

I heard a giggle just then and turned around to see Jeanne standing in the doorway. "He just found it," she told Lindy, my new sister-in-law. Later I learned they'd been making plans for our wedding celebration in Ft. Smith.

There was something else I wanted to research on the computer but I couldn't remember what it was. This wasn't due to the explosion. I've been like that since I was in my thirties. That's why I use up so many index cards making notes. I buy them by the case.

Racking my brain doesn't work, so I signaled Jeanne that I was going out for a walk. She interrupted her call long enough to remind me to take my cell phone in case she needed to reach me. However, that wasn't why she reminded me. I've been known to get lost in a train of thought and end up in an unfamiliar place with no idea how I got there. Jeanne was still checking me out, too.

It was a pleasant night out and the area around our hotel was deserted. A patrol car went by not long after I started walking and I waved as it passed, but the officers were on the radio and didn't respond. Five minutes later another cruiser passed and a few minutes later a third appeared. When it did, I flagged it down and identified myself. Then I asked the officers if this was a part of town I shouldn't be walking. They told me the area was safe enough but that it was rare to see anyone walking here at that hour. Then one of them asked why I was carrying a cane.

"Mostly for safety," I answered. "I walk a lot at night and the reflective tape helps drivers see me. It also comes in handy dealing with dogs, mostly the four legged variety."

The driver smiled and nodded but the officer riding shotgun gave me a strange look. So I explained. "There *are* some sons-a-bitches running around on two legs, too. Especially at night."

"Those are the bad ones, all right," the driver said and wished me a good evening. After that I didn't see another patrol car. Nor did I remember what it was I wanted to research.

Holding the Bag

The next morning Hoagie picked me up at the hotel at nine. He handed me a folder with four eight by ten color photos of the victim and I asked him to take me to the post office. Once I'd sent them off to the Agency by Express Mail I asked Zadovski to swing by the morgue so I could take a look at the victim. Photos and crime scene reports are excellent sources of information, particularly when those who write them are painstaking, but there are other details that can only be seen in person. A corpse can convey a sense of who the person was in ways that pictures rarely can.

Our John Doe was not much to look at. He was short but was neither fat nor thin. As a matter of fact, he looked fairly fit and when I asked the medical examiner about this, she confirmed it. "Except for his teeth, he took care of himself," she told us. "It wasn't just with exercise, either. He was well nourished and used vitamins and nutritional supplements." She smiled at my puzzled look. "No, I'm not being psychic, Dr. Phillips. There was some evidence of supplements in his stomach. All in all, I'd say he was one of the healthier cadavers I've seen. No sign of cancer or anything else."

The good doctor started to say something else, but stopped. When I asked what it was, she told me, "It was just a random thought I had when I first saw him. I wondered why he didn't take as much care with his appearance as he obviously did with his condition. With the right haircut and clothes the man could have been kind of cute." She shrugged. "Judging by the clothes they brought in with him, he bought off the rack at Goodwill."

"I thought he was found nude," I told her. "He was nude in the crime scene photos. I didn't know there were clothes."

"Oh, he was," she assured me. "He was naked as a jaybird. His clothes were in a black plastic bag, along with his shoes. One of my technicians looked at them but there were no bloodstains or perforations, and no gunshot residue. I'm sorry I didn't make that clear."

"It's my fault, Jazz," said Hoagie. "I should have mentioned it. The officer who wrote up the case must have forgotten to include the bag." Seeing my look he added, "He's sick, Jazz, really sick. The day after we caught the case he was out on medical leave."

I wondered why but I didn't press the point. It was possible Hoagie didn't know, though unlikely. The way he told me this suggested the medical leave might be for something like treatment for addiction. This would explain why neither the presence of a bag of clothing nor a report on the contents was included in the file. I could ask the Chief about it later. She could also tell me it was none of my business if it had no bearing.

"So where *is* the bag of clothing?" I asked.

"Oh, we put the clothes in a locker here, except for the shoes," the examiner told me. "We sent those to the state crime lab. I'm the only one with a key to the locker, so your chain of evidence hasn't been broken. Do you want to take a look?"

I looked at Hoagie and he nodded. The examiner took us to a room we could use and a technician showed up a few minutes later with a clear plastic evidence bag. Hoagie signed for it and we put on heavy-duty surgical gloves. These would keep us from contaminating the contents with our own fingerprints and also give us some protec-

tion from sharp objects like dirty needles. This was probably unnecessary since the lab had been over every item,
but it's easy to overlook needles concealed in seams.

I was surprised that the technician who brought us the
evidence bag didn't leave. I wondered why he was hanging around and asked. He told us the medical examiner
instructed him to stay until we were done and to be of
any assistance he could.

When I opened the bag, the first thing I saw was that the
clothes were neatly folded and stacked. I asked the tech
if they'd been as neatly folded when they were brought
in by the police. "Yes, sir, they were," he replied. "I was
the one assigned to run them through the lab. They were
completely clean, like they'd been freshly washed and
dried. There was nothing on them at all. I even x-rayed
for needles."

I must have looked surprised because he added, "Nothing at all, sir. I had a hard time believing it myself. Even
the labels were missing."

"This doesn't make any sense," I told Hoagie. "Why
bring these to the site at all? Our killer didn't use them to
cover the body or for display. So why were they there?"

"Yeah," he nodded. "Why not dump them in a thrift
store bin or the dumpster?"

"I think I can answer that, sir," the technician volun-
teered. "All the charities have video surveillance of their
stores, particularly in the alley behind them. Maybe the
killer knew that and decided that the crime scene was
the safest place to get rid of them. Dumpsters are locked
these days."

"Could be," I said and looked at Zadovski. "Are we
sure these clothes even belonged to the victim? Maybe
they were already there when the victim was dumped."

He nodded. "It's possible. That part of town's full of
transients."

"You don't suppose one of them saw the body dumped

and took off without his bag, do you? We might have a witness."

"How would we ever find him?" Zadovski said, shaking his head. "If I was a transient and saw something like that, I'd be half way to Houston or Kansas City by now. I'd be afraid of the cops blaming *me*."

"Wouldn't you try to recover your bag when the killer left?" I asked.

"No way. He might come back and catch me."

I nodded. "Well, since we're here, we might as well take a look." I took out a long-sleeve shirt and held it up. "This seems a little small for our victim. What do you think, Lyle?" I asked the technician, reading the name on his lab scrubs.

"I'm Slade, sir, Bellamy Slade. I borrowed a clean jacket from Lyle. But you're right. I measured the shirt, and it's two sizes too small for this guy. He'd have a hard time getting it buttoned."

"You found nothing at all?" I asked Slade. "Not even on the bag?"

"Nothing, sir, not even on the inside surface of the bag. It was as clean as when it came from the factory. The outside had all kinds of stuff on it, of course, but nothing out of the ordinary. I catalogued it all but I don't think you could use it as evidence. The detectives didn't bother bagging the bag."

"Right now we're more interested in leads than with hard evidence," Hoagie told him. "Nothing you saw suggested anything?"

The technician shook his head and I looked at Hoagie. "I think this is a dead end. Let's look at the body again."

Two hours later I was back at the hotel. Examining the body didn't give us anything new, and there was nothing else I could do at the moment. I needed to get back to Ft. Smith and Zadovski could do the basic legwork without me. So I left him a list of things I thought we needed to check and gave him the phone numbers he need to get in touch. One of these was the general Agency number and I told him to only use this as a last resort. I explained that whoever answered the phone wouldn't even acknowledge they knew me or anyone else associated with the place. Yet if Hoagie left his name, rank and serial number, the message would get through fairly quickly. I also told him that when I called him back I would not acknowledge getting the message.

Zadovski nodded when I told him this, but frowned.

"All this spook stuff," he said. "I didn't realize you were involved with the Company."

"I'm not involved with the CIA," I told him. "I do research as a consultant that touches on national security. I'm still a sworn peace officer."

"The lines get pretty blurred these days, don't they?" he replied. "All this homeland security stuff seems mostly for show. I hope someone's minding the store. What I've seen is less than overwhelming."

Jeanne was thrilled to hear I was ready to head home. She had us packed and checked out in less than twenty minutes. I think she was afraid the phone might ring and I'd want to stay. The truth is, I was anxious to get back to Ft. Smith. I shuddered to think what my desk looked like after two years' absence and I wanted to talk to Forster, the cranky old priest I visit from time to time. Nothing was on my soul needing his counsel, but I like his company and I wanted his take on the last two years, where my soul went while I was still physically present. He's direct and blunt and pulls no punches. I can depend on him to tell me exactly what he thinks I need to hear, even if I don't want to know.

Tulsa is only about 115 miles from Ft. Smith and the trip normally takes a couple of hours and sometimes more.

Jeanne made it in an hour and a half flat that morning and managed to avoid getting a ticket, too. When we got there she turned to me and laughed. "Goodness, Jazz! I thought you were going to stomp a hole through the firewall."

"This is one of those times that anything I say can and will be used against me," I answered, shaking my head.

"Well, then, I guess it's a good thing I couldn't hear what you were muttering."

"I wasn't muttering," I told her. "I was saying the Rosary!"

This made her laugh again, but when she grabbed me around the neck there were tears in her eyes. "You're back," she whispered. "You're really back. I was so afraid I'd lost you forever."

I suggested we needed to move out of the driveway, even though it is fairly private. She agreed this was a good idea and when we got inside she showed me just how good an idea it was. We didn't get the car unloaded until almost time for supper.

That afternoon I called Forster to let him know we were back in town. When he gave me his new address, I was surprised to learn he was now in an apartment. He's such a private soul I couldn't imagine what it was like living among so many strangers. When I asked about it, I was shocked to find he was in assisted living.

"Things got too difficult to do on my own," he grumped. "I got so run down I was forgetting my medications and my blood chemistry got all messed up. I ended up in the hospital. My doctor told me it was assisted living now or a nursing home in six months."

"The lesser of evils," I thought, not realizing I was giving voice to my thinking.

"Exactly," he told me. "I don't like it but it's more tolerable than being in full nursing care. At least I have a balanced diet now. I had to stop cooking when I started forgetting pans on the stove." He said this with a dry chuckle. "It's pretty bad when the fire department is on a first name basis with your cat. Thank God they allowed me to bring her here."

I found the news distressing. After I hung up I went in my study and sat there a long time, thinking long thoughts. I don't know how long I sat there listening to the clock tick, but after a while Jeanne came in and sat with me. That's one of the things I cherish most about her, how she knows when to tease me out of my moods and when to be quiet.

After a while I told her what was bothering me. I told her that while I was delighted to be back, I realized I was facing an emotional minefield. Even the simplest encounter carried the possibility of being taken by surprise, and this troubled me. I wondered what else was out there, what other important things had changed since I'd been gone.

Jeanne started to say something but then stopped. I understood her dilemma and told her so. There was no way around this, for there was no way of knowing what I'd find troubling and what I could take in stride. I'd been living the last two years in my own little world, a place where all I needed was supplied even before I thought to ask. Nothing ever changed in that little world and I guess it must have felt pretty safe. Yet it was not being alive in the way I understand living, and troubling encounters were simply the price we pay to be fully alive.

I told her all this in even greater detail and when I was done she nodded. "Sounds like you hit the nail on the head. Are you ready for supper?"

I laughed and grabbed for her, but she slipped out of my clutch. "I need to eat," she told me. "I'm starved. Besides, Zilpha and the kids are already on the way."

This was a delightful surprise, one that made my first supper home like having Christmas and a birthday all at once. Over the years Zilpha has become family and her kids call me Grandpa Jazz, a fact which puzzled many of our neighbors at first. There's little doubt that Zilpha and her children are of African descent, or that Jeanne and I are as Caucasian as we can be, and it gets even more confusing when the other grandchildren come to visit.

What is even more delightful is how comfortable the kids are with us. This is because Jeanne and I have encouraged all our grandchildren to take the liberties with us that are their birthright as grandchildren, often over the objection of their parents. So the only thing that would have made my homecoming more joyful would have been for all of them to be there.

After supper it was story time, and that evening even the older kids gathered around as I took down my battered volume of Mother Goose. Not that I read the actual stories. Those are only our starting point and no story we tell is ever quite the same as it was the last time. The reason is that I only start the stories and it is the kids who supply the plot line and the ending. So the story of the three little pigs might end with them climbing up Jack's beanstalk to get away from the wolf, or it might see the advent of a new character like Rambo-Pig who proceeds to clean the floor with the old bad wolf.

That night one the kids wanted to tell the story of Rip Van Winkle, even though it wasn't in the book. I made the mistake of asking the kids to start the story, and it quickly turned into the story of Rip Van Jazz. What blew me away is that the kids seemed to understand what happened to me better than I did.

According to the kids, Rip Van Jazz was beset by an evil witch who blasted his soul into another dimension with an evil spell. This knocked him out and when he came to he didn't know who he was. He didn't even know how to tie his shoes until some helpful fairies taught him. He also did some silly things I'm not about to go into here.

The point is that he had to wander all over the earth looking for his soul until a fairy princess kissed him. When she did, his soul came back and he found his way home. Then they got married and lived happily ever after.

Of course, by the time they were done, there was not a dry eye among us adults. Zilpha and Jeanne had slipped in not long after the story began, and Jeanne blushed like fury when the smallest child looked right at her while she told me how Rip Van Jazz woke up when the fairy princess kissed him. I suggested that maybe we ought to re-enact that part of the story and the kids thought it was a wonderful idea. Yet Jeanne bought them off with ice cream and after that we called it a night.

All week we were swamped with visitors. The second day after we got home, Dee and his wife, Karin, drove over from Mountain Home and ended up spending the night. Karin still walks with a limp and bears scars from the collision, but she seemed in much better spirits than the last time I saw her. More important, it seemed like she and Dee had found a way through their troubles and were closer than ever. The last time I'd heard, things were pretty rocky.

It was good to see Dee again, as it always is, and I could tell he was delighted to have me back. I didn't remember seeing him while my mind was off in Cloud Dingy Town, although we apparently visited quite often. "It was tough, Jazz," he told me. "You used to wander off like that sometimes, even when we were still patrolmen. You'd get lost in thought and were a million miles away, but you could always come back. It might take you a second or two to get your feet on the ground, but there you were. This time it felt like nobody was home."

"I really don't understand it, myself, Dee. I don't remember much about wherever I was. I can remember being at ground zero in Grand Prairie when the bomb went off, and then I was watching a news report two years later in Tulsa. It's really strange. Spooky."

The only one who understood, of course, was Patrick. He flew in one afternoon late in the week with Sam McKee and we spent a couple of hours comparing notes. I found what he had to say reassuring. "A lot of the time I spent in amnesia has come back," he said. "I don't know how much I lost but I think I can recall most of the important things. A good example is the visit with the guy I used to work for, the one who tried to have me killed. I remember small details of the visit but I have trouble remembering his name. It's stuff like that I have trouble remembering."

"I hate to tell you this," I replied. "I had that before the explosion. It comes from hanging around the planet too long."

I noticed Sam McKee was unusually quiet during the visit and I decided to tackle him head-on. As he and Pat were about to leave I asked him, "So what do you think, Sam? You've been awfully quiet. You think I have enough marbles left to play?"

Sam gave me one of those famous McKee smiles. "If I didn't before, I do now," he chuckled. "I never could get anything by you. I think the real question is what Jazz thinks. I get the impression Jeanne was not too happy to see me." He shrugged. "I can't say I blame her. Working for me almost got you blown away."

"I don't think that's fair to you," I told him. "She doesn't like the way I put myself in harm's way. I think she would rather I retire completely."

"And have you underfoot all the time, grumpy as an old bear?" Jeanne was standing in the doorway. Her smile took any sting out of the words. "You are staying for dinner, aren't you, Sam?"

McKee tried to decline, but that was like saying "no" to a glacier. Pat was no help, either. "We're in the Agency plane," he said, looking at Sam. "We don't have to be in

Wyoming until tomorrow afternoon."

"Oh, good!" Jeanne declared. "You're spending the night."

Sometime during all the coming and going I managed to get to the Ft. Smith library. I was amazed to learn they had a copy of *Darkly Dreaming Dexter*. "You're lucky," the librarian told me. "This is a hot item among the young people." She shook her head. "I have my doubts about it but they have the right to read whatever they choose."

There was an open afternoon that week when Jeanne was out and nobody else was around. So I picked up *Dexter* and started reading. At first I was a little put off by the basic premise. It seemed to me that the book was a little too accepting of Dexter's compulsion to kill, justifying murder by limiting his victims to other serial killers. While rough justice may still be justice, I have spent too many years following due process to consider vigilantes righteous.

Unlike a lot of police officers, I understand the need for things like Miranda and for the separation of police powers from the judicial system. Our job is to catch criminals and collect evidence, and Miranda makes for better police work. It protects my civil liberties, as well as those of everyone else. It protects us from abuse by police or vigilantes.

Despite all this, the book was well enough written to keep me reading and I found the fictional character fascinating. I suppose there could be a serial killer like Dexter, but his character is more of a composite than being true to life. While his compulsion is turned toward a specific mission, making him what is called a "missionary serial," Dexter does not fit the missionary profile. Yes, these are inexact descriptions of real people, but in the book it is Dexter's uncle who is the missionary killer. One might say that Dexter is simply the weapon his uncle, a police officer, uses to exact his personal measure of justice.

There were some other things that I found odd about Dexter. One was his asexual orientation. This may be unusual but it is not unknown among serial killers. My experience is that most of them are driven by a desire for power rather than sex, even when sex is involved. That is certainly conventional wisdom when it comes to rape.

Another thing I found interesting was Dexter's work as a blood-splatter analyst. It is true that a certain type of serial killer stays as close as he can to the investigation. Sometimes the killer even "assists" the police by offering suggestions, and Dexter is in a perfect position to do so without raising suspicion. He is part of the investigative team and has access to information no other killer can have.

The third thing I found true to life is that Dexter avoids publicity. While some serial killers do seek publicity and attention, those who do not are the most deadly. I think Coral Eugene Watts, the killer from Texas, is the best example of this. He admitted to having killed more than eighty women over a nine year career that covered a number of states and jurisdictions. Later it was thought he had killed over a hundred.

The point is that Watts did not seek publicity and it was a number of years before he was even suspected. Nor was he convicted of murder until twenty years after he was first imprisoned, and then of only two murders in Michigan. It was only after his first murder conviction that he told three investigators that there were not enough fingers and toes in the room to count the number of murders he had committed.

I sat and thought about *Darkly Dreaming Dexter* for a while. To be honest, I have to admit I found a vicarious satisfaction in the fact he was taking other serials off the street. I know what serial killers do to the friends and family of their victims. I know what they do to whole communities, creating an atmosphere of terror. I fear the backlash they can foster, a backlash that willingly casts aside civil liberties for a false sense of security.

I also wondered if the book might not spawn copycats. Were this so, what felt like righteous vindication would spawn an even greater evil. For all its faults, our judicial system does hold us to certain standards I believe necessary for us to live at peace with one another. Without these we are at the mercy of the mob, and the breakdown of civil order we see in the Middle East today will be our heritage tomorrow.

CHAPTER SEVEN

Close Encounter

She was sitting on the front porch enjoying her first cup of coffee and what looked like a beautiful day when she heard the soft ring of her cell phone. It was set to let her know who was calling, and the distinctive ring was one she used for clients. Other distinctive rings told her when friends called or if it was from a number not recorded in her phone. Those she might answer, or not, depending on her mood. This morning she was only taking business calls.

The display told her the call was from a systop, or system operator, from Tulsa. For a moment she was startled, but she made herself relax. *They can't be onto you yet,* she assured herself. *If they were, they'd send cops, not their systems wonk.* She laughed at the image of this particular systop packing a 9 millimeter Glock. *He'd probably shoot himself in the leg.*

Ten seconds on the phone with the systop reassured her. From what the he told her, she knew she could not talk him through the problem by phone. This looked like a major software glitch. When she learned it had happened just after a peripheral software update, she knew this for sure.

"Are you backed up?" she asked.

"Yes, we played it by the book, thank God. The backup was just before the update and an hour before the system went down. We backed up to an isolated server, too. I just now finished making a second backup on isolated equipment, so we're ready to roll as soon as you get here.

I wish we'd waited until you got here to make the update but the city manager was hot to trot. You know how they are."

She did know, which was why she was an independent contractor now. The pay was not as regular as being on staff, but it was a whole lot better and it gave her time for other things. "Any sign of a virus?"

"Other than the system being down, no. Of course, there are a lot of new ones every week."

"Listen, I can be there in two hours if you really need me immediately," she told him. "Otherwise, I'd prefer to fly in this evening and start then. Is it critical?"

"Aside from the city manager having a screaming hissy? Not really. The main emergency services are still working. What we lost is the central traffic light system and the entire accounting system. Officers are out directing traffic."

"Well, you better warn the city manager that it's going to take most of tomorrow and it's going to be expensive. I better get going. I'll see you about six."

Ten minutes later her phone rang again. This time the call was from Officer Dwayne Simmons in a small city in Texas. How he ever got the job as designated computer guy for his department was a mystery, but she suspected his chief was trying to get rid of Dwayne. At the moment he was having trouble signing onto the regional RISS network.

"Sure, Dwayne, I can talk you through it," she said. "Why don't you give me your codes and password so I can check it out from here first? It might be the regional system."

Dwayne was glad to give her the information. The truth was she didn't need it. The code was the same as he had given her not long before and he'd not changed his password in years. "Dwayne, that sounds like the same password you gave me last time. Why haven't you changed it like I told you?" she scolded mildly.

"Aw, shoot! If I changed it I couldn't remember it," he answered.

"Then why don't you use the name of your son instead of your daughter's name?" she suggested. "Surely you can remember that."

"Yeah, but there's days I don't want to! That boy is a born hell raiser." He laughed and she knew he wouldn't change his password.

How easy it is! She thought. *As long as rural towns pay low wages the only people they can get are people like Dwayne. He's a sweet guy but dumb as dog shit!* She quickly walked him through sign-on. It took about forty seconds and cost his city a hundred dollars, her minimum fee. It also kept her in codes that allowed her into the RISS system, as well as CODIS and NCIC. Thanks to a couple of dozen people just like Dwayne, she always had enough different codes to get in without it being obvious.

Social engineering, she laughed. Her systems skills were the very best but they were only secondary. Without people like Dwayne, and even the systop in Tulsa, she would be out of business, both as a consultant and as a….

The last word stopped her as it always did. She couldn't even think such things about herself without choking up. Though she knew what she did was only to scum who deserved to die, it was still…. Her mind rebelled. It would not even allow her to use gentler terms.

Admit it, Nicole! a savage voice suddenly demanded from within. It was the all too familiar voice of her mother, dead many years before. *Call it what it is! Murder! You're no different from the scumbags you take down!*

She didn't even try to argue. That was fruitless. She knew her mother was right and there was no winning this argument. So she did the one thing that always calmed the savage voice. She began to sing an invocation, the simple words she learned by heart growing up, words to fend off her mother's wrath. These were the lyrics of her mother's favorite hymn.

Come home, come home! Ye who are weary, come home....

❧

I got a call from Hoagie Zadovski toward the middle of the next week. He told me a copy of the file we requested on the murder tied to our John Doe had arrived and he wanted to know if I was planning to be over his way anytime soon. I asked why he didn't just make a copy and send it by Priority Mail. That would get it to me within three days.

"To tell you the truth, Jazz, I want you to see it right away. I was hoping you needed me to bring the file to you." When I asked why, he laughed. "The traffic computer's been down over here for two days and everybody's got a case of the red-ass. The chief has all her regular officers out directing traffic, even the detectives."

"How did you get off easy?" I wanted to know.

He laughed. "I pointed out that I didn't volunteer for traffic duty."

"Well, you're always welcome here, Hoagie. Keep in mind that right now you'll land in a flock of women planning a wedding celebration. I was hoping to have an excuse to head your way."

"On second thought, why don't you?" He laughed. "I'll find us a quiet place to hide."

Jeanne wasn't thrilled to have me headed out on a case again, but she knew I'd been hiding in my study for three days. "You do realize, of course, that if you're gone, I can do anything I like," she pointed out.

"Woman, you'd do that anyway!" I declared. This got a laugh out of her. "I promise I'll stay out of trouble."

"Right," she replied, giving me a kiss on the cheek. "Just keep in touch."

"Like this?" I asked, grabbing her and pulling her close.

She kissed me again, this time on the lips, and my departure was somewhat delayed.

I got to Tulsa just in time to beat the traffic rush. I was dreading the drive downtown, but the traffic lights seemed to be working again. When I arrived at the central police station, the atmosphere was almost festive. The detectives were all back at their desks, telling war stories about traffic duty, and as Hoagie and I walked by a couple of them made good natured remarks about people lucky enough to be retired. Hoagie just grinned at them and said, "How sweet it is!"

Since it was late in the day, no one was using the main conference room. We spread the file out on a large conference table and Hoagie went to get us some sandwiches to munch as we worked. All the health gurus tell us this is not a good idea, and they may be right. Relaxed meals may be better for us, but America eats on the move and crime doesn't take lunch breaks. Not that we were pressed for time. We were simply creatures of habit.

The first thing we looked at was the DNA report. This was a perfect a match and we were both satisfied our John Doe was the killer in Oregon. Next we turned to the medical examiner's report and reading through it was a chilling experience. There were no gunshot wounds to the back of the head and no queen of spades left on the bodies. Yet the placement of every knife wound was almost exactly the same.

"I've never seen anything quite like this," Hoagie told me. "Have you?"

I shook my head. "Never."

"The thing is, we got three hits on the query you asked for based on the MO. They all came in late this afternoon, just before you got here. I wanted us to check this out before I mentioned them. From what they said, the wound type and placement was pretty much the same. So was the DNA chart two of them sent."

"Why didn't they mention this last week?" I asked.

Hoagie frowned. "For some reason the query was delayed for several days going out. I don't know if it had anything to do with our computer system. Then, too, these responses were all from small departments. They may not be that well equipped. I doubt they ran the DNA through CODIS. The reports I have were all based on state crime lab reports."

"Where were they from?"

I moved to the marker pad I'd used before and began writing as Hoagie spoke. "One came in from Utah. Another was from Ohio. Our third was from Louisiana. All had the same knife wounds, but a slightly different MO. That's in addition to the cases in California and Washington."

"Our Tulsa John Doe moved around, didn't he?" I observed. "That's a wide range."

"It couldn't be much wider without going international," Zadovski agreed. "Now we have one in Tulsa, which I guess means we may hear from Tucson, Tuscaloosa or Tacoma next. Take your pick. I wonder what he did for a living?"

"Probably a security guard," I quipped and he laughed. It is a sad fact that in this country we pay the fox to watch the chicken coop. There is such high turnover in security guards that a number of them are felons. "Either that or maybe day labor or construction."

"I think we need to assume there are some killings like this we don't know about," I said. "Maybe a lot of them. They never did track down all the victims of that guy they caught in Texas. Not Coral Watts but the other one."

"I know who you mean but I can't think of his name, either," Hoagie replied.

"Lucas," I remembered. "Henry Lee Lucas."

"I thought his conviction was dubious," Hoagie said.

"Didn't he confess to over three thousand killings?"

"Yes. He was a real screwball. The special task force decided the number was over two hundred, 213 as I recall. The point is that a lot of serial cases are either not known or not identified as such."

"That's comforting," he said dryly. "How do you live with all this, Jazz?"

I shrugged. "I do other things mostly. I've only been involved with maybe two dozen serial cases, and even then only as an observer or consultant in most of them. Financial crime is my passion. I really find a lot of satisfaction taking down a dirty corporation. The bigger, the better."

"I guess it takes all types" he answered. "Why don't you look this over while I visit the head."

"I'll come with you. Will these be all right here?" I asked, pointing to the files spread out on the table.

"They should be," he answered. "Ain't nobody here but us chickens."

Four minutes later we were walking back up the hall when we saw someone coming out of the conference room. It was a tall woman in plain clothes with a visitor's badge like mine and when our eyes met, I saw a flash of something I couldn't identify. It wasn't fear, exactly. It was more like she was startled to find anyone there at all. Yet she recovered quickly.

"I was looking for someplace to spread these out," she told us. There was a thick bundle of papers under her arm. They looked like fan-fold computer printouts to me. "I see you're already using the room."

There was something about the woman that tugged at my memory. She was in her early forties, I thought, and she had one of the most haunting faces I'd ever seen. Her eyes were dark and deep set and her hair was blue-black, like the midnight sky. The navy outfit and white blouse she wore were a perfect setting for her dusky olive complexion, and when she smiled her teeth were bright and even. The total effect was an aura of feminine sensuality that felt like an ocean wave moving down the narrow confines of the hallway.

Yet it was her eyes I found haunting. They were the eyes of a much older woman. Though they were not etched with deep lines, there was something in them that told me she had seen too much of life and had no illusions. They also told me she knew exactly who I was and that she was not altogether happy to see me. It was much later that I realized what I saw in her eyes reminded me of the Ft. Worth assassin.

"Have we met?" I asked, stopping at the door and calling down the hall.

She stopped and turned. "Yes, Dr. Phillips, we have. I handled the technical support for one of your seminars a few years ago. You were quite interesting."

"I'm sorry," I said. "I can't recall the occasion. Surely I'd remember someone as stunning as you."

"How soon they forget," she said to Hoagie, waving to me as she laughed and turned back down the hall. The way she walked reminded me of a jaguar I'd seen in the wild. There was nothing civilized about it.

"Who in the world is that?" I asked Hoagie once we were back in the conference room.

"Oh, that's Marie. Half the detectives are in love with her, including me. She's the one who got our traffic system working again."

"What's she doing over here?" I asked. For some reason I felt suspicious.

Hoagie gave me a surprised look. "She's the expert who keeps our computer system going, too."

"I thought you had a designated officer who did that."

"We do. Einstein keeps our system going on a daily basis. That's not his name, just what we call him. He manages the rest of the city computers, too. Marie is the systems guru he calls in when he's forced to punt. What's going on, Jazz?"

I shrugged and shook my head. "I guess she just surprised me, being in here alone with the open files. I wish I could remember where we met."

"Marie's solid," he assured me. "She used to be one of us."

"A police officer?" I asked and he nodded. "Here?"

"No, I think it was somewhere in Texas. Dallas, maybe, or San Antonio. No, come to think, it was Houston. A real hell hole, if you ask me."

"That's what I've heard," I said, taking a seat and reaching for one of the files. "I wonder why she changed?"

"Are you kidding?" he laughed, flopping down in the chair next to mine. "Do you have any idea what we have to pay her now? It beats getting shot at."

I was still bothered but I dropped it, and we began to go through the cases once again. What is odd is that I didn't make myself a note in the steno book to look at this again.

An hour later there was no doubt in our minds that Tulsa John Doe, as we called him, was the perpetrator for all three murders. The only real questions were who he was and how many more of his victims were still unknown. When we found these answers, if we ever did, we could begin to piece together his career and help clear cases.

"So what's she up to, you think?" I asked. "Our Queen of Spades killer?"

"You're assuming our killer is a woman," Hoagie pointed out. "Why are you assuming that?"

"I don't know," I said. "Maybe because of the calling card. I can see a man choosing a king or maybe a one-eyed Jack. No, make that the ace of spades. Why would a man choose the queen?"

"To mess with our minds," Hoagie reminded me. "Didn't we talk about this before?"

"We did," I agreed. "Call me old fashioned, maybe, but I have trouble thinking of a man as queen."

"Me, too," Zadovski grinned. "Just don't tell the chief."

"You don't have to tell the chief anything," Mendoza said, waking into the conference room. "Call Mendoza old fashioned, too. Serial killers are almost always men." She flashed a grin. "At least, the dumb ones who get caught are. So let's stipulate that 'she' is gender inclusive. What do you have?"

Hoagie brought her up to date quickly. "Where do we go from here?" Mendoza asked when he was done.

"I think we need to put what we know on the network," I said. "We may get more responses to our first inquiry but an update may get someone who's sitting on a potential case off their butt. The more information we have, the better."

"Make it so," the chief ordered, and Hoagie made himself a reminder. "So what's the Queen of Spades' motive?"

"Aside from rubbing our noses in the fact she's caught all of them and we haven't? I think it's vengeance or mission," I told her. "I tend to think she's a missionary although she may have started out for vengeance."

"You think she likes killing?" Mendoza wanted to know. "Or has come to like it?"

"Actually, I don't," I answered. "I couldn't tell you why except she killed Tulsa John Doe before stabbing him. Mutilation seems to be her way of communicating. The whole thing lacks raw emotion. It's very calculated, almost cold."

"I agree," Mendoza said. "On the other hand, I don't want egg all over my face. Let's keep other possibilities open, too." She glanced at her watch. "It's getting late. Are you thinking of heading back to Ft. Smith tonight?"

"I think I may stay over," I said. I explained what was going on at our house. "I'd just be in the way there and something may come in on the wire tomorrow."

⧫⧫⧫

She stopped and looked at her timer, seeing how long it took her breathing to return to normal. Yet she couldn't make out what the display said. Sweat was pouring off her like rain on a tin roof and her headband was so soaked her eyes were beginning to burn. Pulling a towel from her waterproof pack, she wiped her face and looked at the timer again. She was pleased. Her time was better now than ten years ago. She wasn't losing ground.

She turned into the wind and began to walk, cooling down slowly. Sitting down too soon meant leg cramps at this season of life. It was easier to keep going. Later she'd reward herself with a long, hot shower.

She thought about the encounter in the hall as she walked. It was clear the good doctor remembered her, even if he didn't know where or when. Nor was it surprising that he couldn't place her. She looked nothing like she did twelve years ago when she worked the computer during his Power Point presentation. It was in Galveston at a week-long seminar on homicide investigation and she was the only officer there in uniform. Her hair was shorter, her teeth were a mess and she was twenty pounds heavier. Even her eyes were different, for she wore horn rims and no makeup. She wanted to look as much like a man as she could.

The uniform helped. Even cops found it hard to see behind the uniform until they knew you. Add a pair of dark shades and a severe masculine haircut and it was not surprising so few realized there was a woman under the body armor. Those who did wrote her off as Lesbian, and some of the remarks she overheard were cruel. Dickless Tracy is what they called her behind her back, and sometimes in her presence. There were those, too, who didn't bother lowering their voices.

There was a time she wondered why they were so afraid of her. Then she found out. One of them crossed the line, grabbed her from behind. She touched him three times and he was on medical leave for six months. A sharp lawyer and the threat of a multimillion-dollar sexual harassment suit kept her from being fired. Yet the writing was on the wall. She found a job in a smaller department and began to take night courses. Within three years she was a sought-after systems consultant. It was then she began to change her appearance. The only thing that remained was her height.

Yet the funny little man from Arkansas had seen through this. He'd been kind to her during the seminar and asked her to join him every day for lunch. "We're the outsiders here," he had told her, making her laugh. "I'm the great wonk from another planet and you're the only uniform. These guys are Paleolithic. Not many of them have reached the Iron Age."

He had also encouraged her to widen her horizons, to use her mind to find her way out of a cruiser. "They'll never accept you," he told her one day. It was near the end of the seminar. "I'm sure you know that by now. You can do a lot better in the private sector."

That's where she was the next time she saw him, in the private sector. There was a nasty case in New Orleans and they called in Dr. Jazz. She was there when it happened. She won the contract for overhauling the police information system, making their case records electronic. The serial case was the first major case to be kept current by computer and she was the expert on tap. So she knew every move Dr. Jazz made and she was astonished by the intuitive connections he derived from almost no evidence.

As a result, she also took care to stay out of the good doctor's way. The reason was simple. The killer they were after was the one who made the mistake of attacking her one dark night late in the investigation. She touched him four times. He never got up.

Nor did she call the police. The dead man was a respected surgeon, too well connected. While the evidence they found on his body identified him as the serial killer, the police covered it up. Jazz Phillips went back to Arkansas and the New Orleans Police Department never released his final report. It stated in no uncertain terms that Phillips considered the surgeon guilty of all the killings.

The New Orleans slayer was the first of many serial killers she'd taken down. The case was never officially closed until six months later when she fed the police hard evidence they could not ignore. They couldn't ignore it because she fed the same material to the Dallas Morning News. Doing this almost got her caught. It was only her sense of danger that saved her.

Now her sense of danger was stronger than ever. She had no idea what to do about it and she wondered if it was time to burn her bridges and disappear forever. The scheme she had in mind would certainly work, but only once. Even then, she wondered if it would fool the good doctor.

CHAPTER EIGHT

Mail Call

Hoagie had an early obligation the next morning and I grabbed the opportunity to take a long walk. It was a beautiful, warm day without too much humidity, and I made good time. Zadovski was waiting for me when I got back and we had a leisurely breakfast.

While I was out walking, I realized I'd never seen the John Doe crime scene. So when we left the hotel, I asked Hoagie to swing by there on the way. "It's probably a waste of time," I told him. "I just want a feel for the place."

"It's a lot different in broad daylight," he replied. "There's really not much to see, but I know what you mean. The time to really get a feel for it is after dark. The roaches come out in company formation."

The image tickled me. I let my mind play with it while we drove and I laughed aloud. "My strange memory," I explained when Hoagie glanced at me. "Do you remember the Freak Brothers comics? The roaches lined up in company formation in Fat Freddy's kitchen?"

"Of course, I remember them," he said. "I spent a lot of time in Hash-bury then. Who I liked was Fat Freddy's cat."

We were off and running then, swapping memories of that wonderful, crazy period in American history. I spent part of it as a military policeman, serving a tour in Saigon and later in San Francisco and Hoagie had been a surf bum, working casually here and there to keep himself in what he called wildwood weed. "I never did hard stuff," he said. "Thank God for that. What I was into was weed, wine and women, and California was the place for all three. " He paused, then added. "I've always wondered if I've got some love kids out there. I wouldn't be surprised if one showed up on my doorstep some day."

I didn't know quite what to say to this. I was married by the time I hit the Left Coast and was faithful to Nellie. What I wonder is if working around asbestos out there while I was in Vietnam is what caused the cancer that killed her thirty years later. She didn't work directly with the stuff, but she worked in an office housed in the main plant. I remember her coming in with white dust all over her clothes.

As expected, there was not much to see at the crime scene. However, I could understand why transients would hang out there. It had that look and I became convinced the bag of clothes brought in with John Doe belonged to someone else. Where they were set was a good hiding place if someone bedded down nearby. I could also see why whoever owned the bag never came back. It would be too easy to be spotted by the killer. Sometimes they hang around to watch the body being discovered.

It was almost noon by the time we arrived at the central police station. We picked up a couple of subs on the way and when we got there we had a stack of faxes and mail. Right on top of the pile was a CODIS response, but what I spotted beneath it was an Express Mail envelope from the Agency. I knew because the envelope was addressed to me and the return address was from an outfit called the Pan-American Eleemosynary Trust.

Hoagie grabbed the CODIS report and I opened the bulky envelope from the Agency. Enclosed were not only the pictures I had sent but also a rap sheet for one James Allen King, address unknown. I saw right away that this was our man and there was a note in Michael Angelino's handwriting that said the probability of an exact match was 96 percent, plus or minus 3 percent.

Out of curiosity, I skimmed King's rap sheet. There was a list of the usual petty crimes that start a criminal career, but what caught my attention were four arrests on suspicion of rape. None of these resulted in conviction and I wondered why. I made myself a note to check into this when we had taken the case as far as we could.

The interesting thing was that after the last arrest for rape, there was nothing else in the record. To all appearances our man had become a model citizen, not even getting a traffic ticket. He dropped out of sight fifteen years before he was found dead in Tulsa, and there were not even any Social Security records of his existence.

This probably meant that King had graduated from rape to serial killing at that point. He had apparently become very careful and probably had worn gloves to keep from leaving prints. I wondered why he had not been identified from his fingerprints after he was killed. They were certainly on file.

I started to make myself a note to check this but stopped when I saw the fingerprint card. The prints were taken back when ink and paper was still widely used, and whoever had done the prints didn't know what they were doing. The prints on the rap sheet were smudged and of little use in any criminal proceeding. Nor would these prints be much good for positive identification. They apparently had been taken in a small jurisdiction and more than likely had never been added to a state or national database.

Sloppy police procedure had struck again. Sometimes I wonder how we ever put anyone away.

Zadovski was done with the CODIS report and was leafing through our faxes and printouts. I picked it up and when I saw the results, I must have said something. "Sweet, ain't it?" Zadovski said. "It gets better."

The CODIS report positively identified Tulsa John Doe

as the man who left DNA in the bodies of six victims. What we had sent in was a sample from a mouth swab, but the CODIS matches were all from seminal fluid. James Allen King had never been caught because he had learned to take care and to kill his victims. Nor had he been concerned about DNA. When he began his career, DNA identification was not on the radar.

Turning from the DNA report, I looked at the case outlines for each victim and it became even more clear that King, AKA Tulsa John Doe, was the perpetrator. While the wound placement was not exactly the same in every case, it was very close and the same kind of weapon had inflicted them.

I looked up and Hoagie grinned at me. "Give the man a cigar," he said. "I think you're absolutely right about communication. I think our Queen of Spades is telling us where to look."

"How in the world did she know where to look?" I asked, talking more to myself than to him. "She seems to know things that we don't."

To my surprise, Hoagie chuckled. "I don't think so. I think she's like you. She *sees* things others don't see in the same data. I think we're dealing with one sharp cookie."

"Where does she get her information? I think that's where we have to look." Then I had a flash. "She must have access to our records! That's the only way she could know the things she does."

"You think she's a rogue cop?" Hoagie asked.

"It could turn out that way, but I don't think so. I'd lean more toward a medical examiner or a medical technician. Or maybe…. Shit!" I didn't like what I was thinking.

"Don't stop now," Zadovski urged. "What were you going to say?"

"Who has access to any information available?" I asked. "Or even better, who has access to such information without being accountable for going after it?"

"Damn!" Hoagie replied. "You don't pull any punches, do you? Homeland Security is what comes to my mind."

"You get your cigar back," I told him. "That's exactly who I was thinking might swing it."

"Why would Homeland Security go around clearing old cases?" he objected.

"I don't think they would unless they were trying to get dirt on someone. I think I just got a whiff of the Company."

Hoagie got a funny look on his face. "Are you sure it's not some of your people? Maybe a rogue."

I nodded. "It's possible but I don't think so. We don't have rogues." I saw something pass over Zadovski's face and suddenly realized what I'd said. "I'm not part of them, Hoagie. I just work with them so much that 'we' seems natural. I'm just a consultant."

He nodded. "You talk that way about what we're doing here, too. Don't worry about it. Besides, I can think of one reason it's not Homeland Security. How would they ever get around Mendoza?"

Then another thought popped up. "Don't give her too much credit. What if she's a copycat?"

Zadovski looked startled. "You lost me there. I don't know of anything like this."

I asked if he was familiar with Dexter. He said not and I gave him a quick rundown on the book. "That's what this feels like to me," I added. "Dexter finds his victims through his line of work. As a blood splatter analyst he's right there at the center of the investigation and can ask questions without raising eyebrows. He also has access to case information through his crime lab computer."

Hoagie thought about this for a moment, then shook his head. "No, it doesn't fit. Dexter gets all his victims from the same police department. King moved around a lot. He wasn't even known here in Tulsa until he turned up dead."

"All it takes is access to NCIC or RISS," I answered. "I bet I could find a potential victim right now."

"That's pretty secure," Hoagie argued. "You might be able to get in through your spook connections or through one of your old cronies, but somebody else would know about it. And if you made too many queries, that would raise a red flag, too, wouldn't it?"

"Not if I did it right," I said.

"I don't know, Jazz," Zadovski said. "I think that's a little far fetched."

"You're probably right. On the other hand, we seem to have a perpetrator who's operating out of the box. That's how she keeps from being caught."

"So we need to think outside the box is what you're saying," he nodded. "That makes sense but there have to be some limits. Otherwise we're just wasting time." He pointed to the stack of faxes and printouts. "Why don't we look at these first? Then, if we don't get anywhere with standard procedure, we can take a flyer. That all right?"

What Zadovski was saying made sense but I was almost certain it would get us nowhere. There was something tumbling around in the back of my mind that I couldn't quite articulate yet. Until I could, it wouldn't hurt to make the obvious moves. I knew I was still on probation with the chief and if I came across as too flaky, the chief would dump me in a minute. It might take her only two seconds.

We took a quick break and hit the rest of our mail. As we went through the pile, I became ever more convinced I was right. Yet I thought it better to let Zadovski come to this conclusion on his own. The facts would convince him far more quickly than I could and the chief would be more likely to accept an unconventional theory from him. Nor did I have any hesitation in letting him take credit for any bust that resulted. This has been my MO ever since I headed up the Arkansas CID and it has worked well for me.

When we summed it all up, we had quite a collection. We got six more Queen card responses, but these all involved different MOs and there were no gunshot wounds. Four of these victims died of a broken neck and two apparently died from garrote strangulation. The common factor was that all were dead before any other wounds were inflicted.

We also got another four responses where both the Queen card and gunshot wounds were present. What tied these together even more closely was the fact that each of the victims had been shot twice in the back of the head with a .22 and the entry wounds were all close enough be a single hole.

There was no indication that any of the victims was connected to any of the others in these cases. Yet I made a note to check this. Looking at all the cases together, I could see a victim profile with each cluster of cases, but there were significant profile differences between the clusters. There was a slim chance that we might get a strong lead if we could connect the victims within any cluster.

There were other differences among the cases, but none of them were that significant. Out of habit I noted these things in the steno book. Nothing might come of them, but there is always the off chance these might prove important.

Looking at everything we had, what was most significant to me were those six responses we got where a Queen card had been left but the MO was completely different. This told me our Queen had dug up six more serial killers and sent them to whatever reward might be due them. This was confirmed later when Zadovski ran an MO query on these killers and came up with twenty-one different crimes in fifteen different jurisdictions.

What was also evident from these cases was that our Queen had been in business for at least eight years without anyone taking notice. "How did we miss it?" I asked Hoagie. "Not you and me, but all the departments involved. How come no one caught on before now?"

He shrugged. "You know how it is, Jazz. None of these guys were people anyone else missed. Look how few of them have even been identified. I imagine other things came up and the investigations were put on a back burner. That's where they sat until they were forgotten. Nobody ever got around to them again."

"Then how come they even bothered to answer?" I wanted to know. "Why now?"

"Two reasons," he replied. "One is that our query joggled their memory. Either that, or they really wanted the case solved but never had a good reason to open it again. Or maybe they were told to set it aside. A lot of the guys who are chief now were patrolmen or investigators back when. Now they have the clout to open a case that always bothered them."

I nodded but was not convinced. Hoagie grinned and said, "Besides, looks who's asking. Your name went out on the queries and this gave them a chance to run with the big dogs. Do you have any idea how boring a cop's life is in a quiet jurisdiction?"

"Come on, I'm not that well known," I protested. Hoagie broke out laughing.

The result of our work was that the chief called for a task force. Since there were so many jurisdictions involved from different states, the FBI took over. When this happened, I decided it was time to head for Ft. Smith. The Bureau is very good at what it does but task force dynamics are something I don't care to endure. Sometimes these things work and sometimes they don't. Life is far too short to shave with dull razors or fight testosterone wars. So I offered my services to the task force as a consultant, knowing the offer would not be taken seriously. After a couple of organizational meetings I went home to Jeanne and our wedding celebration.

A big factor in my decision was my promise to Jeanne to stay out of harm's way. I'd lost two years as a result of the last task force I served on and I had nothing to prove. The work I'd done for Mendoza satisfied me that I was completely back and still up to the job. That was enough for me. I told myself I'd spent my life working and now it was time to play.

Or so I thought. I plunged into the preparations with a fervor that surprised both Jeanne and Lindy and there was plenty to keep my mind occupied. Running here and there and riding herd on the grandchildren, I forgot about Tulsa. Yet there were times I found myself awake in the wee hours, wondering if this possibility or that one had been explored. I made notes when this happened and I was careful to put them away when I got up the next morning. Out of sight, out of mind. So I thought.

Then I called Tulsa a week before the celebration to see if Zadovski and the chief were coming. We had sent both an invitation but had not heard from either one. I told myself I wanted to make sure they knew how much we wanted them there.

As it turned out, the chief was in Hoagie's office when I called and he put us on the speaker. "We were wondering how long it would take you to call," Mendoza told me. When I tried to explain why I was calling, it sounded lame even to me. We all knew I wanted to know how the case was going, so I asked.

"The navy has a good term for such things," Mendoza told me. "It has something to do with a goat." I heard Hoagie snicker when she said this. "The truth is, Jazz, I wish I'd never asked for a task force."

"I don't see you had much choice," I told her.

"Let me put it a different way," she said. "I wish I had

never agreed to it being here. It's been a waste of our time and resources. You and Hoagie accomplished more in two days than they have in two weeks. It took three days to work out jurisdiction protocols and table seating."

"What in the world are jurisdiction protocols?" I asked, but I had a pretty good idea. The concept is turf protection.

"They are a wonderful way of looking busy while wasting time," Hoagie piped up. "I bowed out yesterday."

"I've decided to run our own investigation," the chief told me. "We can do it on the quiet. Are you interested?"

"Let's talk about it at my place in Ft. Smith next Sunday," I suggested.

"I thought the celebration's next Saturday," Mendoza said.

"It is," I replied. "You can spend the night and we'll talk business on Sunday. Jeanne wants you there and it beats playing golf."

Mendoza snorted. "Who has time for that?"

ॐ

She opened the door and flipped on the light, then let her dog rush in first. The house smelled musty from being shut up for the last week, but it was good to be home. Two major jobs had kept her on the go fifteen hours a day and there had been no time to relax. Now she owed herself a break. After so many days at the kennel, it was obvious that Homer agreed.

She dumped her bags near the door and opened several windows to catch the breeze. Then she turned on her computer, and took a quick shower while it was booting. There was still some sun tea left in the fridge, so she poured herself a tall glass and went into her office. The welcome screen was up, asking for a password and she typed it in. The next screen that popped up was her web browser and it told her she had mail. Typing in another password, she sipped her tea as she looked down the list of messages.

There was nothing urgent there and she keyed in another site on the web. Looking at a table of codes and passwords, she chose one she'd not used in a while and entered the proper information. She was rewarded by another welcome screen that greeted her by someone else's name.

Now that she was into the system, she began to search. There was a lot of traffic since she'd logged in last and it took a while to sift through the general postings. She saw there had been a lot of queries issued by the task force in Tulsa, but from what she could see, none of these represented any real threat. The agent in charge of the task force investigation was a Special Agent named Spinks and he was doing what career law enforcement bureaucrats do best. He was following the standard routines of law enforcement and covering his backside. More important, he was sending the hounds to course the wrong part of the swamp. At the end of the exercise, there would be a massive report no one would ever read, and everyone could go home convinced they had done significant work.

The Queen smiled. This was so predictable. Yet in one sense this was significant law enforcement. The task force *was* clearing cold cases and adding to the cumulative knowledge of serial homicide. The irony was that Spinks was simply following the trail she laid out for them and he was too obtuse to see it. No one would be arrested and none of this mass of evidence would ever be used in trial. Nor would anyone ask why it needed a team of highly paid law officers to do this. Any team of file clerks could have followed her lead and accomplished the same.

She signed off that network and onto another. Yet she could find no trace of Jazz Phillips. Nor was there any mention of him on the blogs she visited. The only thing she found was through vital records, where she discovered he'd recently been married in Tulsa.

Looking at the date on the record, she realized this had happened two days after she dumped King's body. She thought this was rather odd, too much of a coincidence. So she carefully copied down the information on the screen. Even though Oklahoma had no waiting period, and Arkansas did, she wondered why anyone would come to Tulsa to get married. Surely there were places far more picturesque and much closer to home.

Turning off the computer, she sat and thought about what she had learned. With Spinks at the head of the investigation she believed she was safe. With Phillips out of the picture, she should have felt even more secure. Yet when she undressed and got into bed, there was still a light frisson of anxiety at the back of her mind. Tired as she was, it was hard getting to sleep and she was troubled by strange dreams.

CHAPTER NINE

Change of Tactics

The celebration of our marriage was absolutely wonderful. Even Forster thought so. "This is a class act," the old padre told me. "As a rule, I'd rather do a dozen funerals than one wedding." Then he grinned wickedly. "Especially if I get to choose the guests of honor."

Most of our other guests were there when Mendoza and Zadovski showed up and the house was crowded. Jeanne's sister, Lindy, was the first to spot them. "Who's that elegant lady with the college professor?" she asked.

I looked where she nodded and was surprised how svelte Mendoza looked in a dress. I told her as much when I greeted her and damned if she didn't blush. Lindy just gave me one of her looks and rolled her eyes.

"He doesn't even know he's doing it," she confided to the chief. The two of them looked at me like I was a floor lamp they were thinking of buying. Hoagie just grinned and shook his head.

I was rescued by my bride, who told me it was time to put on the brisket. She greeted both Hoagie and the chief with a hug and took me in tow, leaving them in the care of Lindy. Later I saw the chief talking to Sam McKee and wondered what they were saying.

I didn't get a chance to say much to either Mendoza or Zadovski for the rest of the day, but they seemed to be having a good time. I did notice that Lindy was spending a lot of time with Hoagie, which surprised me. I didn't think he was her type. Yet when I asked Jeanne about it, she just smiled. "He reminds me of her first husband," she told me. "A sober one, too. Does he drink?"

"Not much," I told her. "He doesn't even finish his beer at lunch." Later I noticed that they were both missing, and when Hoagie and the chief came for a late breakfast the next morning, he and Lindy seemed to be working very hard to appear very indifferent to one another. Yet there was nothing indifferent about the kiss they gave one another when I happened to glimpse them saying goodbye later. They were in a secluded corner of our formal garden and I spotted them from the only second story window visible from there.

After breakfast, the three of us retired to my study. "This sure beats the station," Hoagie observed, running his hand over the back of a leather chair.

"So where do we go from here?" the chief asked once we were settled.

"Why don't you give me a rundown on what the task force has accomplished?" I asked and Mendoza snorted. Zadovski smiled and filled me in. Aside from digging up a world of information about the victims we had uncovered, and about the Queen of Spades' killer-victims, it wasn't much. Most of the killer-victims remained unidentified, and there was no line on the Queen.

What I found interesting was the profile the FBI spun out of conjecture. I respect the work that profilers do, but like the rest of us, they have their limitations. With most serial killers they are quite accurate, but with our Queen I thought they were off the mark by a country mile.

The profilers described our Queen as a young male of high intelligence between twenty-eight and thirty-five years old. They also thought we were dealing with a psychopath who was not very successful in normal life and who craved attention and recognition. They were not sure of the sexual orientation of the Unsub, as they called the Queen, but felt there was a great deal of anger toward males. They believed the motivation was not sex, but power, and thought the Unsub was operating out of a sense of mission. They also mentioned a high probability of childhood abuse and the inevitable bed wetting.

When the chief asked, I told her my profile for the Queen was different. I thought the age range was older, from the early thirties to the early forties. I was not sure we were dealing with a psychopath, but I had the sense we were dealing with a woman of high intelligence who was probably quite successful in normal life. My sense of it was that the motive was justice more than anger, and that the Queen was not seeking attention. I agreed that she was a missionary killer but was not so sure about anger against males. Unlike her victim-killers, she did not torture her targets. She simply executed them quite efficiently. Nor did I see we had much ground to assume childhood sexual or physical abuse, and bedwetting was not germane.

Hoagie nodded when I mentioned that last item. "I never have understood their hang-up with bed wetting," he said. "If they think a person is motivated by fear and shame, why the hell don't they just say that?" Seeing the look on our faces he added, "Sorry. It's a personal peeve."

The word play was too tempting and I couldn't stifle a grin. "So you're pissed about a bunch of pissers-around pissing and moaning about bed-pissing?"

Hoagie laughed and said, "Yeah! What do they do when they have a suspect, get a search warrant for yellow sheets? I'd tell them to piss in their piss-tolas."

Mendoza shook her head and gave us a dour look. "Let's take five to get our act together, gentlemen. I need a pit stop and a beer."

One thing the task force had discovered was how James King dropped out of sight. This was by changing names after his last arrest. The way he did so was rather simple.

He picked a victim about his size and stature and killed him, stealing the man's identity. How the FBI discovered this was by doing what they do best, overwhelming legwork showing his picture around.

However, this never connected King with the Queen of Spades. Nor had it borne any fruit tracing King's presence in Tulsa. For all we knew, the first time he was seen there was when his body was found.

This got me thinking. There's only one body of agents who are more persistent that the FBI. This is the media and I suggested we might go public with what information we had. I thought the case was unique enough to attract national attention, and exposure with something like *Sixty Minutes* might produce results. Even if it didn't lead to our Queen of Spades, it might scare her off.

"I don't know," Hoagie responded. "Seems to me she's saved a lot of jurisdictions a lot of money. I'm not saying that she's righteous, but she's clearing lots of cases. Some of them are killers we can't touch. I'd give her all the rope she needs to hang herself."

"Doesn't it chap your ass that she's getting away with murder?" Mendoza asked.

Zadovski shook his head. "Not at all," he replied. "I don't see that she's a danger to the public." He held up his hands when Mendoza started to say something. "Let me finish, chief. What she is doing is wrong and we need to stop her. I agree with that a hundred percent. I just don't have the sense of urgency I'd have if she were taking out honest citizens."

"Jazz, where are you on this?" Mendoza wanted to know.

"I agree we need to stop her. That's my primary goal. I don't care if we do it by catching her or scaring her off. I just want her to stop. Justice will be served either way."

"Going public is a big risk," Zadovski pointed out. "The whole department could end up with a black eye if it back-fires. It could also net us ten million false leads. We don't have the personnel to run them all down."

"We could give them to the task force," Mendoza suggested. "They have the people."

"I think they might suddenly find they have more pressing things to do in Pocatello," Zadovski pointed out. "Going public on our own would give them a good excuse to dump the whole case. The press would have a field day."

We worried it back and forth for a couple more hours. The strategy we eventually worked out required a great deal of patience. It also required media cooperation and a lot of trust on both sides. Whoever we used would have to know what we were doing and why. We wouldn't necessarily have to reveal details of the investigation, but we would have to be very upfront about the fact we were holding these back.

There was a reporter the chief knew in Tulsa who she thought might play along. There was a marker she could pull in with a promise of an exclusive if, and a big if, the case was ever resolved. In the meantime, what we could offer was a detailed story on the task force.

Since we were releasing the story unilaterally, we had to be careful not to wound the tender egos involved. So the way we spun it, with the help of the reporter, was that the Tulsa Chief of Police had described the task force as a success. It had identified a major serial killer found dead in Tulsa and had connected this killer to at least seven homicides and possibly as many as a dozen committed all across the nation. However, details were not being released since the investigation was ongoing. This included the name of the Tulsa victim.

When asked who was responsible for the death of the killer, the chief was quoted as saying this was unknown. Given the nature of the fatal wound, a gunshot to the back of the head, she suggested it was possibly a gang execution or a even crime of opportunity. The body was found in an area of town popular among transients.

The first call Mendoza got about the story was from the FBI complaining about her premature release of information. What it boiled down to, of course, was that Ken Spinks, the agent in charge, was torqued because his name had not been mentioned. The chief pointed out that the Tulsa murder was on her turf and that she had been obliged to make a statement. She also pointed out that she had been careful to be sure that the Bureau was shielded from any blame that might arise.

The second call was from the mayor, congratulating her on her good work. What the mayor was seeking was assurance that the serial killer had not been active in Tulsa. Mendoza told his honor that as far as she knew, the killer had not been active anywhere in Oklahoma. The mayor wanted to know more but the chief reminded him the case was still open. She told me later he took this with more grace than she would have expected.

The third call she got was from the chief of a small town in Kansas who had just become aware of the task force. He had a case that sounded like King's work and was mailing her a copy of the file. Apparently the jurisdiction was so small it was not connected even to the internet and the chief was the only officer on the municipal payroll. Where he had heard about the task force was from a county deputy while they were having coffee. The news story had jogged the deputy's memory. The case was twelve years cold.

"It looks like we've gotten away with it so far," Zadovski told me one day when he called. "There's been lots of favorable press and the city council even voted me a reward. It's not much but I'll split it with you if you want."

"I'd just have to pay taxes on it," I replied. "How about the chief? Or would that be conflict of interest?"

Hoagie chuckled. "It might but they voted her a bigger bonus than mine. I bet they'd honor it if you sent in a bill."

"No, I told the chief it was *pro bono* and it needs to stay that way. She did me a real favor taking a chance on me. Has there been any progress identifying the Queen?"

"No, he or she is a pretty sharp cookie. There hasn't been a whisper since you were last here."

"Maybe we got her to stop," I said. "I don't think so, but maybe. That wouldn't hurt my feelings a bit."

"Well, you know how I feel about it. I think she deserves a medal for good citizenship. I know we can't do that, but that's how I *feel*. My granddaughter's safer because of her."

"I hear you," I told him. I had never thought about it like that, but when I put Zilpha and our grandkids into the equation, I understood. "Hopefully, she will stop killing and we won't hear anything more from her."

"Do you really expect that?" Hoagie asked.

I shook my head. "Not really. Once they start, the only way to stop serials is to catch them or kill them. I personally have never known of one who's stopped. On the other hand, our Queen of Spades is not a typical serial. She's an assassin, driven by a mission. I don't think she's a sociopath."

"Remind me," Hoagie asked. "What's the difference between a psychopath and a sociopath?"

"The only difference is how they're spelled. Sociopath is a newer term. It's called antisocial personality disorder now."

Hoagie chuckled. "That sounds like me on a bad morning before coffee."

"What's scary is that it sounds like a lot of politicians, particularly the part about pervasive deceit and manipulation and trampling the rights of others because they can. Look it up in the DSM sometime."

"No shit?" Zadovski asked, dead serious, and I nodded. "That sounds like a lot of cops I know."

"That's the feeling I've had about this all along. I think we are dealing with someone close to law enforcement."

৵৵

She was tired of the killing. Even though they were vermin and deserved to die, she was weary of being the one to do it. The anger that first drove her had disappeared years ago and tracking them down no longer challenged her. There was a sense of satisfaction in getting the job done quickly and efficiently without getting caught but her heart was no longer in it. Now it was something she just did and she felt herself getting stale. This was a sure recipe for disaster.

So it was time to retire. This small piece of land and this old house were hers now. She had always been careful with money, so there was plenty to last her the rest of her life if she wanted to quit nursing poorly designed and poorly used computer systems. It might even be time to quit that. Doing so would be scary because it meant she would be flying blind. There would be no way of knowing if an investigation was moving her way. It might be better to stay in for a year or two and be nursemaid to her Bubbas.

Yet that wouldn't be enough to keep her going, either in mind or in spirit. She was in the prime of life and she needed a challenge. One option was going back to school, but that didn't appeal to her. Whenever she was on a college campus she felt out of place. The new material she studied was interesting enough, but the pace it was taught seemed glacial. She normally devoured the text within two weeks and spent the rest of the time researching, and she found herself impatient with her professors. They seemed to get defensive when she asked questions, and she suspected this was because she had outstripped them in their own fields.

So what was she to do with the rest of her life? She was too old to bear children, and she didn't want to assume the risks of the background check that would go with adoption. There were men in her life from time to time, but none with whom she cared to spend her life. The few exceptions she'd come across were all married and that was a boundary she would never cross. She might kill in good conscience, but breaking up a marriage was completely out. She knew what that did.

This brought her back to her original question. What would she do if she retired? Then a random thought struck her and it made her smile. What might be interesting would be joining forces with the odd little man from Ft. Smith.

Whoa, girl! She told herself. *You really like courting disaster, don't you? He'd have you pegged in a New York minute.*

Then another thought struck her. There was a way she could join forces with him, but she'd have to be extremely careful. With the smallest mistake she'd be toast.

Pouring herself another cup of tea, she began to consider exactly how to do this.

CHAPTER TEN

Out of the Blue

We didn't hear anything more from the Queen of Spades for more than six months. Once I had my desk back in order and my next book outlined, I became restless. I wanted to be doing something more than spending my life in front of a computer display, even one as big and nice as mine.

Jeanne knew what was going on long before I did and suggested I take off for a few days with Forster and head for Dee's fishing camp. He still owned it, even though someone else ran it for him now, and when I called, he was enthusiastic. It had been almost four years since we went fishing and he and Forster got along well.

Time away with the guys improved my outlook considerably. We had an excellent time not catching many fish and telling strange tales around the campfire. The best ones came from Forster, who had spent twenty-five years as a parish priest in Oklahoma and Arkansas. "It damned near killed me when I walked away, Jazz," he told me once in a moment of stark candor. "It was like leaving my family behind, but I had to quit the church to save my soul."

On that particular trip he also told us how he almost became a bishop. "It was not long before I retired," he said, taking a sip of strong camp coffee. "When I was nominated I pulled in a lot of markers and put together a campaign any politico would be proud to claim. We had the votes lined up and only lacked three for a majority among the clergy when the results of the first ballot came back. We were over the mark by ten lay votes and were sure to have the election on the second ballot."

He paused then, lost in thought. When he resumed it was almost in a whisper. "Then the damnedest thing happened. I was in the head standing at a urinal, one of those that goes all the way to the floor. I was alone at first but then someone came in and stood in front of the other one. He laughed and I realized it was my opponent."

"'I guess we two are them who pisseth against the wall, as the Good Book says,' he chuckled. Then he became serious. 'You know, Father, I'm glad you're ahead,' he told me. 'I was half way through Morning Prayer yesterday when I realized this thing would probably kill me. I was shocked how much I want it.'"

Again Forster paused. "As you can imagine, I was thunderstruck. I looked at the man and realized he meant every word he uttered."

"'Jesus!' I told him and without thinking about it, I said, "'Neither do I. What are we going to do?'"

The old man laughed. "What we did was to shock the hell out of the convention. Literally. I moved and he seconded that we do the election the old way. This involved putting all the names of those who were willing to serve in a hat and letting a child draw a name. Whomever that might be would be our new bishop. We added that neither his name nor mine would be in the hat."

"There was a great outcry over this, and much heated debate, but somehow the Holy Ghost got loose that day and that's how we did it. The interesting thing is that the poor bastard whose name we drew became the best bishop that diocese ever had. He didn't want it any more than we did and it turned out that someone else put his name in the hat."

Forster stopped and looked at us fiercely. "He served for fifteen years before the job killed him and I could never have accomplished near what he did."

❧◦❧

Sam McKee called me a couple of weeks after I got back from fishing and invited us to visit him at his ranch in Wyoming late the following week. He had some paper work he wanted me to look over that seemed odd to him, and the aspens were changing. He asked if we had ever seen this and we had not, so we swamped out our motor home and headed west.

Jeanne was a little nervous about this but I told her I would never take another assignment from Sam that put me in harm's way. She smiled when I said this but said, "I know you mean that, Jazz, and it's tempting to hold you to it, but I will never do that. I won't be your jailer. I don't want you to come to resent me."

There was nothing I could say to that. I wanted to say something but nothing came to mind. She was dead right. So I did the smart thing and shut up. Twenty minutes later we were laughing about something stupid we saw on the side of the road, and when we stopped for lunch at a rest area, a nap followed. It took us two hours to get back on the road.

The McKee ranch is near Casper and when we pulled in I did shave-and-a-haircut on the air horn. Most of the family was there, including Sam's older sister, Julian and her husband, and there was barely room for us all around the big dining room table. Somehow we all squeezed in, kids and all, and meals were a bedlam of everyone talking at once. It was wonderful.

The next day Jeanne took off with Martha, Sam's sister-in-law, and his wife Megan. They were headed to Casper to do some shopping, and Sam and I retreated into the study to talk business. His brother, Jack, accompanied us, which was unusual, and I wondered what was up.

There is no question the study was a man's room. It was designed by Sam's dad, as was the whole house, and the thick adobe walls were soundproof. The door was made of wide slabs of closely fit pine and when it was shut, almost no sound could get in or out. I suspect that Jack had also rigged the place to jam any electronic surveillance through the two skylights that illuminated the room with a soft liquid light. The whole effect was an atmosphere of warm security and I found myself immediately comfortable there.

There was a broad wooden desk at one end of the room and a wide worktable nearby. Sam waved us toward chairs facing the fireplace in the center of a side wall and removed a file from a worn leather briefcase next to the desk. He set the file on a low table by his chair and stoked up the fire, adding a couple of logs. Then we sat for a while watching the coals ignite the fresh wood.

After a while, McKee sighed. "I guess we need to get to work," he said, handing me the file. It was about as thick as a ream of paper. "This is for you to go over after I've briefed you. Jack is here to translate electronic speak into something resembling English, but that's not the issue. What I want to know is your take on the situation. The first half of the file is financial reports for companies involved over the last eight years. The second is other information we've gathered from a lot of different sources over the last seven months. Michael wanted to organize it, but I told him to simply put it in the order in which it came to us."

"What am I looking for, Cadre?" I asked.

"I don't know, Jazz. It could be or not. I've got a feeling the whole thing isn't quite kosher, but it's only a feeling. Something doesn't smell quite right."

"I take it you brought me here because you didn't want this information going through FedEx or the mail," I observed and Sam nodded.

"That's one of two copies," he told me. "The other is at our office in Washington. You can work on it in here or out in your rig, either one. Take all the notes you want but don't make copies. I also need you to leave your notes behind when you head home. You'll understand why when you read the file."

"It's going to take me a while to go through all this, Sam," I told him. "There's a lot of information here."

"I'm most interested in your general impressions," he said. "We had a team go through it with a fine-tooth comb, but they didn't come up with much. See what you can do."

I told him I'd prefer to work in our RV and he handed me the worn briefcase to carry it back and forth. "Don't let it out of your sight," he told me. "This is Top Secret, your eyes only." He handed me a key. "This is to that cabinet," he said, pointing. "When you're not working on it, store it there."

"I'm not sure I have a high enough clearance for this information," I told him.

"Sure you do," he grinned. "I'm the one who classified the information. Call me or Jack on the scrambled phone if you need something."

I took the briefcase and headed for our RV. I didn't like all the security falderal, but it's something I've learned to live with working for McKee. I suppose I could feel flattered at being trusted with that level of information, but I'm not. It's a pain in the derrière and I'd rather not be bothered.

Two hours later I called Sam. I'd gone over the file quickly and a quarter of the way through I had a question. The question had not been answered by the time I completed the file. When I asked McKee for clarification, he looked dumbfounded.

"That's it," he told me. "That's exactly what's been bothering me but I didn't know it. What tipped you off?"

"Nothing," I told him, baffled that he'd not seen it. "It was just something that seemed a little odd right from the first." Then I had another thought, one that offended me. "Are you testing me, Sam? Is that what this is all about? Seeing if old Jazz is up to par?"

"No, Jazz, honestly. You're the first person who spotted it. Now that you did it seems rather obvious." He frowned. "I don't know how we ever missed it."

My cop sense told me the man was telling the truth. I can be fooled, and have at times, but I knew McKee pretty well. So I let him off the hook. "Well, sometimes a fresh set of eyes can spot things everyone involved has overlooked. I guess I'm back, aren't I?"

"You are, in spades," McKee said. Seeing the odd look on my face, he asked, "What?"

So I ended up telling him about our Queen of Spades. When I was done, he shook his head. "You get some strange cases, don't you?" Then he asked if I wanted him to look into it very discretely and I told him that would be appreciated.

"I don't know if we'll find anything, but who knows? Our sources of information are different from yours."

The rest of the visit was all fun. Jeanne and I rode horses, smelled the tall pines from the mountaintop, and listened to the wind roaring through them. On one of our outings we found a line camp and made love on the wide bunk in the loft. Not five minutes after we were dressed again, one of McKee's foremen stopped to restock the pantry, and Jeanne and I laughed about that all the way down the mountain.

"He knew!" she said. "He knew exactly what we'd been doing. I could tell."

"He did look a little embarrassed," I agreed. "I guess old married folks like us aren't supposed to do stuff like that in the middle of the day."

We ended up spending a week at the McKee's and then another full week getting home. Not once did I find myself bored in that whole time. Yet when we arrived at home in Ft. Smith, it was good to be there and I looked forward to doing a couple of projects outside before winter set in.

Not long after we got back from Wyoming, other consulting jobs began to come in, and I spent a busy winter in my study and on the phone with those. There was very little travel involved. Then suddenly it was spring and time to put in our garden. So we planted our onions and potatoes on Valentine's Day and our English peas not long after. We also planted some of the hardier new ornamentals.

Then one day a parcel came to me courtesy of UPS. This puzzled me because I hadn't ordered anything and neither had Jeanne. Not recognizing the name of the person it was from, I gently carried it to the driveway and asked our local bomb squad to take a look. They had a new robot, courtesy of Homeland Security, and were delighted for a chance to try it out on a possible threat.

The operation took most of the afternoon. The members of the squad were all police officers who had only a little training and no experience. So they took their time and did it by the numbers.

Jeanne was frightened but I enjoyed watching the officers work from behind a squad car at the end of the drive. Just for safety, we evacuated the houses surrounding us, and a most exciting time was had by all. I thought our neighbors would be scared silly, being mostly elderly folk not long from assisted living. I was surprised when they came to me in a group and asked if they could watch. Three of them even had binoculars along and I later found out they were avid bird watchers.

The officers really didn't like this, but these were important people in town. So we set up behind a tactical Hum-Vee across the street and Jeanne and I joined them. There was an almost festive air about the whole thing, and when the package proved harmless, these neighbors seemed almost disappointed. So did the bomb squad now that I think of it.

The package turned out to contain nothing but papers but the officer in charge offered to bring out their sniffing device to see if the papers were coated with poison or something worse. I was feeling rather foolish by then and told them not to bother. I did ask them to use gloves when they picked up the wrapping and papers. This was so I could develop any latent prints from the papers or the wrapper, but I knew this was useless when I asked. For the first thing I had seen on the monitor when the robot opened the package was a single playing card. It was the queen of spades.

Not wanting to take the papers inside the house, I had the officers place them in a large evidence bag and locked them in a steel evidence cabinet in the garage. I gave the officers an official receipt for the bag and thanked them for their good work. I also told them the papers were from a suspect in a case I was working on and that the danger was real. The officer in charge knew about my involuntary retirement and assured me they were honored to help.

My next call was to Hoagie Zadovski. He had gone back to retirement and was excited when I told him what I had. He wanted me to bring the bag to Tulsa, but I wasn't sure about crossing jurisdictions. Technically, the Ft. Smith PD had jurisdiction since I called them in, and one of their investigators might show up asking to see the evidence. He told me he'd be on the way in an hour and I told him he had a reservation at the Phillips Inn.

I could tell Jeanne was shaken by the experience. She has been around investigations before, but this was her first experience of being even remotely in harm's way. "I know it's not your fault we got that package," she said. "But it was your work that brought it to our home."

I told her I really did understand and she knew this

was true. This had happened to me twice before circumstances brought Jeanne and me together and both times were in this very house. So, yes, Jeanne knew this, but knowing it and experiencing it are two different things.

"I guess we could move," I said. "I don't think that would work, but we could try."

"I'm not suggesting that," she answered. "I'm not sure there *is* a solution." Her eyes clouded. "I just don't want to lose you again."

"I don't want to lose you, either," I said, holding her close. "But we're human. At some point it will happen." We were both acutely aware of this. Jeanne had lost her first husband in Vietnam and I had lost the bride of my youth to cancer. All I can say is that being the survivor is the worst thing that ever happened to me. Nor does it seem fair that we are taught to love life and one another only to lose everything.

One can dwell on this, on the unfairness of life. Yet doing so robs us of the beauty of today and I have come to agree with Forster, the old padre I talk with about such things. The only way to get beyond a sense of loss is learning to be grateful for what we have been given. As he puts it, it's hard to find room for bitterness when one's heart is full of gratitude. This may be a severe consolation, but I find that it does work.

So I took my wife into my arms and held her close. Then I began to tell her all the things I was grateful for, starting with my memories of the time we first met. After a while, she began to do the same. Not long after that we began to laugh and the darkness that came with the morning's scare began to clear away.

CHAPTER ELEVEN

Jigsaw

Hoagie and I laid out the papers in the evidence bag on long folding tables I keep for larger projects. To keep from contaminating them, we used plastic gloves and placed each sheet on long strips of butcher wrap fresh from the roll. While both knew there would probably be nothing we could use on the papers, other than the information they held, good police work means being prepared for the unexpected. The Queen just might have made a mistake. Even a fiber or partial print could lead us to her.

The order of the top half of the stack had been disrupted by the robotic search. The first order of business would be to try to get these papers into their original order and this was difficult. Most of the sheets were photocopies of newspaper articles, but there were also cover sheets explaining the significance of the articles and black and white prints of photographs to go with them. These photos held the most promise of fingerprints but the queen had apparently thought of that. Except for the printing, they were in the same condition as when they came in the box. There was nothing on them, absolutely nothing.

"We might get lucky with the ink," Hoagie suggested.

"We can try but I'd bet it's from one of the most common printer cartridges around."

"No bet," he replied. As it turned out he would have lost.

When we were done sorting I looked at the piles on the worktable. "You know what we have here?" I asked.

"Looks like case files to me," he answered. "Look at the way the bottom half is arranged. They all look exactly like a police report."

"I don't think any of this is from police files," I said. "The cover pages are too well written."

Hoagie grinned. "No, but they're put together with police logic. The Queen knows procedure. All that's missing is a fingerprint chart and the usual forms."

"Let's start with the bottom half first and see if we can figure out what she's trying to tell us."

"That's pretty clear to me," Zadovski replied. "She's telling us where to look for the creeps." Two weeks later he was proven right when the Dallas police picked up the first of the suspects from the package. I actually got a call from one of the deputy chiefs thanking me for sending the information.

She knew someone was sniffing around. Long ago, when she first started hunting vermin, she had set up a network of electronic trip-wires. These were her early warning system, and she was careful to maintain them carefully. Now two of them had been tripped within as many days.

This was not a cause to panic. It had happened twice before and nothing had come of it. What had been tripped this time were distant markers, much like the radar stations on the old DEW Line that warned of a nuclear attack. They put her on the alert, warning her to watch the other markers, but required little else. There was even a parallel to this in the history of the DEW system. One of the stations once reported a flight of geese as a wave of Russian bombers.

She was also aware of the arrest in Dallas. This would lead to the closing of at least a dozen cases if the police followed her leads. Not that they would thank her for this. No, they would be only too glad to take her in, too. Somehow that felt a bit unjust, but that was the law.

Closing down her computer, she made herself a cup of tea. Then she sat on her porch and thought about the electronic trip wires that warned her. One of them was not that significant, but the other could be. Someone was sniffing around the original New Orleans case that got her started. More than likely that would not be a problem if it was someone like a writer researching for an article or a book. Yet if it was that eccentric man from Arkansas, she might be in trouble. There might not be enough evidence to convict her, but he would find out who she was. Then he would find her.

She poured herself another cup of tea and sat for a long time, considering what she should do about Jazz Phillips.

๛

After the arrest in Dallas, there were three more arrests in quick succession around the country. Then it was quiet for a long time and Hoagie and I went over the cases that had not been closed. We both had other things going on in our lives, but we came to know the case details almost by heart. My office in the garage began to take on the look of a task force command center, and a grungy one at that.

"You know what I wish?" Hoagie asked me one day when we were cleaning the place up a bit. Jeanne had threatened to turn Zilpha and some of her other friends loose on the place if we didn't.

I confessed I had no idea, except maybe that the cleaning was done. "No," he answered. "I wish there was some way we could have the Queen working with us without having to bust her. Then we could hit high gear."

"Not possible," I mumbled. "You'd have to get pardons from a dozen states, maybe more. We can't even get them to agree on a common penal code."

"Not necessarily," he said. "I was thinking more in terms of a personal amnesty."

I looked at him over my glasses. He had my complete attention. Jeanne calls this my prosecutor look. "Correct me if I'm wrong, but I think that's called accessory after the fact."

"Not if you don't know details. That's called giving a person the benefit of the doubt." Then he shrugged. "No, forget it. You're right. It would never work." He went back to the file he was studying, possibly for the fiftieth time.

I sat back and thought about the situation. The truth was that I'd had the same thought two days before. Then an obvious solution came to mind, one worthy of McKee's best hair splitting. "You know, Hoagie, I can talk about stuff like this because I've had a hard lick on the head. Anything that might be used against you could be torn up by a first year law student."

"That's what I was thinking," he replied. "Anything you might say could be put down to brain injury."

"It's an interesting concept," I said. "I don't think a judge would buy it, but who knows what a judge is going to do? The trick is staying out of the courtroom completely, but that begs the question, too. The real question is if you could live with it. That's the rub."

He nodded. "I've lived with things like this before. Not as bad but still major felony level. How about you?"

"As a brain-damaged soul I can tell you I think I've lived with the same kinds of things you have. Of course, I may be wrong. My circuits were scrambled."

"So what do you think?"

I sighed. Nellie used to tell me when I did this about half of the air was sucked out of the room. "Hoagie, I think we best sleep on this a long, long time. I personally consider this a hypothetical consideration we're kicking around. It's not possible in the real world. Let me think about it for a few months and I'll discuss the ethical aspects with you. You do understand we need to keep this all very hypothetical?"

"Oh, absolutely. All I'm trying to do is get inside the mind of the Queen, you understand."

"That's what I thought," I replied. "I didn't think you were suggesting conspiracy."

"Good heavens, no!" He declared, grinning. "I surely hope I didn't give you that idea!"

The next week, all hell broke loose in Tulsa. The mutilated body of a young woman was found displayed on a park bench near the center of the city. Unfortunately the press arrived before the first squad car and the person who found the body talked to a reporter. The good news was that we had a witness's statement on tape. The bad news was that she had told the reporter all about the queen of spades displayed between the victim's mutilated breasts.

Three days later it happened again. This time the killer called the press and simply told them a big story was breaking at such and such location. He also said that the police were not using radio but cell phones, and this was clever. News people monitor the police channels with a scanner so they can send a team to fires, accidents and crime scene. To avoid tipping them off, police now use cell phones.

As a result, the television crew got there first and found the body. They were the ones who called the police and they were able to film the whole scene before the first squad car got there. They were also smart enough to change the video tapes in their cameras when they heard the first sirens. When the investigators demanded the camera tapes as evidence, all they got were the secondary shots. These showed that the camera crew had been careful not to violate the crime scene. What was also very clear was the queen of spades playing card between the bloody breasts of the victim.

We knew right away, of course, that this was a copycat. The victims were young females, for one thing, and the wound pattern was much different. Nor was there any bullet wound in the back of the heads, or anywhere in the bodies. It was clear to me that each victim was terrorized before they were killed, and both were raped. We were able to get seminal fluid from both victims and there were bruises consistent with rape.

The problem came when the press immediately labeled the perpetrator as the Queen of Spades killer. When the chief held a press conference, she was asked if there had been more than two Queen of Spades victims, her answer was less than satisfactory. "Not as far as we know," she told them. "It may be that there are more victims out there we don't know about. This particular killer has only struck twice as far as we know." She repeated that phrase, "as far as we know," three more times during the interview.

The press could tell there was a lot she was holding back and they pushed for answers. When they did, the chief told them it was an ongoing investigation and neither she nor her investigators could comment. When they asked her who the investigators were, she introduced Hoagie and me. Since she used my title, most of the reporters assumed I was with the medical examiner's office. Yet one of them recognized my name and the next day the banner headline read, CITY CALLS JAZZ. The next line said, NATIONAL EXPERT AFTER QUEEN OF SPADES. There was also a short blurb on my career at the end of the story.

I had only been on the case a couple of hours when the chief called the news conference and I would have preferred to remain anonymous. There was little I could do until the basic police work was done, but I owed Mendoza several favors and I agreed to let the chief introduce me as an investigator. I did so to take some heat off the investigation. Calling me in showed due diligence on her part. Having to do this is an unfortunate political fact of life these days.

Since Zadovski was supervising the investigation, I took off for home once I'd visited the crime scenes and looked at the bodies. There was nothing unusual about either, but both victims did have defensive wounds on their arms and hands. This confirmed what I had known all along. There was a lot of rage expressed in these crimes, both in the slashing and in the brutality of the rapes. Unlike our Queen of Spades, the copycat's primary motive was power and the crimes were definitely sexual. There was also a toe missing from these victims, a small detail the media overlooked and one that we held back.

Whoever the copycat might be, he was clever enough to stop at two killings in Tulsa. One definition of a serial killer is someone who commits three or more murders separated in time, and with only two crimes, the investigation was not hot enough to get the FBI interested. Not with someone like Ken Spinks running the Tulsa office. I'd known Spinks a long time and I'd never known him to do any more than he had to do, except grab for glory.

This was a blessing since we didn't have to deal with interference from the man. Spinks almost blew the whole case the first time I ever tried to work with him, and I'd had to burn some markers to get him reassigned. He had done the same thing the next time I ran into him, but fortunately I was working for Sam McKee. The Agency had jurisdiction and I was able to conduct an effective investigation.

Of course, this almost got me killed but that's beside the point. Had I known the outcome, I would have gladly let Ken Spinks have the case and the coma that came with it. I hate to admit I believe the world would have been a better place those two years. Yet it is very unlikely Spinks would have ever been that close on the heels of the bomber.

Though I stayed home in Ft. Smith, Zadovski was in touch with me at least once every day. These were long calls, for he not only kept me up to date, but we also kicked around ideas about the case. As we talked, I kept track of our progress on a marker board in a corner of the garage.

One day a letter arrived from a law firm in Kansas City. At least, that was the name on the elegant printed envelope and I opened it without question. Inside there were two items. One was a single sheet of plain white paper. It was a copy of an article about the latest Tulsa murders with a single line of print below it. The message read, "As you know, this was not me." The other item in the envelope was a playing card, the queen of spades.

I sat at my desk for a long time thinking about this. Why had the queen sent me this letter? How did she expect me to respond? Aside from having the envelope and the paper run through the lab, along with the playing card, what did I need to do? After puzzling almost an hour nothing suggested itself, so I picked up the phone and called Hoagie.

I brought him up to date on my end of the wire, and when I was done he whistled. "Sounds like you're right, Jazz. The lady is trying to communicate with you but I can't figure why, either. Let me sleep on it and maybe I'll come up with something."

"Think about how I can communicate with her, too. She may know something we don't."

Hoagie chuckled. "I expect she knows a whole bunch we don't. You think she knows anything about our copycat?"

"I think that if she doesn't, she will soon. She seems to be able to go places the police can't. Either that, or she's quicker on the uptake." I paused and Zadovski must have sensed I had something else to say. After a moment I decided to grab the thistle firmly. "This copycat worries me, Hoagie. This guy is a rage killer and I want to get him stopped before someone else dies. We may not have another body in Tulsa but there will be another one somewhere soon. To save lives, I'm willing to take whatever help I'm offered on whatever terms I can get."

It was his turn to be quiet. "I believe we talked about this once before," he said. "I gather that you've slept on it long enough. I'm ready to move ahead any time you are."

"As I mentioned then, we need to be very careful to set it up right. Why don't you head my way and we'll go fishing?"

Later that week an article appeared in the Tulsa paper. The reporter who helped us out before was delighted to do so again and I had no problem promising her an exclusive interview when the case was completed. "I need to be sure you understand what I'm promising and what I'm not. The case needs to be resolved to my satisfaction before you do the interview. The other thing is that the article needs to be about my professional work. My personal life is off limits."

The story appeared on the first page of the paper although it was not the banner story. The article read like this:

JAZZ AFTER MAN UNSEEN

Tulsa, Oklahoma. National homicide expert Jazz Phillips today asked the public's help catching a potential serial killer. The profile of what he calls the Playing Card killer, to prevent confusion with another killer who was never caught, describes the killer as being a single Caucasian male between twenty and thirty-four years of age. He is left-handed and of average intelligence and works in a service occupation, having a history of frequent job changes. His neighbors describe him as a quiet man who minds his own business and he is very polite in normal conversation. He is short in stature and of average build, and is someone who others normally overlook. "We're looking for the man never seen," Phillips said recently. "This is someone you wouldn't normally remember and this is the killer's basic disguise. He's the neighbor you'd never suspect and the man who's always forgotten."

Phillips added that his main concern is to get this killer off the street as soon as possible. "We're trying to save lives and we need the public's help. We're willing to accept help from any source and no questions will be asked except to clarify the information given."

An anonymous police hotline has been set up at the toll free number listed below and those who prefer can write Dr. Phillips in care of this paper. All written responses will be kept completely confidential.

For the first few days after the article appeared, the police hotline was swamped with calls. These were recorded and the information was carefully assessed by a team of detectives led by Hoagie. About a dozen good leads came from this but none of them panned out. By the second week the response was down to a trickle and only one part-time operator was taking the occasional call.

The real fruit of this article was a letter in an envelope of a different law firm. There was only a single sheet inside with a picture of a playing card. This one was a one-eyed jack and the message was short. It reminded me of a telegram.

NICE ARTICLE. GOOD WORK. WILL BE IN TOUCH SOON.
NO CARD TRICKS, JAZZ, OR THIS WILL END. Q

I read this through again just to make sure I hadn't missed anything. What I found interesting was that the one-eyed jack was the knave of hearts, not of spades. I wondered what this meant. I hesitated to read too much into it, but I was sure the change was made for a purpose. This might be anything, but I suspected the Queen did this knowing I would figure it out.

I was sitting in my study when the letter came and I started to ask Jeanne what she thought. Then I changed my mind. I had no idea how Jeanne might respond. She had been very quiet ever since the bomb scare.

Then I had another thought. This was sent to me and I was expected to figure it out from a man's point of view. So I sat down and did a little thinking, trying not to get too far under the surface. I am prone to doing that and sometimes it backfires.

I went through a breathing exercise Forster had taught me first. This is used to prepare a person for meditation and when I was done, I let my mind float. I conjured up the image of the jack of hearts in my mind and simply held it there, waiting to see or hear whatever came. I've done this before with evidence I didn't understand. It has always worked.

This time I was so recollected, so deep in meditation, that I fell asleep and didn't awaken until Jeanne came in and woke me for supper. Seeing the jack of hearts propped on my desk, she laughed. "Are we feeling romantic, darlin'? Or is this some new kind of solitaire?"

I mumbled something inarticulate and reached for a hug. An hour later she grinned at me and said, "Well, I do declare, Dr. Phillips. I believe I smell supper burning in the oven. I guess we'll have to order something in."

Looking at her, I made a decision. Murder could wait, even serial murder. "Woman, I'm hungry! Let's call in an order for ribs from Lee Roy's and rent a silly movie. I don't care what it is so long as it isn't serious and doesn't involve crime or cops."

That's how we ended up watching a strange French movie with subtitles, eating ribs and drinking microbrewed beer. Neither of us could figure out what the movie was about, but it didn't matter. What mattered was that we were alive and together at that moment. Half way through the movie we stopped watching and turned to other things we found more compelling. I have no idea how the film turned out.

CHAPTER TWELVE

Odd Bedfellows

The morning was absolutely beautiful. As she sat on her porch sipping her tea she listened to a mockingbird driving the other birds crazy. This one seemed to have a better repertoire than most, and she wondered where it heard some of the calls it was singing. She knew some mockingbirds migrated as far east as Boston, returning in the spring. The interesting thing was that some of the other mocking birds, the ones who remained, seemed to resent these "southerns" when they arrived home.

Sure enough, another mockingbird swooped in and began an attack. Yet the southern was a bigger, more aggressive bird and after a short, loud skirmish, chased the other off his turf. Then the southern resumed his perch but remained silent. She wondered why.

Pouring herself another cup of tea, she returned to the porch and thought about the situation in Tulsa. She wondered how the investigation was going. So far she had stayed out of it, though she had done some careful research. This had not turned anything up so far. The identity of the killer remained unknown and there was no trace of him she could find anywhere else. It would be helpful to know what the police had discovered, but there was no way of finding out without taking an unnecessary risk.

What would be even more helpful is if I could talk with the good doctor directly. She smiled when she thought of his response to her last letter. It had appeared in the personals column of both the Tulsa paper and the one in Kansas

City, and it was sweet.

> **How I miss the queen of my hearts. Please get in touch. All is forgiven. We can work this out. Your Jack.**

The message seemed very clear and she was sure the typo was deliberate. It was tempting to give the good doctor a call. She knew his personal cell phone number, courtesy of the Tulsa chief of police, who had written it on her blotter beside his name. She also had a device for distorting her voice, making it sound like a man, and there were ways to keep the call from being traced immediately. Yet she was afraid to try. What could be coded, like the sound of her voice, could also be decoded, and she knew the good doctor had resources far greater than anything the Tulsa police department could muster. Why take the risk?

Smiling to herself, she pulled on a pair of surgical gloves and took some paper and an envelope from a special box she never touched with bare hands. Nor did she ever lick the envelope. It was too easy for investigators to pick up DNA from the saliva in the glue.

❧

I was in Tulsa visiting Hoagie when the next letter came. We were reviewing the copycat file, taking a closer look at some of the dead ends. Occasionally this will generate a new lead, or at least stimulate new thinking, but the detectives Hoagie chose were the best Tulsa had. They were not only thorough, but also articulate, a combination too infrequently found among local investigators. Many come up through the ranks and police speak is what they know best.

The first issue we had to consider was that the DNA found in the victims was from five different sources. This was not surprising since the victims were both hookers, but it made it difficult to identify their killer. Only two of the donors were identified. Both of these were soldiers of an army reserve unit in town for training exercises and their alibis were rock solid. Members of their unit had seen both victims alive after the two men had been with them. Then, when the second victim had been dumped, they were both on maneuvers in Utah.

Another dead end was the relationship between the victims. From what we had found out, they were not friends or roommates. Nor was it clear how they were connected or why they were together. The two soldiers picked them up in a café where they were eating supper. The two women normally worked different parts of the city and while one of them was well known to other hookers on the street, the second victim was not. She was much younger, just turned nineteen, and the detectives had discovered where she was staying. She had arrived in Tulsa only two months before she was killed and she did have a record, which is how we found out where she lived. Yet she was never booked under her birth name and we never discovered her identity, where she was from or how the two became known to the killer.

The first victim *was* known and had been around Tulsa for a couple of years. She roomed with another woman on the same stroll but no one had seen her connecting with the other hooker or with a john. One minute she was there talking with the others, and then she wasn't, but her roommate didn't worry when she failed to return that night. The roommate assumed her friend had scored an all-night trick and had no idea what had happened until she talked to detectives the following day. Nor did she know where her friend was from, or her legal name, and she was not acquainted with the second victim at all. As far as she knew, there was no regular man in her roommate's life.

The first victim was only known to the other hookers by her street name, which was Dovey. Unlike the other victim, Dovey did not have a record, at least not one we could find. There was no record of her DNA in CODIS and no record of her fingerprints. Nor were there any missing women named Dovey on either our NCIS query or on a Who-Where search.

Since our victims were prostitutes, we were not even sure if our killer had left DNA or not. I suspected he had not. But a DNA match was a possibility and we had to keep it in mind. Nothing had come up on the original CODIS search, but it was possible our killer did not have a record. With that much anger, one would think at least something would pop up, but nothing did.

The other strange thing was that our perpetrator did not leave any trace evidence behind, at least none we could find. There were no hairs, no fibers that could not have come from the crime scene and no physical evidence aside from the playing card and the condition of the bodies. There is almost always such evidence and the only explanation we could think of was that the bodies had been carefully cleaned just before they were dumped.

While this was possible, the medical examiner told us it would be very difficult to do. Sometimes small fragments or foreign fibers are embedded in the wounds. Yet this time they were not. When I probed, the medical examiner allowed that the bodies could possibly have been cleaned with a high pressure sprayer or something similar. He couldn't say that for sure, but there was tissue damage that might be consistent with that. When I asked what else could do the same damage, he couldn't think of anything.

After that, Hoagie and I began referring to our "unsub" as Mister Clean when we were talking together. We even put this clean victim factor out on the networks and got several responses. Yet none of them worked out and together they didn't make a pattern. The MOs varied widely as did the victim profiles. I suppose this could have been a result of television shows like the *CSI* series that goes into great detail about forensic evidence.

This is what Hoagie and I were talking about when my cell phone rang. I knew right away it was Jeanne by the sound of the ring and wondered why she was calling. We had talked just a couple of hours before and she knew I had a meeting with Hoagie to discuss the case.

When she answered my call her voice was different and I knew right away that something was wrong. "You have a letter from a law office in Little Rock," she told me. She read the name of the firm but I didn't recognize it.

I wondered why she'd called but I didn't ask. "Put it in my inbox, sweetheart, and I'll look at it when I get home. It can't be that urgent." I had a pretty good idea who it was from but I didn't say anything.

There was a long pause. Then she said, "I don't think it's from a law office."

When I asked why not, she replied, "The postage is two stamps, not a postage meter. One is a first class stamp—the old one—and the other is a penny stamp."

"It must be a small office," I said lightly. "A one-horse operation."

There was another long pause. "I did a bad thing, Jazz. I thought it might be something important and I opened it."

"That's no big deal, Jeanne. You've opened my mail for a long time. What's wrong?"

"I think it's from her, your Queen of Spades."

I didn't like the way she said that. She sounded jealous and jealousy is something I had never experienced with her before. I didn't know how to respond, so I asked, "How do you know?"

"By what it says." She read it to me. "'Saw your message. Too much is at stake. How can I trust you? Q' She also put a queen of hearts on the message before she copied it. Why did she do that? I thought she was the Queen of Spades."

I noticed that the Queen was writing complete sentences, which was a change. "I don't know. I think she was trying to tell us something but I'm not sure. The queen of spades is one thing and the queen of hearts is another. What do you think?"

There was an even longer pause and I was about to make sure Jeanne was still on the line when I heard something. It was a muffled sound, like she had her hand over the receiver and I realized Jeanne was crying. "I'll be there as soon as I can," I told her.

"No, Jazz, don't do that. I'm just being a silly woman. You stay there and finish your business."

"You and me is my business," I declared. "I need to be with you as soon as I can. I'm on the way."

"No," she said. "Let me come there. There's some garden club business I need to take care of in Tulsa. Doing it in person will be easier. That's why I started to call in the first place, to let you know I'd be there, but then I saw the letter and opened it."

"I'll call the hotel and tell them you're coming."

"I already did, silly man," she said, and I knew things were all right again, at least for the moment. It was clear we needed to talk but for now we were pulling in the same direction.

Hoagie had left the office when it was apparent this was a personal call and I found him talking with some of the detectives. They looked my way when I came into the room but I said nothing about the letter. "I've got a hot date in town tonight," I told Zadovski. "Any suggestions for really good Chinese?"

They debated this for a couple of minutes but the consensus was a place called Tulsa Big Wong. "You've got to be kidding!" I said but they assured me it was the truth. It was also true that Tulsa Big Wong was run by the nephew of the owner of two Chinese restaurants in Dallas. One was called Big Wong, and the other, New Big Wong.

I filled Hoagie in on the new letter when we got back to his office. I also told him Jeanne's first response and he nodded. "I understand where she's coming from, Jazz," he told me. "You've been giving the Queen most of your attention. No woman would like that. Have you been talking about the case with her?"

I shook my head. "Normally, I do but not this time. Part of it's the way the case has developed." Then I realized what he was pointing out with the question. "Well, shit! No wonder she's jealous," I said and he nodded.

"I always talked to my wife about my cases," he told me. "I know we're not supposed to, but I did, anyway. She saw some things I didn't and it was one way of keeping her involved in a big part of my life." He grinned. "She kept me up to date on all the gossip at her beauty shop, too, and damned if she didn't know what was going on around town better than I did."

The Tulsa slasher struck again that night. This time it was not in Tulsa, but in Lawton, a small city in the southwestern part of the state. Why the killer chose Lawton is anybody's guess, but the thing Lawton is best known for is its proximity to Ft. Sill, a large military reservation where the US Army has its field artillery school.

It was a week after the Lawton murder that Hoagie and I were invited there for a consultation. We drove down in my Crown Victoria and like my other friends, Hoagie gave me a hard time about my choice of rides. "A white Crown Vic with plain tires? Couldn't you find something that looked a little more like a police car? About the only difference between this and a cruiser is red lights and the leather upholstery." Seeing my grin, he nodded. "I bet you have red lights behind the grille and a siren, too."

I pushed a button and he laughed at the sharp whoop. Then I pushed another button and treated him to the sound of my air horns. "I use that one when someone cuts me off," I told him. He just shook his head.

The investigators in Lawton were glad to see us. One of them had attended one of my workshops and I remembered him well. He was another one of those who asked good questions. His partner was a bit reserved at first, perhaps expecting me to strut around like a Prussian general, but he warmed up soon enough.

I suggested it might be helpful if they gave us an overview of the case. I told them I was just as interested in their impressions as I was in the facts in evidence, and as they spoke I made notes. These were mostly about things I needed clarified. As far as I could see, the detectives had done a thorough job with the investigation and I told them so.

When they were done, there was no question in my mind that it was the same killer. The victim was a young woman in her early twenties of about the same height, build and coloration of the two hookers in Tulsa. She was not from Lawton or any of the surrounding towns and her fingerprints were not on record. Nor did she match any missing persons report in the national system. As a last resort, the investigators ran her DNA through CO-DIS, but no one was surprised when nothing came up there, either.

The closest anyone came to identifying the woman was a pump jockey at a truck stop who had seen a woman of her description having supper by herself the night before the body was found. He remembered her because she had asked for directions to the base. Yet none of the guards at the gates remembered seeing a single civilian woman that night and this was confirmed by their review of surveillance tapes. They were also good enough to check whether either of the soldiers tied to the Tulsa victims had been at Ft. Sill, but both had been with their unit in Utah continuously.

Since he had been the last known person to see the woman alive, the local investigators gave the truck stop worker a hard look. They discovered quite a lot about the man that was not generally known, but his alibi was ironclad. He was on an early release program from prison and was wearing an ankle tracker. The GPS in the tracker showed the man had not been within two miles of the place where the body was found. Nor was his crime consistent with serial murder. He had been convicted of bootlegging. That may sound like something out of the Prohibition era of the thirties, but there are still dry counties in Oklahoma and Texas, and bootlegging is still in the criminal code.

The most convincing evidence that it was the same killer, however, was the condition of the victim's body. The medical examiner was certain the perpetrator was left-handed and the wound pattern was almost identical to that of both Tulsa victims. There were some small differences, like the normal variation in a person's signature, but both medical examiners were convinced it was the same person who inflicted the wounds in all three victims.

One odd difference between these cases was that the Lawton killer had chosen to display his victim in a cemetery. Nor was the body arranged like the Queen of Spade's victim. This victim was carefully laid out against the largest monument in the cemetery, much like the bodies had been arranged in Tulsa. Once again, there was a queen of spades card between the victim's mutilated breasts and there was also a toe missing.

Fortunately, the media had not heard the grisly details of the Lawton killing. It was an off duty policeman who found the body and he knew enough to call the investigators directly by cell phone and to keep his mouth shut. The police were able to seal off the cemetery quickly and the crime scene was not visible from the road. So the incident was contained for the moment. The local paper had done a story about the murder but had accepted the transient murder theory that was offered. All the police were holding back was the fact that this transient murder might be connected to others, and the brutal details of how it was done.

There were some other consistencies with the Tulsa slashings. One was that the Lawton victim had been murdered somewhere else before the body was displayed in the cemetery. Like the others the body had also been carefully cleaned and there was almost no trace evidence. Nor did we ever discover where any of these killings had been done.

One thing that was different was that the body had been in cold storage, frozen. Some of the internal organs still held ice crystals when the medical examiner did the autopsy. Consequently, there was no way to estimate when the victim died. There was no freezer burn, but this could mean that the body was either tightly wrapped or that it was not frozen that long. The point is that this victim could have been killed *before* the two in Tulsa. The pump jockey had not been able to positively identify the Lawton victim as the woman who had asked for directions.

The fact that the victim had been killed somewhere else and that the body had been frozen also made the case less pressing for the local police. The information was passed along to the local paper as part of a case update, and the subsequent story focused on this. It gave even more credence to the transient killer theory and the owner of the paper was glad to be able to give his friends and neighbors some reassurance. Of course, anyone who really thought about it much would not have been reassured at all.

The biggest question in my mind was why Lawton had been chosen for a dumping ground. The local investigators had wondered this, too. The town is about eighty-five miles southwest of Oklahoma City, putting it almost two hundred miles from Tulsa. All of this was by freeway and could easily be traveled in three hours, even keeping close to the speed limit, but this was an extremely long way to haul a victim. It suggested that the perpetrator might live somewhere in between, and it seemed to me that Oklahoma City might be a good place to start nosing around. It was about half way between Lawton and Tulsa and large enough to give the killer a great deal of anonymity.

Starting in Oklahoma City meant looking for our needle in a haystack, but there were large areas of the metropolitan area we could rule out for the time being. It was doubtful that our guy would live in the suburbs, though it was possible. Living in the suburbs requires a level of income I didn't think our killer could sustain. Nor would it be easy to be a single male there without standing out. Suburbs are family turf and it's hard to disappear there or remain anonymous. Transitional neighborhoods in the inner city are much better for dropping out of sight and remaining invisible against the background, and I suspected it would be there we'd find our copycat. As it turned out, I was right, but not in the way I imagined.

CHAPTER THIRTEEN

Blunt Talk

The slasher was torqued. Not that it showed. Anyone who didn't know him well would only see the calm surface of his untroubled face. They might even think he was a bit slow or even retarded. It took him a moment or two to answer even the simplest question, as if he had to puzzle out what the speaker had said.

The truth was that he lived in two worlds. One was the ordinary world of everyday life where he got up in the morning, went to work, and came home to a simple meal late in the afternoon. Nor was it a full time job. Sometimes there wouldn't be any work for several days, but it didn't matter. He was very careful with his money and rarely spent half of what he brought home. All he had to worry about was paying taxes on his place, buying gas for his van, and his light bill, which never ran high. Everything else he might need was bought at the thrift store or garage sales, or salvaged from the stuff people paid him to haul to the dump.

The other world was where he really lived. This was his private world, a magical place where he was king. This is where he spent most of his time, even when he was working. His job was one he knew well from years of practice, and it took very little conscious thought to do it. His hands knew exactly what to do, and even though he worked with razor-sharp tools, he never cut himself. Others did, quite often, but not him. He had no idea why this was but the question never troubled him.

There were intrusions from the outer world from time

to time. Sometimes these were simple, like answering someone else's questions. This was like going to the door to see who rang the bell and what they wanted. He did the least he could to deal with the intrusion and then shut the door on it.

Most of the time this was simple, but at other times it took more effort. Sometimes the Enemy sent agents to his door while he was at home and he had to pretend to be ignorant of who they were. If they were alone, it was simple to deal with them, but if they came two by two, like the well dressed young men from Utah, it could get tricky.

Either way, it was best to act quickly and decisively once he let them in the door and while their backs were turned. He kept a heavy sock partially filled with sand by the door for this purpose and he knew just how hard to strike without killing them. Then he could bind and interrogate them at leisure. He even had a special place for this, the place he used to slaughter hogs for his neighbors. Nor could their screams be heard through the rags he stuffed in their mouths.

Of course, he knew not to leave any evidence of this for the Enemy to find. So when he was done, he hosed them down thoroughly with the high-pressure sprayer his uncle had used to clean the floor. Then he would wrap some of them with heavy black plastic and put them in the freezer under a couple of hundred pounds of pork. Or if there was not enough room in the freezer, he could always cut them up and feed them to the hogs. The whole process took less than an hour and when he was done, nothing was left. Just to be sure there was no way of identifying his victims, he always knocked their teeth out and cut off the tips of their fingers. The fingertips went into the hog feed and he threw the teeth into the river.

Once this was done, he could return to his inner world,

calm and serene until it was time to go to work. He was always surprised how fast time went by there, and it was always sad to leave. There were even times he thought of killing himself so he could remain there forevermore. Yet he never did. Somehow it didn't seem right to leave the outer world behind until he was sent to another place. He had no idea of where this other place might be or whose voice might call him there, but he was convinced that he would know when the time came.

Of course, there were other times the outer world intruded and he had to stay there for long periods of time. He became irritable when this happened, though he was careful to never let this show. He knew others thought he was retarded and this made him laugh inside. Let him get them in his special chair and see if they laughed then. He liked to imagine what this would be like, particularly with the women. They acted like they were too good for him, just like the hookers did before he showed them the money. They sure didn't laugh after that, and just to teach them a lesson, he made them each watch as he mutilated the other.

As bad as the hookers were, they didn't compare to that other whore, the one who called herself the Queen of Spades. That's who he'd like to get his hands on. The gall she had, coming after him! She wasn't even a cop, either. He didn't know how she came across him, but give him five minutes alone with her and he'd know. He'd know a lot of other things, too, like her tolerance for pain.

Thinking of her tolerance for pain he returned to his magic world and an hour passed while he thought about what he'd like to do to the Queen. There were ways he could make it last for hours, or even days.

❧

Hoagie agreed with me that Oklahoma City was a good place to start looking for our copycat. He had a good friend in the police department there who was willing to help us out. The understanding was that if we caught our killer in Oklahoma City, any arrest would be to his credit. Apparently he was something of a free soul and was always behind the eight-ball with his chief.

We drove up from Lawton that evening and took rooms at a quiet place with a good restaurant where Jeanne and I often stayed. Hoagie called to arrange for us to get together with his friend late the following morning. Having nothing else to do, we found a mall where I could walk some laps while Zadovski browsed a bookstore. When I was done I joined him and was delighted to learn we shared a liking for the short stories of a particular writer who was almost unknown outside his native state.

The detective friend's name was Leland Blunt, though he preferred to be called Lee. When I met him, I understood exactly why he was in trouble with his chief. I had trouble believing he was even a policeman, much less a sergeant.

Lee Blunt looked and acted like a recent refugee from a central European war zone. He was a dark little man, short and wiry, dressed in dirt-stained jeans and a dark flannel shirt. Over this he wore what looked like an insulated vest, even though it was a warm day, and on his feet were grimy work boots that had seen better days. This whole ensemble was topped off with a worn leather newsboy cap that flopped over almost to his ears, and his straight black hair stuck out from underneath at odd angles. Nor did he make it a practice to shave every day.

Yet what struck me at first was the way Blunt acted. He avoided looking me in the eye and mumbled when he spoke, his head turned away as if he was talking to someone else. He was also restless, glancing around here and there as he spoke and his feet were always moving. To me he looked guilty as hell of something and came across as someone on the make.

Hoagie laughed when I told him this later. "Wait until it comes down to a bust," he told me. "You won't believe it's the same man. He's fast off the line and looks them in the eye when he reads them Miranda. You wouldn't think it, but he has the highest conviction record in the force. That's why his chief hasn't fired him."

I was surprised when we met Blunt in the parking lot of a suburban shopping mall rather than at the central police station. I wondered why he wanted to meet us there and asked him. He glanced at me so quickly I wasn't sure I'd seen his eyes and told me he tried to avoid the central station whenever he could. "All those frigging cops!" he said. "Makes me nervous as hell."

Hoagie thought it might be helpful for Lee to show us the most likely areas where our killer could disappear. He told him what we were after was a feeling for the area. "He has to have someplace where he can kill his victims, clean them up and keep them in cold storage," Hoagie said. "So we're looking for a stable base of operations. He has to have access to a house or a building he can afford to keep over a long time and it needs be out of the way."

"An abandoned meat packing plant would fit the bill," I said. "Or an old grocery store with a meat locker. The main thing is that he needs access without drawing attention. I'd guess he drives a pickup with a topper or a trade van."

Lee nodded. "A few places come to mind." He pointed toward his car. "I'll drive."

Seeing the condition of his rusty rattle-trap I offered to let him drive mine. The back seat of his car was cluttered with old coffee cups and fast food wrappers and it looked like the ashtray was full of dead butts. I wasn't sure how clean it might be, but that was not the issue. I'm not particularly squeamish when it comes to a crime scene or searching trashed apartments, but the smell of stale French fries and aging cigarette butts turns my stomach.

Blunt looked at me like I'd lost my mind. "Driving that white Crown Vic would out me in a New York minute," he said. "I might as well take red lipstick and write 'cop' across my face." Then he added, "This old thing may not look like much but it can outrun any cruiser the chief has. A few assholes have learned that the hard way."

Seeing my reluctance to climb in the back seat, Hoagie told me to sit up front. "I don't mind Lee's pet rats," he told me. "What we have to worry about is the Department of Health impounding this wreck."

When I climbed in the car, I was pleasantly surprised. The air was fresh and smelled faintly of wood smoke. Lee looked at me for the first time and grinned. "It's strictly for effect, Jazz. I don't even have to lock the doors when I park it." Later I found out that the food wrappers had been smudged for effect but had never been used, and what looked like a dirty ashtray was filled with wood ashes and smudged cigarette butts that had never been smoked. I've heard of undercover police officers going to great lengths to build a cover, but never to the extent of Lee Blunt.

While we drove I described what the killer we were after might look like and Lee nodded. "Sounds like about half the assholes on the street. Only he ain't no street bum. Knowing he's a lefty is useful. It weeds out about nine out of ten suspects." He chuckled dryly.

When Hoagie asked what Lee had come up with looking through missing persons reports, Blunt shook his head. "Not much. We've got a lot of missing women in the file, but not many who look like your victims. The time frame's not right, either. To fit the ones we have, this asshole would have to have been active for more than ten years."

"That's possible," I told him. "I don't think it's too likely, given the rage he vents on his victims. It would be hard to control but he may be able to do so. I can name you at least a dozen serials who could, and did."

"What a fucking world!" Blunt muttered. "Most of them are here in this country, aren't they?"

I nodded. "By far. Go online and search for serial killers by country. You'll find more in the United States than in the rest of the world combined. The FBI estimates there are more than fifty active right now and the number is growing."

"What do *you* think?" Blunt asked. When he did, he held my gaze.

"I think they're being too conservative," I told him. "There are a lot out there we don't know about."

"And your Queen of Spades is taking them down?" I was surprised at the question, but nodded. "Well, good for him," Blunt said. "We need all the help we can get."

I didn't know how to respond. "That's one way of looking at it," I finally said.

"Aw, hell, Jazz, I know that isn't right. That's how I feel, not what I'd do. Still, I'm glad I'm not the one hunting him. Unlike this asshole we're after, I'd find it hard to give a damn if we ever caught the guy. You figure he's gay? You know, choosing the queen of spades rather than the ace?"

"Just among us girls?" I asked and he nodded. "I think the Queen of Spades is a woman."

"Whoa!" he said. "She must be tied to a victim somehow." I was impressed how quickly he had come to the same conclusion I had.

"That thought occurred to us," Hoagie responded. "She's definitely a lady with a mission."

"God tells her to whack them?" Blunt asked.

"I don't get that sense of it. I don't think she's religious or even crazy at all. I think she's trying to point the police in the right direction so she can retire." I filled him in on the different MOs and why I thought this.

When I was done, Lee whistled. "Sounds like she has access to case files, too. You think she's a cop?"

"We don't know," I told him. "Hoagie thinks so but I'm not so sure. She may be something like a criminalist or someone in the medical examiner's office."

"A darkly dreaming Dexter-ine," Blunt quipped.

"Exactly, but I don't think she's a copycat. It's strange, but I have this feeling I should know who she is."

"No shit?" This time it was Hoagie speaking.

"Yeah," I said. "I meant to tell you about it but we got distracted with the Lawton case. It's been in the back of my mind for several days now, but I can't quite get it."

"I hate it when that happens," Lee said. I noticed that the longer he was around us, the better his grammar became. "I know the best thing is to leave it be and let it come in its own time, but I have a hard time doing that. My mind wants to pick at it and that doesn't help a damn bit."

We spent all afternoon looking at possible places our copycat might hole up. When we left I thanked Lee for his help and told him I'd ride in the back seat next time. He laughed and told us he'd keep an eye on the spots we'd seen. Then he asked us if we were really convinced the copycat was in the city.

"Why do you ask?" I wanted to know.

"This doesn't feel like a city guy to me," he said. "He could be but I get the feeling he's holed up somewhere out in the boonies."

"Any idea where?" Hoagie asked. "That's a wide area to try to cover."

"Yeah, but there are fewer people there and he'll be easier to spot. If it was me I'd be looking at a meat processing plant or one of those places that butchers your game for you. It could even be a taxidermist. The point is, this is seasonal work and it would give him lots of time for fun and games. With those kinds of places there's always blood around and I'd bet a big freezer, too. Don't they freeze the meat after they package it for you?"

Neither Hoagie nor I had any idea. Neither of us hunted but it stood to reason. I made a note to call a game warden I knew to find out for sure. He might also have some other ideas we could use for finding our man.

We told Lee we'd keep in touch and headed for Tulsa. Neither of us was in a mood to talk and we were content to ride in silence. There was something nagging in the back of my mind, pushing against the edge of awareness, and I tried to figure out what it was. It was a memory of something I had seen, but I couldn't recall where or when.

I must have been quiet for a pretty good while because I heard Hoagie whisper, asking if I was asleep. "No," I told him. "I was just thinking."

"That's what I thought. I could swear I smelled insulation burning."

"I have an idea I know who the Queen is," I told him. "It's like I have all the pieces of the jigsaw puzzle but nothing quite fits together yet. I even have a vague picture in my mind but I can't quite make out who it is."

"Can you give me some of the details?" he asked. "That might help."

"Well, we're looking for someone who has access to police information. It could be a file clerk or some officer's wife, but I'm sure it's a woman. Like I told Lee, it could be a lab tech or a criminalist. It's definitely someone who's hiding behind a mask of normality, and I think I may have even seen this person at some point."

"Was this awake or in a dream?" he asked. "Some of my dreams are really vivid. And even at my age, some of them are…quite interesting." He smiled, but there was a bitter-sweet edge to his voice.

I was too focused on the Queen to respond just then. A few moments later I realized he was thinking of his late wife. Yet the moment had passed.

"I *think* who I've seen is an actual person but someone I didn't notice," I told him. "At least, not in connection with the case. Yet I must have noticed them or I wouldn't have this feeling, would I?"

I shook my head and rubbed my temples. "I don't know. It could have been a dream. I've got to stop thinking about this. It's giving me a headache." I glanced at Hoagie and he nodded. Yet there was a faraway look in his eyes and we finished the trip in silence.

୭∘ଓ

She closed the web browser and shut down her computer. Though it was getting late and almost time for bed, she went into the kitchen and fixed herself a cup of tea. This time she chose chamomile, dropping the bag into a cup of water. Her mind was chomping at the bit like a two year-old at the starting gate. But she forced it to slow down, focusing on the cup being heated in the microwave. Only when her tea was done and she was seated in her favorite chair did she consider what she'd learned online.

She knew about the Tulsa slashings, of course, but the one in Lawton was news. The details sent over the police network told her this was the same killer. It also told her this was no simple copycat.

While imitation may be the most sincere form of flattery, she knew this was *not* what the killer had in mind. She was being mocked. For there was no doubt in her mind that the message was to her, not to the police. Using her trademark the way he had, as a grotesque parody, he was issuing a direct challenge. For he was not only telling her that he knew what she was doing, but he was also saying he was coming after her.

She thought about this. The simplest response would be to take the vermin out as she had so many before. It would be a challenge since he would be aware she was stalking him, and he might well get her first. This was a risk she was willing to take, but she had to make sure he was caught if he did. This would be the tricky part and she would need help.

Once again she thought about the odd policeman from Arkansas. She wondered if he might be willing to help her. He was no ordinary policeman, but that could work against her, too. Up to now, there was no way the eradication she had done could be tied to her, personally. At least, there was none she knew about and that was the rub. For if there was anyone who could find a fatal connection she had overlooked, it would be the good Doctor Jazz. Knowing who she was would give him a strong lead and a place to start digging. Once he did, he'd surely find her.

Normally she would have given this more thought, or at least slept on the decision, but the copycat made the situation urgent. She needed help and she needed to act before she lost her nerve. So she booted up her computer again and began to write. When she was done, she once again pulled on surgical gloves and took down the box of untouched stationery.

CHAPTER FOURTEEN

Royal Mail

I drove home to Ft. Smith when Hoagie and I got back from Lawton. I could have stayed the night, and Jeanne said I should when I called to let her know I was on the way. I suppose it might have been more prudent to do so, but I wanted to hold my bride in my arms. I'd only been gone for three days, but it seemed like a month.

It was good to be back and there was work waiting for me on my desk. Word of my recovery had filtered out and two offers for seminars had come in two days before. One was in Florida, thankfully in late January, and the other was in New Hampshire during the summer. I wondered if I could persuade the New England people to re-schedule for late September so we could see the leaves. On the other hand, there was no reason we couldn't take our motor home and simply stay until the leaves were over. Jack McKee had set our RV up with better phone and computer connections than Air Force One, or so he claimed. So I could run my consulting service from almost anywhere.

While I try to keep the business from running me, I sometimes find myself much busier than I want. There was something Sam McKee wanted me to look at right away, so Jeanne and I flew to Washington and spent two weeks there. I did keep in touch with Hoagie while I was gone, but there were no new developments in any of the Oklahoma cases.

There was a letter waiting for me when I arrived home. It was from a law firm in Amarillo, Texas, and it had been postmarked the day after we left home. When I saw it, there was no question in my mind who it was from. The postage was exactly the same two stamps, but this time it was cancelled in Baton Rouge.

Once I'd read the letter, I showed it to Jeanne. I asked her to take a look at it and tell me what she thought. The message was simple. The implications were not.

> Jack, your Q wants to retire. Copy-
> cat is making it difficult. Q is will-
> ing to be the bait but needs your
> help. The price is total amnesty.
> Will you help? What guarantees
> can you give? Please reply ASAP. Q
> needs to act soon.

As always, the message had been photocopied, but this time it was in color. There was no mistaking the red and blue image of the queen of hearts. Nor was there any signature.

"I don't know what to say," Jeanne told me. "The message is pretty clear. She wants your help and she's willing to take the risk of helping catch this copycat. I assume it's that awful slasher in Tulsa and Lawton."

I nodded. "What about the price? She's asking me to overlook the fact she's taken out at least six victims."

"All of them were serial killers, weren't they? She hasn't killed anyone else?"

"Not as far as we know. She may have."

"Then ask her," Jeanne suggested.

"I will, but how will I know she's telling the truth? Even more important, how do I know she'll stop killing?"

"Well, you *can* be fooled," Jeanne smiled. "After all, you married me." Then she turned serious. "You did so knowing I married a serial killer, too. They weren't my crimes but I could have been an accessory. You didn't even bother to ask me that."

"And I won't now," I replied. "Murder is not consistent

with your character, even as an accessory."

"Well, it may shock you to know that several times I considered taking the rustiest, dullest knife I could find and cutting Henry's throat. I didn't but it wasn't because I was afraid I'd get caught. I didn't because it would have meant losing you."

I must have looked doubtful because she said, "It's true whether you want to believe it or not."

"You wouldn't have lost me," I assured her. "I would have picked you up at the prison door."

"Kinky man, into prison sex, are we?" she asked arching an eyebrow, and I had to laugh. "The point is that you're a good judge of character, dear man. You took a chance with me and you took a chance with Zilpha, too. Even though you knew she was guilty."

"Between you and Nelly, I didn't have much choice when it came to Zilpha. Besides, all she was guilty of was petty theft. We're talking multiple murder here."

"No, we're talking about killing snakes, poison snakes," she answered. "That's how I see it. It may be legally wrong, and morally, too, maybe. But I think it's righteous."

I started to argue but she put a finger lightly on my lips and looked at me gravely. "You did ask what I thought. You shouldn't ask if you're not willing to know."

She was right. I did ask. "Well," I told her, "I'll risk it again. What do you think I need to do about this?" I held up the letter.

"I think you need to help her if you can. That means keeping her secret. If you can't do that, then you need to say no."

"I don't know how to do that. Even if I agree to her terms, I don't know how to set it up. I'll need help and I don't want to involve Hoagie."

"Well, it's simple," Jeanne smiled. "You have me."

"Jeanne, we're dealing with a multiple murderer here,"

I said, aghast. "It's too damned dangerous."

She looked at me like a schoolteacher bracing a truant. "I seem to remember you were dealing with a serial killer the last time and you almost got blown up. Are you telling me it's fair for you to take risks like this and tell me I can't? You didn't have to deal with the consequences, Jazz. I did. Have you heard me complain?"

I opened my mouth to argue but there was nothing I could say. Like it or not, she was right, at least about herself. So I did what smart men have done since the beginning of time when confronted with a righteous woman on the warpath. I kept my stupid mouth shut and carefully considered what my wife had said. As things turned out, it saved my life.

ॐॐ

The Queen was nervous. This was not a feeling she was used to now, not for many years. What was behind it was simple fear, but it was fear on two fronts. One source was the copycat, but she was not that worried about him. There were precautions she had taken and these would keep her safe. It was the other source that haunted her. She would rather face a dozen copycats than to let down her guard enough to trust another human being with her safety. This was particularly true with someone she didn't know that well. While she could still back out up to the last minute, she knew she wouldn't. That's what scared her. The die was cast and she'd stick to her decision, come what may.

Even so, the decision might be taken from her. More than a week had passed since she posted the letter. Even assuming the mail had been delayed, the good doctor surely would have gotten it by now. He'd had ample time to reply and his answer should have been in the classifieds already. He could be answering with his silence and she found herself relieved and disappointed, too.

Now time was running out. The only other course that was safe to follow was to go it alone and take action. Unless she heard back from Dr. Jazz very soon, that's exactly what she'd have to do.

Not that she'd been idle while waiting. There were preparations that had to be made either way it went and the research she'd done on the Internet had been fruitful. There was a response to something she said on one of the blogs that caught her attention. The discussion was the original Queen of Spades and one of the postings came from someone who seemed to know more than he should. It was possible that this was a policeman, but she thought not. Something about the way the message was written told her it could well be the copycat.

☙❧

While I recognized that Jeanne presented a strong argument, I still couldn't bring myself to respond to the Queen in any other way than I had for thirty years as a policeman. I saw my job as finding evidence and apprehending criminals, not making decisions about whom to prosecute or not.

I said as much to Forster when I went to talk to him about my dilemma. He listened patiently, as he always did, and when I was done, he thought about it a while. "Didn't you ever make deals with criminals?" he asked me.

"No," I told him. "Never."

"You never let someone off from a misdemeanor so you could go after someone else for a felony? How about your snitches? Did you make deals with them?"

He had me there. Not only had I let a misdemeanor slide, but I had let a lesser felony go to nail a more serious violator. Nor was I alone in this. The practice is quite common in law enforcement and snitches often save up information they have for when they are arrested. They swap the information for a lesser charge, if not for being let off completely.

I told Forster as much and he nodded. "I thought so, but let's take it a bit farther. Don't prosecutors offer people like hit men immunity so they can go after the big players who run the organization?"

"Yes, but I'm no prosecutor. I'm an investigator and it's not my place to make decisions like that."

"Wait a minute, my friend. You're no longer a policeman. You are a *retired* policeman and have no burden of vows taken." He was referring to the oath I took as a new law officer more than thirty years before.

"I'm still a sworn peace officer in Arkansas," I told him.

"That's not exactly true," he pointed out. "You told me they revoked those credentials when you were in a coma. Am I missing something? Have you been reinstated yet?"

I told him I had not, even though the papers were in process, and he continued. "Were I a Jesuit, I'd also point out that you were never a sworn police officer in Oklahoma, just in Arkansas. As I remember, you once told me the reciprocity is very limited."

"You're being very legalistic," I pointed out.

"Of course I am!" he snorted. "We're talking about the law and splitting hairs is what the practice of law is all about. There are no absolutes under the law. Have you never known the law to be morally wrong?"

I thought about this. The man was right and I told him so. The Jim Crow laws of my own beloved Arkansas were a case in point. Enforcing such laws was morally wrong, even though it had been my sworn duty as a law officer. I was fortunate to have never been called upon to do so.

"Your dilemma is not a legal one, my friend," he said gently. "It's a moral one. The question is what course is the most righteous and righteousness has little to do with the law."

"So what's the standard? How do I know?"

"Generally speaking, the accepted standard is the greatest good for the greatest number. However, the highest standard is asking what is the most loving thing to do. When we ask that, we are face to face with God and we may be required to break the law to enable a greater righteousness."

"So helping the Queen, and on her terms, would be the most loving thing to do?"

"I think so," Forster told me. "It would certainly seem the greatest good for the greatest number. On the other hand, my ass is not on the stove. I don't have to live with the consequences. Listen to your heart."

"I was afraid you were going to say that. You always do. I believe my heart is telling me to go for it. That goes against everything I have ever been taught."

Forster nodded. "Righteousness often does. Conventional morality is based on fear, and rightfully so. Without it things would be even more chaotic than they are. Yet, the higher law is the law of love, which sometimes requires us to sacrifice our most closely held beliefs for what is righteous."

"'Seek ye first...?'" I asked.

"Exactly, but the righteousness must be the righteousness of the Kingdom, not the morality of the village." Forster paused and I knew there was something else he wanted to tell me. So I waited and saw him make up his mind. "Jazz, I think this thing is so righteous I'm going to make you an offer that does put my ass on the line. You can use me as a channel of secure communication if you can't do this any other way. Yet, at some point, you are going to have to come face to face with your Queen."

I nodded. "I appreciate it, but you're right. I think it would be better to be directly in touch from the start."

"So you're going to take her offer?"

"Are you kidding?" I asked him. "I'll never hear the end of it from you and Jeanne if I don't."

⊹⊱⊰⊹

There had been no word from the good doctor. Now it was time to act. She had a good idea where the vermin was and she had a basic plan for taking him out. There would be risks because her copycat was no dummy. By now he surely knew she was after him and he would be setting up his own defenses. She had a good idea what these might be and she had plans for avoiding each of them. Yet it would be better for her to force him to engage on her terms, and on a battlefield of her choosing. Nor would it be difficult to get him to do so. The sharpest sword in her armory was patience and, driven as the man was by his own bloodlust, he would never be able to outwait her.

Logging off her computer, she made a pot of tea and began to make a list of things she needed to do. One thing was to find a place where she could set her trap. Right where she was would be ideal, but the farm had been in her family for generations and her fondest memories gathered here. She loved the place far too much to compromise the web of security she had so carefully woven around it. For once she used it as a battleground, she would have to leave forever. She wanted to avoid this if she could.

Another consideration was weapons. She would have to bring a pistol along, though she preferred a knife or her bare hands when she could use them. Most of the time she could not and she smiled when she remembered the first rule of combat. Never bring a knife to a gunfight. She had to assume the copycat would have a pistol and she must, too.

This posed some limitations. Bringing a gun meant the ground she chose had to be within driving distance.

There were several good possibilities and all of them had assets and deficits. She would have to think which would work best and plan accordingly.

Then, too, there was the question of how to let the slasher know where she could be found. It would be best if he thought he had found this out on his own. So she couldn't make it too easy and she couldn't make it too hard. This would take some thought and once again she wished she had the good doctor from Arkansas for a friend.

Logging onto her computer again, she spent an hour going over the plan, trying to work out wrinkles and working out every detail she could conceive. Not trusting memory, she wrote these out, making cryptic lists that would make no sense to anyone else.

To be even more sure, she encrypted the file, using a complex password to limit access. While the code could be broken by someone with the resources of the federal authorities, it was doubtful anyone could make sense of her notes. What they would find is what appeared to be a volume of secret family recipes for cooking southern food.

Thinking of this, she smiled. She wondered what the good doctor might think of the code name she'd given him. It was a compliment, being one of her favorite foods, but she doubted he would appreciate being known as Sweet Potato. Okra was how she referred to herself. Hoagie was called String Bean.

Having done this, she started her web browser and went to the blog she knew the slasher was watching. For the last couple of interchanges he had invited a response via email, but he had been very clever. He'd couched the invitation by extending it to anyone who wanted to discuss the previous thread more, and he had given what she knew was an alias address. Two days ago, using a computer that could not be tied to her, she had begun the process of becoming acquainted. Within the next few weeks she knew he would ask to meet her in person and when he did, she would have him.

ཚ◌ཚ

He had her! At least, he thought he did and he'd find out soon. Someone he was sure was her had responded to his invitation to exchange email. The blogger's handle was Dagwood, and that was the e-mail address, too, but the responses all sounded like a woman. *Or maybe he's gay*, he thought. Well, if Dagwood turned out to be a guy, he'd never make the meet. He'd stand the asshole up!

Or maybe he wouldn't. He had never killed a man before, but why not? A gay man might be like killing a woman and it would give him a chance to perfect his plan, even if it wasn't as much fun. Or if a woman showed up who wasn't the Queen, that would be all right, too. He'd have someone else to play with and leave for the cops. Then it occurred to him that even if his playmate turned out to be a man, he could carve the dude and leave a calling card, just to mess with their minds.

He thought about all this. It wouldn't do to seem too eager. That's what he'd be watching for, himself, someone too anxious to take things too fast. So he'd wait a day or so to answer. No, he wouldn't wait two days. Tomorrow evening would be good enough and when he got her reply he could check out her computer. That was simple enough and if it turned out to be one that couldn't be traced, like his, he'd have a pretty good idea it was the Queen.

Opening a word processing program, the Copycat began to compose his reply. When he had it perfect, he'd cut-and-paste it onto an email and send it out tomorrow evening.

Dashed Plans

The first meet was set. It was possible the young man she agreed to meet was not Tripe, the code name she used for the copycat. This was the disadvantage she labored under. There would be no forgiving herself if she mistakenly killed a bystander. She would rather risk having the perpetrator's blade at her throat, and this made things difficult.

Once he pulled his knife, of course, or whatever he used, he was hers, even if she seemed unarmed. The trick was to see him pull it. Yet it was more than likely he would try to disable her first, either hitting her with a sap, as he had with the Tulsa victims, or by drugging her food or drink. Since they were meeting at a public place, she was sure he would try drugs, if he made a first move at all. He might wait until the second meeting.

Once again she wished she was not alone with this one. The best way to trap him would be by seeing him drug her drink, and if she had it on tape, it wouldn't matter even if he won. She would at least die knowing he would be caught.

Yet she didn't want to die and there was no way to have someone else run the recorder without exposing herself to being caught. She had no doubt she could survive life in prison but she would rather run the risk of being killed.

The only other option she could see was to have someone else play her part while she laid in ambush, but she would have to bring them into the plan. Even if they agreed, there was always the risk the ambush might fail and she would end up with their death on her head.

No, it would be better to take the risk with someone else as the watcher, but who could she ask? Anyone bright enough to consider would see through a bogus plan in a moment. Anyone not that smart would not be reliable. They would be as big a danger to her as to the copycat. She might end up getting them killed, too.

No, it was better to do this alone. Yet there were still some things she could do to tip the balance in her favor. One thing would be to cancel at the last minute, delaying the meeting for at least a week. This would irritate the copycat and might push him into a mistake. At the very least, it would whet his appetite for vengeance.

This would also give her another week to come up with more contingencies and a better plan. There were other things she needed to do, as well. One of these was keeping herself fit and she slipped on shorts and her running shoes.

She was about to leave the house again an hour later when her eye fell on the mail that lay forgotten on the entry table. She frowned when she saw it. There was only the paper and a flyer that had come the day before and she had intended to read the paper once her chores were completed. Yet when they were done, she simply forgot and had started something else. While it wasn't a big deal, she didn't like it. Overlooking details like this on a project could get her dead in a hurry.

She started to leave the paper until later, but something made her stop and pick it up. Without even reading the headlines, she turned to the classified section. When she saw the ad in the personals, she could hardly believe her eyes.

> Queen of my heart. Your wish is my command. By-gones will be completely forgiven. You have my word of honor. Your Jack.

Nor could she believe her response. Dropping the paper, she slumped to the floor and began to weep. For the first time in too many years, she was not alone.

৯৩৯

I was in my study trying to puzzle through a form letter from the Social Security people. Apparently they had not paid me $83.15 they owed me for some reason I didn't really understand. They were going to mail me a check unless I wanted them to deposit this to my account but I had to let them know within ten days. What I found amusing was the part telling me I had a right to dispute this and how to go about doing so. As if anyone would.

I had just put this missal into the file for my CPA when the phone rang. I knew it wasn't Jeanne or the Agency because they have their own rings and I almost let the voice mail intercept the call. Then curiosity got the best of me and I answered, thinking it might be another job.

"Good morning, Dr. Phillips," a man's voice greeted me. It was rich, a pleasant baritone. "I hope you're well."

There was something familiar about the voice though I did not recognize it. Suddenly a face came to mind, a woman's face, and I remembered exactly where and when I had first met her. I also knew she was the Queen, but it took me a moment to figure out she was using a voice changer.

"Hello?" the voice asked. "Are you there?"

"Good morning, Nicole," I said. "It's been a long time." This time there was a long pause on the other end and I wondered if she'd hung up. Not knowing what else to do I plunged on. "I'm well but I hope you are, too. You sound like you're coming down with a cold."

There was another silence followed by a throaty chuckle from the other end. This time it was a woman's voice that responded. "So you've known all along. Silly me.

Why did you decide to take my offer?"

I thought complete candor was best. "I just realized who you were when you called just now. I knew I'd seen you before when we passed in the hall in Tulsa, but there's been a lot of change in the last ten or twelve years. It took me a while to connect Marie the computer analyst with Officer Nicole Tracy."

"Oh, yes, that was me and I remember our lunches. Yet it's hard for me to remember Dickless Tracy these days. You helped her become Nicole Verassi."

Something else tickled my mind. "Yes, there was a strange case down there about then, too. No, it was two or three years later. A surgeon was killed and it turned out he was a serial killer. Not that the police ever admitted it. He was pretty well connected and they stonewalled. It's one of the few cases where I've walked away."

"Yes," she told him. "I remember the case. I was doing the transition to electronic records for the New Orleans PD."

Then I knew something else. I don't know how this happens, but it does and I have learned to trust it. Maybe it was something in her voice, but I knew. "Yes, I always thought it was one of his victims who killed him," I said. "No one ever came forth but that's what I thought."

"I suspect you may be right," she answered. "Look, I don't like doing business over the phone. Too many electronic ears may be listening, including the guy you're after. Is there somewhere we could meet?"

"Well, you know where I live. Would that do?"

There was another throaty chuckle from the other end. "Yes, we could meet there. I'll try not to create such a fuss as I did the last time."

"You were here?"

"Yes. I was the attendant helping the old lady who asked you if it would be all right if she watched."

"I'm glad you want to be friends," I told her and I was

rewarded with another chuckle.

"I'll be in touch, Dr. Phillips," she said, and hung up.

❧

The copycat was livid. How dare the bitch cancel their first meeting? Did she think he was stupid enough to believe such a brainless excuse? Grabbing a boning knife he swore as he savagely attacked a side of beef hanging by the cutting table. Jabbing and slashing, he reduced the side of meat to shreds, calling it every obscenity he could imagine. When he was done, he dropped onto a wooden crate and sat there, breathing hard.

"Shit!" he gasped. "Shit! Shit! Shit!"

Then he realized he'd made a bad mistake. Looking around, he was relieved to discover the shop was still empty. He should have never come to work this morning. He never called in sick but that's what he should have done after he read his email. Now he'd have to grind most of the side of beef into hamburger or sausage, and there wasn't much time before the others arrived.

Throwing the half of beef onto the cutting table, he set to work in a frenzy. Though he was exhausted from his attack on the meat, the bitterness of his disappointment fueled his haste, and when his boss arrived an hour later, he was done. The meat still had to be packaged but there was no evidence left of his savagery.

"My God!" his boss declared when he walked in and saw the copycat sitting there, pale faced and exhausted, his apron splattered with red stains. "You look like hammered shit!"

"I think I'm coming down with the flu," the copycat told him. He pointed to the pile of meat sitting on the packing table. "I did get that side cut and ground but I didn't get it wrapped yet."

Looking at the cutting order, the boss shook his head. The cutting was all wrong, but he didn't say a thing. It was hard to find a cutter as good as this who'd work for the miserable wages he paid. The man was very reliable, too. "You better go on home, boy. You're liable to cut a finger off, the state you're in. Take a couple or three days off if you need it."

The copycat nodded, so weary he could barely make it to his battered van. Yet remembering the email that set him off made him angry all over again. Driving on nervous energy, he made it home and fell into bed.

It was the middle of the afternoon when the slasher woke. His body felt like he'd taken a beating, especially his arms and shoulders, but the rage was gone, at least for now. He knew it would come back soon, like it always did, but at the moment he was at peace. The only thing that troubled him was his lapse in judgment in going to work but he'd covered his ass on that. He was always lucky like that, but he knew he couldn't rely on this. Just when he did was when his luck would turn sour.

As drained as he was, he was also ravenous. Wolfing down a Dagwood sandwich, he allowed himself two beers and half a box of cheese crackers. Then he drove himself into the city, stopping at a cyber café where he checked his email. There were several of these in the city, and free computers at the public library, but he was careful to never use the same one more than twice before using another.

Reading the message that set him off, he felt irritated but not angry like he had been the day before. The family emergency might be real. This would probably mean the woman who logged on as Dagwood and signed her email as Lovelace was not the Queen.

For a moment he considered simply not responding and letting her go. Yet he liked the way she described herself so he could recognize her when they met: slender, blonde, and five-foot four. Those were the ones he liked best and she would make an easy target. Doing her, or him if it was a gay man, would also prod the Queen to action.

Making a decision, he began to craft a response. "Sorry to hear about your uncle. I hope he gets better soon. We can get together when you get back." He signed it Messermann, a German surname which meant "meterman" if you looked it up in a dictionary. Yet there was a darker translation, for it also meant "knife-man."

৵৽

I sat and thought a while after the Queen rang off. There was not much I could do until she called back except try to find a lead on our copycat. So I went back through my notes, looking for anything out of the usual.

All I found were a few odd questions I had about the case. One of them was about the condition of the second Tulsa victim and I called the ME. I caught her in the office, which was unusual, and asked her what I wanted to know.

"Yes, Dr. Phillips," she answered. Unlike people in the police department, she refused to call me anything else. "One of the bodies had been frozen before being displayed. Didn't you see that in my report?"

I told her I had looked for this but somehow had missed it. "Oh," she answered. "I was coming down with something that day. I was sure I dictated that in my report, but maybe I didn't. I'll check and correct it if I didn't. The second victim was definitely frozen before she was found. There were still ice crystals when I dissected her liver and her core temperature was lower than air or ground temperature."

"I also noticed you found some bruises on the back of both victims' heads," I asked her. "Do you have any idea what caused those?"

"Those bruises were on all *three* victims," she answered. "They were all in the same area and all were caused before the victims died. Because all of the women had thick hair, there were not any distinct marks on the skin, and I'd guess that they were made by something heavy and fairly soft."

"You're thinking of something like a home-made cosh, maybe a soft leather one filled with shot?"

"Exactly," she replied. "Only I think you're being too sophisticated. A leather cosh is a concealed weapon. A sock filled with a little sand would do just as well and your man could always dump the sand."

I chuckled. "You should be doing my job," I told her.

"Oh, not for a minute," she told me. "I'd rather deal with a corpse any day. Dead people don't shoot."

I thanked her and hung up. The way she said this seemed funnier the more I thought about it and I was still laughing when Jeanne came in to ask what was so funny. However, she didn't appreciate the dark humor at all. "She's right, you know," Jeanne told me sternly. "The dead don't stick you with knives or throw bombs, either."

"I can't argue with that," I told her. "It's a strong argument for what our Queen's been doing." It was on the tip of my tongue to point out that she was the one who was urging me to cooperate with the Queen. Nor did I like the resentment I was feeling toward Jeanne at the moment. "Maybe I need to be with myself for a while," I suggested.

"Maybe you do," she answered, with more asperity than I'd ever heard from her, and left the room.

I went out for a long walk, taking my cell phone with me. I do my best thinking while I walk. When I'm upset, as I was just then, I find it calming. I couldn't blame Jeanne for feeling the way she did. Were our positions reversed I'd probably be even more vocal than she. I even thought about talking to Forster about it, but I knew what he'd say. As he has told me a dozen times before, when we are resentful, the source of the problem is best seen in the mirror.

My feet took me to a favorite bench along the Arkansas river. It's about two miles from the house and I sat down to rest a while before I started home. Yet watching the water is hypnotic and I stayed far longer than I intended. When the phone rang, it was Jeanne, worried about me. She asked if I wanted her to come and get me.

I glanced at my watch. It was getting late and I told her I was hearing some barbecued ribs calling my name. I added I would be glad to wait if she already had something cooking for supper. She told me that was what was on the grill and they'd be ready in about an hour. She knows her man well and cooking my favorite meal was her way of apologizing for being short with me.

When I got up my legs let me know I'd not been walking enough lately. I was still rubbing out the kinks when my cell phone rang again. Somehow I knew who it was before I answered.

"Dr. Phillips?" the familiar voice asked.

"Why don't you call me Jazz?" I asked. "Everyone else does. Dr. Phillips sounds like foot powder."

She laughed. "I'm a little too old fashioned," she admitted. "Why don't I call you Dr. Jazz, instead?" I allowed as how that might be all right. "The reason I'm calling is to make an appointment," she told me. "I think it's time for us to talk face to face."

"I think so, too, but I think we need to set some ground rules. We can wait and do that when we get together, but I think that needs to be our first order of business."

"Would day after tomorrow be convenient?" she asked. I told her it would. "At your place?" she asked.

I thought about it a moment. Jeanne was planning to be out of town and I didn't want us meeting at the house without her around. "I think somewhere else might be better at first. I think it might be a bit more secure."

"That's a good way of putting it," she agreed. Then she laughed. "You know what this reminds me of?" I told her I didn't. "A couple of cats checking each other out very carefully before coming into claw range."

"I would have said a couple of dogs," I told her without thinking of how it might be taken. She laughed and I suddenly realized the image this might evoke. I started to apologize, trying to clarify, but she laughed again and I found myself feeling very self conscious.

"I'll give you a call about three or so," she said. "We can decide where to meet then." She laughed again. "Two dogs?" she said, snorting, and hung up.

I found myself very unsettled by the call. I looked at my watch and realized I needed to get going to be home in time. So I set off at a brisk pace and as I walked I thought about how I felt. It took me a while to figure it out and when I did, I was even more unsettled. What I realized was that I liked the sound of Nicole's laugh a little too much.

CHAPTER SIXTEEN

First Meet

I was as nervous as a cat with kittens when the day after tomorrow arrived. Jeanne had left early for Hope, needing to take care of business with the lawyer there. From Hope she planned to go on to Monticello and stay over for a garden club event there the following day. This event would go late into the evening and I encouraged her to spend the night there rather than driving into the wee hours alone. I even offered to rent a car and meet her in Little Rock.

To keep my mind off my meeting with the Queen, I went for a brisk walk down to my favorite place by the river. I took along a good book and I was soon completely lost in it. It was a collection of short stories by a well-known British author, all from his time spent in prison, and I found them fascinating. What I found captivating was how civilized British prisons seemed to be. I wondered how long those prisoners would survive in the American penal system.

I wasn't particularly concerned about the time, but all at once I realized it was getting late. I glanced at my watch and saw that it was twenty past three, but I also became aware of someone sitting on the other end of the bench. I looked and was startled to see Nicole sitting there cool as a cucumber and laughing silently.

I looked at my phone, thinking I had missed her call, but I saw it was on. I was so flustered that all I could think to say was, "How long have you been sitting there?"

"About twenty minutes," she smiled. When she did

I had thoughts running through my mind that I didn't want to be there. "You were so engrossed I hated to disturb you."

I wondered if she had any idea how disturbing her presence was to me. Then I remembered my manners. "Please, excuse me," I told her, turning and offering a hand. "It's good to see you, Nicole. It really is."

When she took my hand it felt like I'd touched a live wire. Yet somehow I kept from twitching or jerking it away.

"It's good to see you again, Dr. Jazz." She smiled and I could see in her eyes that she knew what a devastating effect she was having on me. Yet I didn't have the sense she was trying to seduce me. She was simply aware of the tension between us. "It's been a long time, hasn't it?"

"It surely has, Miss Nicole," I replied. She was surprised when I called her that but not unpleasantly so.

"Goodness," she said. "We're being rather formal." Then she shrugged. "Perhaps it's best."

"Perhaps so," I answered. "You seem to have done well. I think being out of uniform agrees with you. You must enjoy what you're doing these days." I immediately regretted my choice of words. I hoped she had taken it as I intended.

"Actually, I'm thinking of retiring," she told me. When she said this I became aware of just how soul weary Nicole was.

"I beg your pardon, " I told her. "I wasn't being tacky. I was referring to your computer business."

She gave me a wry smile. "So was I. There is not much fun to be had for me there these days." Then she frowned and when she did, the day seemed less bright. "Look, Dr. Jazz, there are some preliminaries we need to get out of the way. Then we can speak freely."

"All right, Miss Nicole," I answered gallantly. "I guess we can talk here as privately as anywhere."

"Leave your book and your jacket on the bench. Your phone, too." She slipped out of the light jacket she was wearing and handed it to me. "Check the pockets and whatever else you want," she told me. I did so and found the jacket clean. "Now hand me yours." This time I smiled. I had anticipated this and there was nothing in the pockets for her to find. I handed her my book and she flipped through that quickly, too, taking time to look down the back.

"All right," she said. "Now I need to check you for a body wire. Let's go where there's more privacy. Your stuff will be safe here." She pointed toward a decorative hedge that stood between us and the river. We moved behind it and I saw it was only chin high. We could see the bench clearly.

"Slip your shirt out of your pants," she told me. When I had complied, she stepped close and ran her hands up my back and my sides, and then across my chest. When she was done she checked my arms carefully. "Now I'm going to have to get sort of personal," she warned me. Quickly she ran her hands up and down my legs, then over my buttocks and across my stomach. "Sorry," she said, then ran her hand under my testicles and checked each side. The effect was so electrifying I thought I would lose it.

"I beg your pardon," I told her. "There's no controlling the reflex."

"I take it as a compliment." She smiled and her eyes told me she was telling the truth. "Now tuck your shirt tail in while I'm blocking the view. When you're done, we'll switch places."

She took my place with her back to the hedge and I stood between her and the river. I was glad there were no boats in sight and no pedestrians on the path by the bench. When she nodded I checked her arms and legs first. Then I ran my hand over the back of her sweatshirt.

"Under the fabric, Jazz," she insisted, so I ran my hands over her back, along her shoulders and down her sides. I was surprised she was not wearing a bra, not even an athletic one.

"Check the buttocks, too," she told me and without thinking I slipped my hands under her waistband. Her eyes grew wide but she said nothing. All I found was taut muscles and smooth skin. I removed my hands quickly and started to step back when she told me, "check the front, too. I want you to be as sure as I am." When I flushed, she smiled. "It's all right, Jazz. It's business, not sex."

That was fine for her to say but I was as steamed as a clam. I stepped forward and quickly ran my hands under her top, then over her belly and breasts. There was no wire there, nothing but wonderful soft woman. "All my front," she told me when I was done and I ran the back of my hands over her lower abdomen and between her legs. She shuddered when I did so and blushed. "Sorry," she told me, echoing my own words. "That was reflex, too."

I smiled. "Well, as someone recently told me, it's business, Nicole, not sex."

She chuckled, a deep, throaty chuckle that seemed to touch my soul somewhere very deep. I smiled and turned to look at the river and a moment later I sensed her standing next to me. "Your wife is a very lucky woman, Jazz," she told me.

"I am, too, Nicole," I answered. "We suit one another well and are very happy together." I looked at her and smiled. "I'm glad we're finally on a first name basis."

She chuckled again, but said nothing. We stood there a long time in comfortable silence, watching the river flow. Then I heard her sigh. "We better talk so you can get home to your wife." I nodded and we moved to the bench. Rain clouds were gathering to the west and the light was beginning to fail.

"Are you sure you don't need to let her know you'll be a bit longer? Maybe you should give her a call."

"Actually, she's out of town," I said. "That's one of the reasons I wanted to meet somewhere else."

"Oh, I thought you were protecting her," she replied.

"I am," I said. "Obviously from me." Even though it was business, I knew how I had responded and it felt like I'd betrayed Jeanne.

"Be gentle with yourself, Jazz. It was pure reflex."

"I wouldn't try to sell that to Jeanne in a million years. The fact is, I responded and that means there's something I can't share with her. That troubles me more than you may realize. Besides, I felt it the first time I ever talked to you on the phone. Maybe even when I saw you in the hall in Tulsa."

"So did I, but it won't go any further than this." There was iron in her voice and I knew she meant what she said. Yet I also knew we'd better not spend much time alone together. Iron does have a melting point.

"That's the first rule. The second is that I will not tell you anything that will make you an accessory in any way. When you ask me something I cannot answer without compromising you, I will remain silent. You also need to understand that I will tell you everything I know in one way or another. I may tell you where to look but you must not ask me how I know what I do, or press me for an answer. There are other innocent people indirectly involved who I will not compromise. That's the third rule. We'll work out any others as we go along. Agreed?"

"Absolutely," I said. "So how are we going to catch this asshole, partner?"

For just a moment I thought Nicole was going to cry. It was at that moment I realized just how lonely she was and how isolated she felt. It was all I could do to keep from taking her in my arms to comfort her, but I knew where that would lead. So I took her hands in mine and simply held them. When I did the floodgates let go. She bent over and wept the way I wept when Nellie died.

At some point a passerby came over and asked if my wife was all right. I told the lady my sister had just had some very disturbing news. A few moments after the lady moved on Nicole sat up, wiping her eyes with my handkerchief. "Your sister?" she snorted. "Couldn't you come up with anything better than that, Jazz?"

I shrugged. "I thought it was better than calling you my cousin. They know my wife and the last time I used the p-word there was a hellacious cloudburst."

She rewarded me with another throaty chuckle and a wry smile. "Damn you, Jazz. Why did you have to be so...Jazz?"

The question stunned me. That was one of the first things Jeanne had asked me not long after we met.

❦

The bitch never got back to him. He sent a couple more emails but there was never an answer. Then after a couple of weeks, he sent another. This time an answer came back from the mail daemon. The message told him his email could not be delivered because the address was no good. The bitch had bounced him.

This enraged him, but he didn't fly off the handle like he had with the side of beef. He spotted a potential victim and began a careful stalk. When he saw a chance he took her and when he was through with her mutilated body, he fed her to the hogs. He rarely hunted this close to home. The last thing he wanted was to give the local yokels a mandate to get off their fat asses.

This calmed the raging beast within him, but he still hungered for revenge. How dare the bitch ignore him. If he ever found out who she was, she would pay dearly.

Then he had another thought. There was a way he could really score and his kill would be a long way from home. The only threat he really felt was from that expert from Ft. Smith. So maybe it was time to take out the famous Jazz Phillips, but first he wanted to make the man suffer. He knew exactly what to do to accomplish this.

❧

I was home before dark. Nicole and I spent almost two hours exchanging information and coming up with the basic outline of a plan. We also set up communication protocols. Since there was no way we could cover every possible contingency, we didn't try. We simply covered the basic issues and agreed to a plan we could refine as things developed. We also agreed not to take unilateral action if this could be avoided and to make major decisions together. When we were done it occurred to me that the last two items were the formula for a successful marriage.

One point on which we disagreed was about Jeanne's involvement. "I understand where she's coming from completely," Nicole told me. "If I were your wife, I'd feel the same way." There was a strange note in her voice when she said this but I ignored it and she pushed on. "But I don't know what kind of training she's had, Jazz. You and I are professionals. We're trained police officers. She's not and that could get somebody killed, especially her."

"Oh, I agree completely. On the other hand, she is very competent with logistics. She also knows who to call if we need quick backup."

"No other police, Jazz," Nicole told me, shaking her head. "That's a deal breaker."

"These people are not police," I told her. "They are people I work with from time to time. They are involved in national security." Seeing the look on her face, I added, "They are not CIA or NSA. They are people who do what you have been doing but on a larger scale. They go after dirty multinationals, not individuals. There are some exceptions to that, but very few. You couldn't ask for better backup."

"Are they aware of this meeting?" she asked. For the first time that day she looked uneasy.

"Not at all. They are simply an arsenal I have in my personal quiver," I told her. "They would do just about anything Jeanne asked them."

"An arsenal you have in your personal quiver?" she asked, grinning. I could see that she was about to say something more but then she changed her mind. "They sound like interesting folk, but I think we need to limit our team to thee and me. You can let Jeanne know what's going on but we need to keep her out of the line of fire."

Now I was home and the place seemed terribly empty with Jeanne gone. I was tempted to call Lindy, my sister-in-law, but she's a therapist and would know something was out of sorts. Nor would she give up until I told her exactly what was bothering me. So I ended up calling Forster and asking if he wanted some company.

"Do *I* want company?" he asked. "It sounds to me like *you* need some company. Come on over and I'll beat your ass at cribbage." One of the things I like about Forster is his matter-of-fact use of earthy expression. There is nothing pretentious about the man.

Knowing me as he does, Forster was well aware something was eating at me. Yet he's a patient man and we had been playing for an hour before he picked up all the cards and put them back in the box. "You're no fun," he told me. "I don't know what's going on but your mind's not in the game. What do you need to get off your chest?"

I shook my head. "It's so damned silly."

Forster nodded. "Human behavior usually is. Knowing you I'd guess it involves a woman. Is it Jeanne or someone else? Perhaps your Queen."

"It's the Queen." Without going into details, I told him

about our meeting and about the electricity between us.

Forster shook his head. "I don't know how you do it, Jazz. A youngster would call you a chick magnet, but that's not altogether true. The women you attract are the best. They may or may not be the most beautiful, but they *are* the real deal. We used to call this being authentic."

"I don't know what to do," I told him. "I don't want to feel this way."

"I don't want to feel old, either," he snorted. "When I do I at least I know I'm still alive." He frowned and then continued. "As I've told you before, we don't have much choice over how we feel. It just happens. What we have control over is how we respond. It sounds to me like you have the matter well in hand."

"Well, what do I tell Jeanne?"

"Absolutely nothing!" His response was so intense I almost flinched. "Jeanne already knows how you feel. That's why she's jealous. Don't rub her nose in it. Knowing her, she will come to terms with it fairly soon. Just don't give her any farther cause for concern. That means not acting guilty. You have done nothing wrong, Jazz. You've simply responded as men often do to the right woman."

So I told him about checking one another for a wire. Nor did I omit details this time. When I was done, he laughed. "No wonder you're so consternated! You feel guilty because you enjoyed it and wanted some more." I nodded. "So you found out once more that old Jazz is human. So what? I should be so lucky. I seem to remember your feeling this way when first you met Jeanne."

"That's what scares me."

"For God's sake, man, relax! The point is that you didn't seek this out. When it happened, you stayed within bounds."

"I damned near didn't," I argued. "When I felt her bare butt in my hands I didn't want to let go."

"I would imagine not! You may have skated pretty close to thin ice, but you didn't go through. You saw what was coming and veered away. Trust who you are, man! Trust who you are!"

CHAPTER SEVENTEEN

Bad Day at Little Rock

Trust who you are. That was my last thought before I fell asleep. Nor did I dream, which surprises me, looking back. I lay down, tired from the long walk to Forster's and back, and dropped off immediately. The next thing I knew I was wide awake, aware that something was terribly wrong. I looked at the clock and it was just past three and I got up and checked the house. The alarm was armed and I shut it off before I went outside and looked in the garage. Jeanne's car was not there.

I went back into the house and checked our voice mail. It told me there were no new messages and I hung up. I was about to go back to bed when the phone rang. When I answered, it was Lindy. She had awakened alarmed, just as I had, and her first thought was us. I told her Jeanne was not home yet, but before she could answer, the phone signaled an incoming call. I asked Lindy to hold while I took it.

The call was from the state highway patrol. There had been an accident and Jeanne had been taken to the emergency room in Little Rock. The officer gave me the number to call there and I wrote it down. I thanked him for calling and told him I was on the way. He cautioned me not to drive too fast and end up in the hospital, too.

I hung up without thinking but the phone rang to remind me I had a call waiting. When I picked it up Lindy was on the line and I told her what had happened. I gave her the number at the hospital and she told me she would get the first flight out.

When I called the hospital, they put me through to the ER quickly. They told me Jeanne had been taken into surgery and asked if they had my permission to treat her. I told them to do whatever was necessary and gave the clerk my cell number. I told them I was driving in from Ft. Smith and would be there as quickly as I could.

I keep a bag packed for unexpected trips and I was out of the door within ten minutes. On the way out of town I called Zilpha to let her know what was happening and asked her to look after the house until I got back. Then I called Jeanne's oldest son and asked him to call his siblings. I told him I'd call the minute I knew something.

I was only fifteen minutes out of Ft. Smith when a patrol car came up behind me with his lights on. I started to pull over but the officer pulled up beside me and signaled me to follow. He kicked up the pace to around ninety and I turned on my emergency flashers and unleashed the Crown Vic. It roared to life and it wasn't long before I was a safe two seconds behind the cruiser. When I looked at my watch going through the doors of the emergency room, I had been on the road for one hour and fifty-two minutes. That includes street time to the hospital. Door to door was a hundred and sixty miles.

When I got there the surgeon came out to talk to me and he was not very optimistic. I phoned Lindy and caught her at the airport. I told her verbatim what the surgeon had said. It would be touch and go for at least forty-eight hours, and even then Jeanne might never come out of a coma.

When I got off the phone I saw someone I knew waiting to talk to me. He was wearing an Arkansas Highway Patrol uniform with captain's insignia on the collar. The last time I'd seen him he was still a rookie at the CID and I was surprised he had switched back to patrol.

"Hello, Jazz," he greeted me warmly, offering a hand. "I'm sorry to hear about your wife. What do the doctors say?" I told him it didn't look good and he nodded. "I've got to ask you some questions. It's a rotten time, but I've got to ask."

"Go ahead," I said. I wondered what he needed to know.

"We looked at the car. There was some evidence that someone might have run your wife off the road. Are you still retired?" I told him I was consulting on a serial murder case in Tulsa. "Have you had any threats recently?"

"Nothing at all," I replied. "We had some excitement a couple of weeks ago when some case files arrived in a package we weren't expecting. We didn't know who sent it so I had the bomb squad check it out before I opened it. It was embarrassing when it turned out legit. Other than that, there's been nothing."

The captain nodded. "Why did you call the bomb squad? I know it was an unidentified package, but why did you think it might be a bomb?"

"Some of the people I consult with are involved in homeland security. I was almost killed by a bomb doing a job for them. I was in a coma for several weeks."

"Who are these people?" he asked.

"Captain, I can't tell you that. I'm not allowed to because it's very sensitive work involving national security. I don't think this is tied to my work for them, but I assure you they will find out. Can you tell me what happened?"

The captain thought about this for a moment. I knew he didn't like it but I also knew he didn't get to be a captain by bucking the powers that be. "It looks like the crash happened a couple of hours before anyone found the car. We're guessing it was around midnight. She was traveling north toward Little Rock on the four-lane out of Pine Bluff. Her car went off the road at an overpass on a turn. It rolled a couple of times before it landed right side up in a deep drainage ditch. It's lucky there wasn't water in it or she'd have drowned. A little bit after two a trooper spotted the skid marks and investigated and he almost didn't see the car. When he did, he took a look and found only one person in the car. She was behind the wheel and he thought at first she was dead. When he saw she was alive he called for an ambulance and they brought her here. That's when we notified you."

A doctor came out of the surgical suite and walked over to me. "Are you Mr. Phillips?" he asked. I told him I was and he gave me the news. "The surgery went better than we hoped but there was a lot of head trauma. She's in intensive care now and she's on a respirator. She's stable at the moment but we almost lost her twice on the table. I wish I could offer you more hope, but I can't. You can see her now but only for a couple of minutes."

"What about brain damage?" I asked.

"We don't know how extensive it is," he answered. "We do know her neck and spine do not appear damaged, so there is a good chance she will not experience paralysis. With the brain itself?" He shook his head. "We just don't know."

A nurse led me into the area where they were tending Jeanne. When I first saw her she was so bruised and bandaged I hardly recognized her. A respirator was busy keeping her lungs functioning and there were a number of tubes and wires attached to different parts of her body. The only part of her not covered or bandaged was her right hand and I took it in mine. It was cold and felt lifeless. "Hello, sweetheart, it's Jazz," I told her. "We've got a lot of good people looking after you."

There was no response. Nor had I expected one. To me it felt like nobody was home and I wondered if she was gone. The only sign of life was the flickering pulse line on a green monitor by the bed. This told us her heart was beating on its own. The rate seemed a little slow to me but the blood pressure seemed pretty normal.

The nurse patted me on the arm, letting me know it was time to leave. "I've got to go now, sweetie," I told the still face that looked so pale. "I'll be back in a little while."

The captain was waiting patiently when I stepped out of the ICU. "I need to make some family calls," I told him. "Is there anything else you need to know?"

"No, but I need to show you something," he said, taking a plastic evidence envelope out of his jacket. "We found this on the dash." When he held the envelope out I could see it held a playing card, the queen of spades.

"The chicken-shit was stalking her," I said. "I should have known!" It was almost two hours later, getting close to eight in the morning. After calling Lindy and the kids, I talked with the captain for three-quarters of an hour. When he wanted to know more about the case, I gave him Hoagie Zadovski's number. "I'm pretty scattered right now, Steve," I told him. "Hoagie can give you a better picture. Who we're after is a real asshole."

"There was no way you *could* know," Nicole replied when I called her. "I'm the one he's after and I underestimated him. So if anyone is to blame, it's me." She paused and her voice changed. "How is Jeanne?"

"No change," I answered. "I was in with her five minutes ago. You know, the only good thing about this is that Jeanne didn't suffer like the others. We're lucky he thought she was dead. God, if he'd cut her up like them...."

"He didn't," Nicole reminded me. "Hold onto that. It's the reason she's still alive."

"You know, she wanted me to get out of this business. I've almost been killed four times and she was worried about me. I should have listened to her."

"No, Jazz! Listen to me! You're not to blame. Jeanne had a choice and she took you knowing exactly what you do and what the risks were."

"She knew the risk to me, not to herself!"

"Damn it, Jazz! Listen! Am I going to have to come down there and kick your ass from Little Rock to Memphis to get you to hear me? You're being as stubborn as a...mule! " I was stunned by the number of expletives she was able to cram in between "stubborn" and "mule." Then she fired off an even more impressive volley between "get off the" and "self-pity pot!"

"Are you still there?" she asked after a moment of silence.

"I'm in shock and awe," I told her. "You must have been at the top of your class at mule-skinner school." Suddenly I felt very old and very tired. "I'm sorry, Nicole," I said. "I need to hang up. I just now hit the wall."

"Get some rest," she told me gently. "Find the most comfortable chair they have and get some rest."

We laughed about this exchange later, but it was the next thing she said that really touched me. "You and Jeanne will be in my prayers."

I managed to hold on until I got to the chapel. Then I tried to pray and lost it completely. I wept so hard I passed out and that's where Lindy found me two hours later, slumped between two pews.

I woke a week later in a hospital room. At first I couldn't figure why I was there, but when I saw Lindy I remembered. Her face told me all I needed to know. Jeanne was gone.

They never did figure out what happened to me in the chapel. The closest the doctor came to a diagnosis was either a mild stroke or a hysterical reaction to stress. Yet there was no sign of a stroke and when he learned I'd been in a coma after an almost lethal explosion, the doctor shrugged and said it could have been some kind of relapse. He advised me to take it easy and let other people handle things. I thought that was excellent advice and did so.

The next ten days are a blur. I do remember the funeral, which was held at the Episcopal Church in Ft. Smith. Jeanne was a member there and I frequently attended services when I was in town. The curate did the funeral and Forster gave us the words of hope. Yet I found little consolation in these. The unfairness of life ground on my soul, though I was grateful for the short few years Jeanne and I had. I also made myself scarce after a brief appearance at the reception, pleading illness and retreated to my study.

There was no interment since the body which once housed Jeanne was not available. After the autopsy had been done, at my request, the remains were sent to the crematorium. So I never saw Jeanne again after that first visit to intensive care and perhaps that was just as well. That caused some odd complications later on but I was content to remember Jeanne the way she was the day she left Ft. Smith.

Once the funeral was done, I turned the estate matters over to our attorney and arranged for any bills to be sent to the trust department of our bank. I also took care of other things, like arranging for a cleaning service once a week and canceling the paper. The last thing I needed was a daily reminder of how shitty the world can be.

Over the next six weeks, a lot of people came to see me. I am told I was polite but very reserved, almost distant. Even the grandchildren seemed reluctant to approach me and I spent most of my waking hours either in my study or walking by the river. More than once I found myself on the edge of the levee, thinking how simple it would be to just let go and let myself drown.

Eventually the visits began to grow fewer. Then they came to an end and I was relieved. At some time during that period Jeanne's ashes came from the funeral home and I set the urn on a bookshelf near my desk. I had chosen the wood to match my desk and I spent a lot of time in silence, looking at the urn and at Nellie's picture, wondering why I was alive.

Occasionally calls would come, asking me to consult, but I let the answering service take them. Yet I never checked my voice mail box and never returned them. Nor did I bother to turn on the cellular that McKee had given me. When people came to the door, I never answered, and I never checked my email. The only person I saw was Zilpha, who came to check on me every day and make sure I ate the food she brought. Some days I simply forgot, and she scolded me gently. I also made sure I was out when the cleaning service came, but Zilpha was good enough to supervise them, too.

I rarely used my car those days. I walked everywhere I went, mostly to the river to watch the water, and to the assisted living complex to see Forster when I wanted company. For the first couple of visits he tried to engage me in conversation, but when my responses were vague, he got out the cards and the cribbage board. Then we would play in silence, only speaking to call out our points. Later he told me I would always tell him goodbye and thank him for the visit. He added that during that whole time, he never won a single game. This was odd since he'd always won more often than not before.

CHAPTER EIGHTEEN

Gift of St. Nicholas

One day when I was walking to the river it began to snow and I realized several months had slipped by. I looked at my watch, which Zilpha kept set correctly, and saw that it was five thirteen on a Friday afternoon, and the sixth day of the month. Yet I had no idea what month and had trouble remembering the year. When I got home I picked up the phone and called Zilpha. She told me it was December but I was too embarrassed to ask the year.

Later that evening I went out again. It was still snowing and my feet led me to the river where I stood and watched the reflections from lights on the far shore. I thought about my camera, wished I had it with me to catch the light. I even had a title if the picture turned out as I wished: Reflection on St. Nicholas' Day. Yet I couldn't seem to move my feet to go and get it.

I don't know how long I stood there. It was dark when I arrived and I hadn't looked at my watch. Nor could I seem to rouse myself to look. My feet felt cold as ice, but for some reason it didn't bother me. I thought about this a long time. I had read somewhere that death from hypothermia was very gentle once the initial icy shock was over, and I was sure the water I was watching was cold enough to do the trick. Yet I still couldn't get my feet to move.

I don't know when I became aware of the presence by my side. I was so focused on the play of light on the water, and on thoughts of departing this world, it took me a long time to even turn my head and look. When I did so I saw a dark figure huddled in a navy pea jacket with a knit watch cap pulled down over its head. Then the figure turned to look back and I recognized the eyes. Yet I couldn't put a name with it. Then it occurred to me that this dark presence might be the angel of death.

"How long have you been standing there?" I asked. My voice sounded old and rusty and I wondered if the figure was really there. My mind seemed as frozen as my feet.

"A couple of hours," the dark figure answered. "I was afraid you were finally going to do it tonight."

"To do what?" I asked, but I knew the answer.

"To throw yourself in. Your overcoat looks heavier than usual. What do you have in the pockets?"

I reached in my pocket and pulled out a roll of quarters. I did so again and found another roll. Then I found a third and a fourth, and when I reached in the other pocket I found four more. I had no idea where they came from and no memory of putting them in my pockets.

"That's a lot of video games," the angel said, giving me a wry smile.

"It would seem so, wouldn't it?" I answered, recognizing the voice. Yet I wasn't sure whether it was coming from my head or from the figure. I wondered if I had stood here so long I was freezing to death. "How are you, Miss Nicole?"

"Cold as a well driller's ass," she told me and I felt myself smiling. It felt like my cheeks were going to break. "Could we go somewhere a little warmer?" she asked.

"Of course," I answered and tried to turn. Had she not caught me I would have fallen on my face. My shoes were frozen to the ground.

Nicole took charge then. She got me out of my shoes and kicked them loose. Then she started to put them back on but when she saw my feet, she wrapped them in the long scarf that hung around her neck. Then she called a cab, promising a large bonus if they got there in five minutes or less, and she picked me up and carried me to the curb. She told me later I felt no heavier than a small child.

As it turns out, I was lucky. There was no frostbite but the slow process of warming my feet was intensely painful. It was the pain that brought me back, and after a while I began to question Nicole.

"On the shore you said you were wondering if I was finally going to throw myself in," I said and she nodded. "How long have you been watching me?"

"Ever since you came home from the hospital," she answered. "It's been a little over seven months now."

"That long? Where do you stay?"

"I have an apartment in town. I usually stay there unless I'm worried about you. Then I stay here."

"Here at the house?" I asked and she nodded. "How do you keep from running into Zilpha?"

"She thinks I'm a ghost," Nicole said, smiling. "I found your secret hiding place. I slip in there when she comes in while I'm still here. Hasn't she said anything?"

"I don't know," I told her. "I can't seem to remember too much of the last six months. I seem to have been walking around in a daze. The last I remember is going to the hospital and talking to the doctor about Jeanne. Then you and I talked and you told me to get some rest. I seem to remember the funeral but not much else." I wondered what secret hiding place she was talking about but forgot to ask.

"You've been sort of out of it," she agreed. "Are you sure you're back?"

"Nicole, I'm not sure of anything except that my feet hurt and so do my fingers."

"We'll get a doctor to see you tomorrow. I'll stay over."

"I better call Zilpha and tell her I have a house guest."

Then I remembered. "My partner."

"Maybe you'd better explain it's from your consulting. Tell her I'm your gofer."

When I could bear to stand on my feet, Nicole helped me walk around the house a little to get circulation going. I was still chilled, so she put me in a hot shower and stood by to make sure I didn't fall. Somehow this didn't embarrass me. "You're thin, Jazz," she said as she dried me off. "You've lost a lot of weight. Your body still feels like ice."

Nicole wrapped me in fresh towels and led me to my bed. I could see there were fresh flannel sheets on the mattress and a thick, light comforter. "No," she told me. "Don't put on pajamas. You'll warm up faster without them." She helped me lie down and tucked me in. "How's that?"

"I'm still cold," I told her.

"Well, there's something else we can try." She switched off the light and I could see her stripping off her clothes. Then she walked around the bed and got in the other side, fitting herself up to my back like a spoon. "How's that?" she asked.

"Like I died and went to heaven," I told her. Once again I heard her deep, throaty chuckle.

After a while I dozed off. When I woke up I was on my back, warm as toast. The tips of my fingers and toes were still a little tender but it was not that bad. Nicole was propped on her side, looking at me in an odd way. "How are you doing?" she asked softly. I could feel her wonderful breasts against my arm.

"I'm doing great," I told her. "I seem to be reflexing."

"That's odd, I am too," she whispered. "Maybe we better do something about that."

"You know, Nicole, I'm old enough to be your father," I whispered softly. It was early the next morning and we were lying in one another's arms. I looked at her features in repose and was struck by just how beautiful she was. I wondered, not for the first time, why she had chosen to sleep with me. I had no doubt she had saved my life and I was grateful to wake and find her still beside me. Yet I wondered what in the world she could possibly have seen in me.

I decided she must have been moved by pity. Nor did this offend me. I dreaded the moment she would walk out of my life forever, but I was grateful for her presence now. Even more, I was grateful for the way she shared herself with such total abandon. We'd made love like there would be no tomorrow, and in the gathering daylight I realized she would soon be gone.

Then she opened her eyes and the warmth in them told me she would at least be here for the day. Then she smiled and said, "You know, Jazz, I'm old enough to be your lover, too." Then her eyes grew wide and she said, "Goodness, I think you're reflexing again."

A while later she looked at me and said, "You need to know something. You can tell me to leave, and I will, but I will never leave you willingly."

I must have looked dubious because she added, "For such an intelligent man, you can be awfully dense. I fell in love with you when we first had lunch in New Orleans. You were the first man who ever affirmed me, and if you had asked, I would have gladly had your baby. I wish I was still young enough to do so now."

Anything I might have said then was interrupted by the sound of the kitchen door opening. I was out of the bed in a flash and threw on a bath robe. "Good morning, Zilpha," I called. "I meant to call you last night. I have a house guest." I glanced back toward the bed but there was no sign of Nicole.

Zilpha stuck her head around the kitchen door. When she saw me her look of surprise turned into a knowing smile. "A *house* guest?" She asked, glancing at the door of my room. I don't know how women know these things, but they do.

Just then Nicole walked out of the guest room, rubbing her eyes. It's on the other side of the hall from the master bedroom and I had no idea how she got there. I don't know where she found it, but she was wearing one of Nellie's old robes. "Good morning," she said, smiling at us.

I made introductions. "Oh," said Nicole. "I thought you were the airline with my luggage."

Zilpha was not fooled for a moment. "I didn't know you were expecting a house guest, Jazz."

"I surprised him," Nicole told her. "He doesn't answer his phone so I took a chance and flew in. He doesn't answer the door, either, so I let myself in. He was sure surprised when he got home." She looked at me and shook her head.

"I bet he was," Zilpha said. "You're one of his associates?"

"I'm his partner, actually. I decided he's been hiding in his study long enough."

"Amen to that," Zilpha replied. It hung in the balance for a second or two. Then she smiled and nodded. "I'm glad to see someone has managed to get him going again. Are you here on a case?"

"That was my excuse. Mostly I wanted to see for myself how he was doing. Not well, I'd say. He looks like he lost a lot of weight."

I decided enough was enough. "She *is* my partner, Zilpha. Or she was until I went AWOL. Nicole saved my life last night."

"You were down at the river again?" Zilpha asked. I nodded and she looked at Nicole and then back at me. "You're lucky she showed up at the right moment."

I decided that complete candor was best. Zilpha is like

a daughter to me and she deserved the truth. "It wasn't luck, Zilpha," I said. "She's been keeping an eye on me a long time. Several months."

Zilpha looked at Nicole. "How were you able to do that?"

"I decided to retire," Nicole told her. "I was getting burnt out and it wasn't much fun without Jazz around. I decided to make Dr. Jazz my last case."

"Is he all right?" Zilpha asked her. It was clear I had been cut out of the assessment.

"He needs to see the doctor today," Nicole told her. "His feet were almost frostbitten last night."

"My shoes were frozen to the dock," I corrected.

Zilpha nodded. Then I saw her make the connection. "I saw your coat in the kitchen. Did you have all those quarters in your pockets?"

I was pinned in place by the look of both women. "I don't suppose you'd believe I was looking for state quarters for the kids?" I offered.

Zilpha shook her head. "You *are* better if you can lie like that, Jazz Phillips!" She declared. Then she relented. "Why don't I fix us some coffee? We can wait for the airline to show up with your bag."

"I actually have an apartment in town," Nicole told her. "I didn't think he should be alone last night." She shrugged.

Zilpha smiled. "Maybe you need to keep an eye on him for a few more days," she said.

"Amen!" I said and both women glared at me.

That was the beginning of my recovery. There was still a world of grief to go through. The most innocent things could set me off without warning. One day I was cleaning out a pantry cabinet and I came across the apron Jeanne wore the first day she fixed us a meal in what would become our home. It was my old barbecue apron, stained from many years of use and she had teased me about it. Seeing this, I broke down once again, weeping as hard as ever. Yet the weeping never lasted as long as it had the last time, and after a while it was not so intense.

I wondered why I'd not done this before, but I knew the answer even as I thought the question. I would have if I could have, and before I could do anything, I first had to decide if I wanted to live. It had taken almost a year to make that decision and now I had a partner to stand with me in my grief. No one can ever do the grief work of another, but Nicole lent me her strength and provided a warm haven for my battered soul. She tells me I could have done it without her, but thank God I didn't have to go it alone.

☜☞

The bastards set him up. The woman was as good as dead and he was on the way home. When he forced her off the road he thought he saw a second head pop up, but things were moving very fast and he couldn't be sure. Yet when he searched the hillside, there was no sign of another passenger. There were some plush pillows scattered over the car and he decided it was one of those. Checking the woman's pulse, he found it very weak and he decided not to mark her. Even if she lived he could take care of her later. So he had dropped the card and once he was back to the van he stripped off the plastic gloves. After he'd gone fifteen miles, he threw one of them out the window. Ten miles more and he tossed the other one. There were more in a package behind the seat but it was unopened. There were also a couple of greasy ones in the tool box, along with an oil funnel. He could honestly tell anyone who asked that he used them for changing his oil.

It was a long way home from where he forced the bitch off the road and he was tired. A couple of times he almost fell asleep at the wheel, and once he almost ran off the road. This happened about fifty miles from home and a couple of deputies saw it. The red and blue lights went on and when he pulled over, the deputy who came to the driver's door asked him if he'd been drinking. He tried to explain he'd almost fallen asleep, but the deputy told him to get out of the van.

They did the usual things. He was able to touch his nose with his finger and to walk a straight line without stumbling. When he did, the deputies attitude became friendly. "Be careful, son," one of the deputies told him. Then he pulled a half pint of whiskey out of his jacket pocket and took a hit.

"We use it to wake up," the other deputy explained. He cracked the seal on another half pint and offered it to him. "Want a hit, son?"

He tried to explain he didn't drink but the first deputy became surly. "You too good to have a drink with me, boy?" The other deputy jabbed the half pint into his face. Trying to fend off the blow, he raised his arms and the deputy slapped the bottle into his open hand. His fingers closed involuntarily and he found himself holding the bottle.

"Answer me, boy!" the first deputy said. To placate the officer he took a sip and swallowed. Then he gasped as the raw liquor burned all the way to his stomach. The two officers laughed and each took a drink out of the first deputy's bottle. "Ain't so bad, is it?" the first deputy said. "You're wide awake now, ain't you?"

"Yes, sir," he answered. "I'm wide awake."

"That little sip won't get you home," the second deputy said. "You better take another. Make it a big one. That will really wake you up."

Trying not to offend the officers, he did as he was told. The whiskey still burned going down but this time it wasn't so bad. Smiling, the first deputy got up and came close, sniffing his breath. "Earl," he said. "It appears we got a drunk driver here." And before he could respond, his hands were cuffed behind his back. When he tried to protest, the second deputy pushed the open bottle in his mouth and tipped it up and he was forced to swallow or drown. About half the bottle went down his throat and the other half spilled onto his shirt.

"Goodness," the first deputy said. "I'm surprised he can still stand up."

"You're drinking whiskey, too!" he challenged the officers. "And you're on duty!"

"This, boy?" the first deputy asked, holding up the bottle he and the other drank from. "This here is tea. It helps keep us awake."

The judge was no better. Even though it was a first time offence, he was sentenced to eleven months and five hundred dollars fine. Since the sentence was less than a year, he would have to serve it in the county jail. And since he didn't have cash to pay the fine, his van was impounded and sold for pennies on the dollar at the next sheriff's auction. While it was sold to someone else, a week after the auction it belonged to the second deputy. He used it for a fishing van.

CHAPTER NINETEEN

Return to Duty

There came a day when I began to make some calls and to return others. I had decided to retire for good, but I had friends I had shut out of my life far too long. The first call was to Dee, of course, and the second was to Sam McKee and Patrick. Then I called Hoagie, who had gone back to retirement and was trying to keep up with his granddaughter. "Damned if she doesn't out-fish me, Jazz," he said. "She knows the game better than I do and I've been working on it all my life."

"Well, her teacher deserves a lot of the credit for that," I reminded him. "I suspect he doesn't try as hard as he once did, either."

"Winning doesn't seem to mean so much any more," he agreed. "What I enjoy is the game. I'm glad she's still willing to hang out with this old fart."

"Speaking of old farts, it looks like I'm about to be a father for the first time."

"You and Tony Randall," he laughed. "Who's the lucky lady? Anyone I know?"

"As a matter of fact, I'm the lucky one. I'm sure you remember Nicole. You may remember her as Marie."

"The computer whiz? Wow! You just broke the hearts of half the detective force," he laughed. "No shit? Congratulations, Jazz. It couldn't happen to a better man. When did you get married?"

"Well, officially we haven't," I told him. "Now she wants to wait until after the baby is born. I can't seem to change her mind."

"I don't imagine you can," he agreed. "She was always a hard headed lady. She never rubbed your nose in it, but once she made her mind up, that's the way it was."

"There's something else I wanted to ask you," I told him. "Have there been any more developments with the Tulsa slasher case?"

"Not a thing," he replied. "I've monitored that pretty close and there's been nothing even remotely related. Our man seems to have dropped off the earth."

"We should be so lucky," I replied. "What do you think?"

"I don't know. Maybe he tangled with the wrong victim and they took him out. I have lines out in a six-state area but there's been nothing that caught my attention."

"He could be in jail," I said. "Or a mental institution."

"Well, let's hope it's jail. I don't want to see him get off on a plea of insanity. I want him shut away forever. Or given the needle. I imagine that's what you'd like."

"No, I don't see any good in that. It won't bring Jeanne back, or any of his other victims. Besides, it's cheaper to keep him in prison than pay for his lawyers on appeal."

I could almost see Hoagie shaking his head. "You're one of the few cops I know who's against capital punishment. It must get kind of lonely out there."

"Well, you know what our prison system's like," I pointed out. "I think life without parole is worse punishment than killing them. Not many people I know want to stay inside when their time is up."

"Yeah, there's always the hope of a well-placed shank and a long, painful death, too."

Unlike Hoagie and Dee, Sam McKee was not convinced I needed to retire. He was never pushy but he wasn't very subtle, either. One day he and Patrick showed up out of the blue, and when I went to the door they were carrying this huge ice cream cake shaped like Pike's Peak. As McKee told me, if Mohammed wouldn't come to the mountain, then they had to bring the mountain to him.

McKee charmed the devil out of Nicole, of course, and he told me later he thought she would make a great agent. "She has that same quality Willie Dill has. I'd sure hate to get on her wrong side."

"You have no idea," I told him, piquing his interest, but I left it at that. "Right now she's busy having my child."

"That doesn't mean you couldn't look over some documents, does it?" Sam asked. "You won't have to go anywhere," he assured me before I could decline. "I'd either overnight them or send them by messenger."

"Sam, I almost went into a coma again the night Jeanne died. I don't want to risk it. I've been given a third chance and I don't want to blow it. I have a child on the way."

He nodded. "I understand completely, Jazz. The only reason I stay in this game is to make this world a little better for my children." I must have looked skeptical because he gave me his infamous grin. "Who am I kidding? I love it, Jazz. I flat love it, God help me, but there are times I'd like to step down, too. It's like a cold. I'm usually over it in a week."

The next morning McKee and Patrick left. "Are those men the backup you talked about the first time we met?" Nicole asked me. I told her they were, along with a number of others. "Why did they come here?" she asked.

"Sam wanted to see for himself how I am," I answered. "He's also a good friend, but that's why he showed up. He brought Patrick because he survived the same kind of coma I did the last time I worked for McKee. They want to know if I'm fit for duty."

"The serial bomber?" she asked and I nodded, wondering how she knew about that. She gave me a mischievous look. "I still poke around the Internet, Jazz. You have quite a reputation out there. The current speculation is whether you have really retired."

"I hope so," I told her, but there was a lingering doubt that asked what it would hurt to look at some documents for Sam McKee. When I looked at the mother of my first child I saw that she was aware of that doubt, too.

"You're an old fire horse, aren't you, Jazzbeau?" she asked, using her favorite pet name for me. Yet it was more of a statement than a question. "I think the fire bell just rang and the old horse is ready to run. That's all right. Answer it if you need to."

"It got Jeanne killed," I told her. "I'm not going to take that risk with you and Jazz-ette."

"How do you know it's not a little Jazz-beau?" she asked. "Would you be disappointed if it was?"

"Only if he's not like his mom," I answered, giving her a gentle hug. "I love it when you talk Cajun." She answered with a kiss and things got a little intense.

૨૦૭

They were out to kill him. There was no question about it. Six months after they shut him away another inmate came after him with a knife. Nor was it a shank. It was a high quality lock-blade with a double edged point that could gut him swinging either way.

Lucky for him the punk thought he was a weak sister who didn't know how to fight. When the punk grabbed him and tried to shove the blade under his sternum, he seized the punk's arm and diverted the strike into the punk's liver, clamping his hand over the punk's mouth to silence his scream and twisting the blade back and forth to do all the damage possible.

There were a dozen witnesses, all other inmates, but no one would admit they saw a thing. Nor were his fingerprints on the weapon, though the punk's were all over it. All they had was the punk's blood on his jumpsuit but it was the same judge who shut him away the first time who handled the case. When he asked for a lawyer the judge just laughed and sentenced him to twenty years for involuntary manslaughter. The judge also got him placed in the maximum security Cummins Unit in Lincoln County.

That was a mistake. It was at Cummins his luck changed. When he arrived he asked to see an attorney. The request was shuffled back and forth for weeks and nothing was done until a news reporter somehow got wind of his case and asked to interview him. The request was denied and the journalist had a field day, reporting on a prisoner who allegedly was given a twenty-year sentence without benefit of legal defense.

All of a sudden a major law firm was interested in his case, smelling a large settlement for false imprisonment. Such cases are hard to win in Arkansas, but the publicity generated business for the firm and a settlement was reached. He was not released, but he was given a new trial in a different venue.

Almost two years had passed since his arrest, more than half of it in unwarranted solitary confinement, and he was awaiting trial. While he waited he made sure he qualified as a model prisoner. He did what he was told and never allowed his anger to surface. He took it out on the free weights in the hour a day he was allowed to exercise. He also worked out in his cell and was up to a thousand push-ups a day, using only his arms to lift himself and with his toes lightly touching his cell wall for balance. When he was released, as he knew he would be soon, he'd be ready to strike.

છ∞ઉ

Our child was born that fall, a healthy boy who arrived in this world in the early hours of September 7, nine months to the morning Nicole first came to my bed. I was told the poor child looked like me, but he had his mother's eyes and her dark complexion. Next to his mother, he was the most beautiful thing I had ever seen. At Nicole's insistence we named him after me, but I insisted we call him Jack. I also insisted we give him the middle name of Nicholas.

Coming home from the hospital I told Nicole we needed to set a date for our wedding. I was surprised when she seemed reluctant and asked her why.

"We have a wonderful thing already, Jazz," she told me. "I don't want to mess with it. You're on record as Jack's natural father and I could not be more committed. You may throw me out but I will never willingly leave you. We can have Forster bless our union and baptize Jack, but let's leave it at that for now. We can get a license later if there's need."

"I want to give you every legal protection I can," I replied. "Arkansas doesn't recognize common law marriage."

She smiled at me. "Silly man, they have to recognize them from other states. All we have to do is spend a week or two in Oklahoma and sign the register as man and wife."

"Why not make things simpler and get married here?" I asked.

The look she gave me almost broke my heart. "There is no statute of limitations on certain things, Jazz. You know that. I will not do anything to make you an accessory, not even by implication. As much as I would like to be your legal bride, I will never put you in danger."

"We can move to Brazil," I told her. "There's no extradition there."

"Do you really want to learn Portuguese?" she laughed.

"Sweetie, for you I'd learn Russian," I said.

I even looked into immigration to Brazil. The biggest problem was my age, although my financial assets were probably enough to make up the difference. I also talked to Forster about it. He treats everything I tell him as confessional, and has for years, and I'd hate to be the prosecutor who tried to make him break the seal of silence. Forster would hand the prosecutor his head on a platter.

"That's one solution," he said. "On the other hand, there is always the possibility they might change the law. *Ex post facto* might protect you but that's a legal nightmare. At this point in your life, I think a geographical solution would create more problems than it solved. Why don't you live down there for a year or two and then make a decision?"

So that's what we did, though it didn't take a year to find out what we needed to know. After six months we were ready to come home, though it was a wonderful experience. For one thing, we both became fairly fluent in Brazilian dialect. It became our personal language with each other and we rarely lapsed into English. I don't know why, but speaking Portuguese seemed to have a romantic effect on us both, and the biggest reason we came home when we did was for the birth of our second child. She arrived at Christmas, a dark headed little angel who had her dad wrapped around her pinkie without ever trying. We called her Marie Jacqueline.

❧

Taking down the two deputies and the judge had been almost boring, though torturing them had not. None of them had ever seen him coming. One of them had managed to get a hand on his gun and he had been rushed, but the end was the same. When they woke up they found themselves bound and gagged in his special chairs, not unlike condemned prisoners just before they put the juice to Old Sparky.

Once he had the deputies secured, he left them in the darkness of the cellar he used for his dungeon and captured the judge. This was pathetically easy and he made the deputies watch him do the judge so they would know what was coming. He loved to smell the stink of their fear, to see it in their eyes as he first took his pleasure and then slowly emasculated the man. Then he cut the man loose and made him stand at attention before picking up the knife and unleashing his rage.

Once the judge was dead, the slasher carefully placed the body on a sheet of black plastic and carefully cleaned it with the high-pressure washer. Then he wrapped it and dumped it in the freezer, hefting the dead weight like it was no heavier than a small sack of feed. Doing this, he was careful not to let the plastic wrap touch the floor.

"You stink," he told the deputies, taking the sprayer and washing away the urine and offal beneath their chairs. "Didn't your mothers ever potty train you boys?" he asked, laughing. There was no anger in their eyes now, only naked fear. Without warning, he turned the high pressure spray on their genitals, not enough to injure them but plenty enough to hurt.

The slasher laughed, remembering how their bodies clenched against the stout wood. "There," he told them, smiling. "All clean now. Anything you boys have to say to me?" Both deputies shook their heads, terrified. "Then nighty-night, sweethearts," their captor told them. "Sleep tight and don't forget to say your prayers."

❧

Coming home was not without flies in the ointment. There was a tax issue waiting for me, prompted by an overzealous auditor who challenged some of my expense deductions. The tax lawyer took care of that and the revenue people ended up having to pay me more than the attorney's fees. Yet it was stressful dealing with this.

Then there were house repairs that needed urgent attention. Zilpha and the kids had moved in while we were out of the country, so the place was cleaner than when I lived there. Still, the place needed a new roof, the carpet was getting old and several rooms needed new paint.

Nicole and I tried to convince Zilpha to stay in the house after we got home. She told us lovebirds with new children needed all the space they could get. So the best we could do was get her to live in the apartment over the garage. Since we were planning to be in New England most of the fall, she agreed to supervise repainting and installation of the carpet, as well as the roofing, and to remain as housekeeper, too.

Those were all minor things. Another was not and it tempted me to head back to Brazil. It came in the form of a personal visit from the state police captain who had talked to me in the hospital in Little Rock.

The captain came by to warn me of a possible attack. "We found some more of those queen of spades cards," he said. "Three of them, to be exact. Two of them were on county deputies found near Rosston. They were cut to pieces and their genitals were mutilated. The other was on a county judge found near Hot Springs. He was cut up exactly the same way. All of them appear to have been sexually violated and all of them were displayed in different graveyards."

"Were the deputies in uniform?" I asked. He told me they were naked, as was the judge. All were from the same county, one on the Oklahoma border.

I asked some more questions and the answers were all affirmative. "How did you know those details?" he asked. His voice was no longer friendly. It carried an edge of suspicion.

"Except for the sexual violation, those are the exact same things we found with three victims in Oklahoma. The bodies were washed clean, leaving no trace evidence, the slash wounds were made by a left handed perpetrator, there was some evidence the victims had been gagged, and a queen of spades card was left on the victims. Two of the victims there had also been frozen and kept in cold storage, but not long enough to produce freezer burn. The difference, and I think it's significant, is that the other victims were all women and we don't think they were sexually violated."

"One of our victims was frozen, the county judge." He thought for a moment. "You think we're dealing with a homosexual?" he asked. I saw a muscle bulge in his jaw.

"I don't think so. I think the sodomizing may indicate that the killer was angry with his victims. It sounds like a very personal crime, to me, possibly by the same killer as in Tulsa. I suspect the motive in these three crimes is revenge. Do you have a suspect in mind?"

"We are looking at several possibilities," he told me. "It seems like the judge and these two deputies were in cahoots. They had a real sweet game going, arresting people for DUI and then ripping off their assets. There was a case recently where these same three players put a man away for twenty years for murder. They did it without letting him have legal counsel. Didn't you read about that?"

"I'm afraid not. Between dealing with a tax problem and house repairs, I haven't been keeping up much."

"Yeah," he said, his voice more sympathetic. "Then here I come bringing you bad news."

"Not at all," I assured him. "I'd rather have the warning than not." Then I had another idea. "Listen, why don't you phone Hoagie Zadovski in Tulsa? He was the other investigator and I think he can give you more recent information than I can." I gave him Zadovski's office number at the Tulsa PD and his home number, too.

The captain thanked me. "One more thing," he said. "That guy that was sent up without a lawyer is free now. The jury let him off for self-defense. He acts so nice butter wouldn't melt in his mouth but I think he's a nasty piece of goods. You need to watch out for him. Between you and me, he's the one I like for killing the judge and the deputies. You might want to check his picture in the papers. His name's Victor Quentin Shupe."

I thanked him and rang off. Then I went online and looked up the case. When I saw a picture of the perpetrator, a chill went down my back. I'd seen the man recently in Ft. Smith. He was the butcher who handed me my meat that very afternoon. I grabbed my pistol out of desk and made sure there was a round in the chamber. Then I went looking for Nicole and Jack, locking doors and windows as I went.

I found them in Jack's room and told Nicole what was going on. She wasted no time, gathering baby Jack up and following me down the hallway and into my study. Once we were in there, I locked the door and showed her the picture of the man in the papers. When I did, she turned pale. She had seen him at the grocery store, too.

ॐ∽ॐ

The killer was on the road, headed home. He knew the detective had seen him and the woman had, too. He'd made sure they looked at him, going so far as to engage them in conversation. Sooner or later they would put it together and realize who he was and why he was in Ft. Smith.

He liked them knowing. Sooner or later he'd take them out and he liked them not knowing when. Let them stew in *his* prison for a while. He had all the time in the world and could afford to wait. And if he needed to feed the beast in the meantime, there were always lots of unsuspecting targets to feed his hogs.

CHAPTER TWENTY

Manhunt

We got out of town fast. I told Zilpha what was going on and asked her to take her family to Hope. Then I phoned her brother and let him know. He's a policeman with the Hope PD and he said she and the kids could stay there until it was safe to come home. I told him we were mounting a full scale campaign to bring this monster down, but I didn't know how long it would take.

"It could be a week," I said. "Or it could be two or three months. I just don't know."

"You want me to take leave and help you get him?" her brother asked. "I've got a good bit of time coming."

"No, I need you to be sure Zilpha and the grandkids are safe. I do appreciate the offer and I may take you up on it, but right now I'm good for help. I've got to find him first. He was in Ft. Smith but he isn't now."

I knew Nicole had a place somewhere in the Ozarks but I never had been there. When we arrived I was quite taken with it. "Why don't we just move here?" I asked. "It looks like a wonderful place to raise kids."

She smiled. "I had a wonderful time here while I was growing up. It belonged to my aunt and she left it to me. It was a place I could get away from the craziness of the rest of my family."

"You've never said much about them." I wanted to know all about her family, of course, but early on I got the idea that Nicole simply didn't want to talk about her childhood. This made me wonder what had happened. I knew it must have been pretty awful from the little she said.

"I appreciate the fact you never asked much, Jazz. It's very painful to remember. There wasn't much in the way of child abuse that didn't happen to us. One of my therapists called it toxic." She gave me a wry smile. "That's one of the reasons I don't want to marry. You deserve a lot more than damaged goods, Jazz."

"Don't ever let me hear you talk about yourself like that!" I told her. I was surprised at the heat in my voice, and so was she. Yet, I meant every word of it. "You're one of the most beautiful and loving people I've ever known."

"Right," she said, sticking out her index finger and making her fist a pistol. "A real angel of mercy."

"That's right," I told her. "You could have tormented them but you chose not to." This was as close as we had come to talking about her work as an exterminator.

"I think we're getting on dangerous ground, Jazz."

"Are you worried about mistreating our children like you were mistreated?" I asked. She nodded her head. "I'm not." I went on. "We will talk about these things, wife, as often as we need to, and they will not happen again. As your husband, I cannot be compelled to testify against you."

"You're not my husband, not legally. You're my husband in my heart, but not under the law."

"The hell I'm not," I told her, grinning. "We're in Oklahoma now, Nicole. We just moved here with aforethought and the intent to cohabitate. We also consider ourselves wife and husband. That's all it takes here."

She gave me a look that I'd come to know well. "God, I love it when you talk official like that," she told me, molding herself against me. "I think our children need a nap."

A while later I was leaning on my elbow, looking down

into her wonderful eyes. "I think we just cohabitated, wife."

She smiled. "That was my impression, too, husband."

"There is a small issue I need to talk with you about," I told her. "It may be a little late to ask, but how many children do you want?"

"At least a dozen," she said, then laughed. "I wish you could have seen the look on your face. I'll be serious. Two is plenty. I never expected to even have one. And don't worry. The third is not on the way. When we had Marie, I asked the doctor to do a temporary block. We can have it reversed, but she advised against it. I meant to tell you about it sooner but we've had other things on our mind. I hope you're not mad."

I thought about it. "It's your body, Nicole. You're the one who has to make the ultimate decision. I'm your husband, not your master."

"Oh," she said looking disappointed. "You're not into leather and bondage?" For a moment I thought she was serious. Then she laughed. "Gottcha. That's twice in five minutes, Jazzbeau."

"Well, you're not the only one with surprises," I told her, getting off the bed and digging an official looking blue folder out of my briefcase. "Have you ever seen an Oklahoma marriage license?"

Her eyes got as big as saucers and I handed her the folder. She opened it and looked inside. Then she frowned at me and said, "This isn't a marriage license, Jazz."

"No," I nodded. "It's a college annuity for Marie."

"You turkey!" she laughed and nailed me with a pillow. I never could figure out how she knew which way I'd duck. When I'd asked her about it once she shrugged. "I don't know, Jazz, I just do. I've always been able to do that." To demonstrate, she pointed at a grasshopper and picked up a rock. She threw the rock an instant before the hopper jumped. It was a direct hit.

It was about a week after that conversation that we formalized our common law arrangement. Details of these things is almost always printed in a local paper, so we drove to Joplin and flew to Amarillo. There we rented a car and drove up to Guymon, the county seat of Texas County, Oklahoma. We were in luck because the judge was in town and only too happy to do the deed. When he asked what brought us to Guymon, I told him it was a spur-of-the-moment thing. We were in Amarillo and Texas had a waiting period. We gave our home address as Ft. Smith, Arkansas.

That wasn't the real reason for Guymon, of course. I chose it because it was as far away as we could get from where we were and still be in Oklahoma. Arkansas doesn't have a waiting period, either, but I didn't want the killer to know we had married. I was certain he would use the information against us if he could.

Since we were in Amarillo, we drove down to Canyon to see Palo Duro and spent the night in Amarillo before flying back to Joplin. Neither of us had ever seen Palo Duro before and little Jack was fascinated with a horned toad we saw. Marie mostly slept when she wasn't eating or being burped.

After we had been home a week Nicole and I began to talk about ways we could most safely trap the slasher. Since we knew who he was and where he lived, she suggested going on the attack as she had before. As much sense as this made, I couldn't bring myself to consider it seriously. From where I stood, this would be premeditated murder and I simply could not condone that. To me it had to be a clear case of self-defense, and that meant the killer had to make the first move.

I had no qualms about shooting to kill, of course, but only if we were pushed into such a situation. I was also willing to fire first without warning at the smallest hint of a threat. When she asked what that meant, I told Nicole that we could shoot to kill if the asshole set foot on our property or made any threatening move.

I also considered giving Sam McKee a call. He is always strapped for agents, but I knew he'd send the best he had if I asked. Yet then I'd feel obligated to the man and I really did want to retire. I was tired of crime scenes, ballistics reports and autopsy results, and I was getting tired of going after dirty companies, too. Having children seemed like a full-time job to me, a delightful one at that, and I was looking forward to being a soccer dad and attending recitals. I had never had that and watching my grandchildren, I was aware just how much I had missed.

Then, a couple of weeks after we got back from Amarillo, I got a call from Hoagie on my cell phone. He was excited. "We've got the son-of-a-bitch, Jazz!" he told me. "A team is on the way to search his place, and they have a full crime scene team and a mobile lab with them. So if there's one speck of evidence, they'll find it."

"How did you get probable cause to search?" I asked. This had been a problem. On the books our suspect was clean as a whistle and his wrongful conviction made it very difficult to go after him without the appearance of harassment.

"Remember that scam the two deputies and the judge had going? The ones who sent him up for twenty years?" I told him I did. "Well, one of the deputies ended up with the confiscated van our killer had and he never got it back. Then someone dropped the ball and it was never searched until I asked about it. At that point the Arkansas CID impounded it and ran it through the lab. They found traces of human blood, which would have been enough for a search warrant, but they also found a single drop of blood our perp overlooked. It matched the DNA of the second Tulsa slash victim, and that gave us a warrant for the man, himself. A couple of hours from now he should be in custody."

Hoagie had to get going but he promised to call when it was done, and I told Nicole the news. She didn't seem too excited about it and neither was I. We would believe it when we heard back from Hoagie, and even then there was the uncertainty of the legal process. We had both been disappointed by it too many times.

ॐ•ॐ

He was running late. He was rarely on a schedule, but he liked to do the same things at the same times every day. It gave him a sense of order in a chaotic world, and it helped control the beast inside him. He also liked to limit his exposure, and at the moment he was carrying a fresh load of special food for his hogs. Like so many of his victims, this one had fallen into his hands at a rest area on the interstate. Now she lay in the back of his new van, tied and gagged, and he was anxious to get home to play.

Topping a hill two miles from his place, he saw it was lit up like a Christmas tree with red, white and blue flashing lights. Pulling over to the side of the road and turning off his lights, he took out a pair of binoculars, and looked through them. He counted twelve official vehicles. Most of them were police cars but he saw one that was a white van like the one he was driving. Taking another look through the glasses, he could read part of the lettering on the side. It was the medical examiner's crime scene van. The one next to it was much larger and was identified as a mobile lab.

"Shit!" he declared, and then apologized to his passenger in back. That was the strongest expletive he allowed himself most of the time and only when alone. It was certainly not for use in mixed company, not until it was time to unleash the beast. When the beast roared, raging free, obscenity flew liked splashed mud.

Carefully avoiding the brake pedal, he turned his van

around and headed the other way. Once he was over the hill he turned on his lights and headed for his second haven. No small creature in the wild ever allowed itself only one way out if there was any choice. Not if there were larger predators around. He had set up this second refuge years ago and had carefully taken care of it on a regular basis. This, too, was how he found a sense of order and peace in a chaotic world, and when the hunters gave up and turned to other things, he would strike again.

∞∞∞

I knew the moment Hoagie called it wasn't good news. It was something in his voice that told me this, and so it was. "We had everything in place, Jazz," he said. "We had twenty officers and a crime scene crew, and we moved in carefully. We even had a couple of guys with binoculars on a hill watching the place and his truck was there. It was right at sundown and we waited until we were sure he was there. When one of the lookouts saw a light go on in the barn, we moved in fast. He wasn't there. The light was on a timer."

"Rats!" I said, absorbing the news. "It sounds like you made all the right moves, Hoagie. It happens sometimes."

"Yeah, but this dude seems uncommonly lucky. It makes me think the devil takes care of his own."

"Or her own," I said. "On the other hand, bad luck sent him to prison, which is how we know who he is. What did you find when you searched the place?"

"Oh, we found a real slaughterhouse. There was all kinds of blood in cracks in the floor. Most of it was animal but a lot of it was human. It was too much to come from accidental cuts, way too much. It won't surprise me if we get a lot of different DNA samples."

"So the raid was still successful, then. You got plenty

of evidence."

"We got a room full, everything from knives and meat saws to grinders and sausage stuffers," he told me. "The guy ran a custom meat cutting business during hunting season, so a lot of this could be explained, but there was other stuff. There was this chair like a cane chair with no bottom and arm and leg straps just like the electric chair Texas used. It wasn't wired to a power source but there was lots of blood soaked into the wood and I figure it was what he used to torture his victims. Then there was this big thing about the size of a whiskey barrel, only with spaced slats instead of staves. It had blood stains, too, but they didn't look that old. It had hand and feet fetters, too, so God knows what he used that for. I don't care to speculate."

"Did you get any good fingerprints?"

"Oh, yeah, hundreds of them. There wasn't any doubt it was the same guy either. Yet the only reason the guy was in the system was the false bust that sent him to prison. So we did get lucky, there. He was completely clean except for that, not even a traffic ticket. We also got his DNA, but that didn't match anything we have except prison records."

"Well, I hate to sound pessimistic," I said.

Hoagie finished the thought. "Yeah, I know. We probably won't catch him until he kills again. He's probably holed up for a while somewhere we don't know about."

"Take a look at his papers," I suggested. "See if you can't find something that isn't accounted for by the place you raided. I think he's a fairly organized guy most of the time and you may find a tax receipt or something like that." Then I paused. "Listen, I don't know why I'm telling this. You know the moves as well as I do. I'm just itching to get a look at his papers. I think we may find him."

"Unfortunately, the FBI has them," he told me. "Since

it's an interstate investigation, Spinks took charge." I was surprised he seemed so calm about it.

"That means we may hear by Christmas," I said bitterly. "Two years from now!"

Hoagie chuckled. "Yes, but damned if some of his papers didn't get stuck to my foot, Jazz. I found them in an unlikely place, one where Spinks and company never thought to look. Believe it or not they were hidden in the bottom drawer of a filing cabinet in the tractor shed. The top drawers were filled with car parts and junk, and so was the front half of the bottom drawer. I did mean to mention it to Spinks, but I seem to have forgotten."

"Well, shame on you, Hoagie!" I laughed. "What did you find in them?"

"I haven't really looked at the content yet. I made copies and turned the papers over to the Tulsa lab. I thought you and I might look at the copies together. Seems like our man paid his taxes just like any law abiding citizen, and these looked like tax receipts. They're lumped together by year."

"We've got him, Hoagie," I said, getting excited. "I'd bet dollars to donuts we find something that leads us to where he is now."

Tulsa was only a couple of hours away and Nicole decided to come with me. There were some things she wanted for the kids, stuff we didn't have time to bring from Ft. Smith, and I think she was itching to get out of the house. The cabin was perfect for one or two people but it felt cramped for us four. Two little ones take up a lot of cubic space and living in the Ft. Smith house by ourselves had spoiled us.

Hoagie was delighted to see Nicole and he won little Jack over right away with some sleight of hand. I always thought I was good with grandkids, but Hoagie was a master. When it came time to leave with his mother, Jack wanted to stay with us. Hoagie had to bribe him with a promise of ice cream when Jack and the ladies got back.

"You really lucked out there," he told me when Nicole had left. "I always thought she deserved better than that son-of-a-bitch she had for a dad. Did she ever tell you about him?" I shook my head. "Well, I'm not going to tell stories out of school," he continued. "He had a record and it was for some pretty dirty stuff—worse than drugs."

"I take it he's dead?" I asked.

Hoagie nodded but didn't say anything more about the man. "I'm glad she's got a good man and two sweet kids. I was worried about her."

I started to ask him to explain, but the look in his eye stopped me. Then it happened, one of those intuitive leaps Dee tells me I'm famous for making. I realized that Hoagie knew everything I did and maybe more, and that he would never, ever betray Nicole. "I'm glad she has you for a good friend," I told him. "I'm glad I do, too. Now, didn't you mention some papers that stuck to your foot?"

It took us three hours to go through the receipts, but we struck a vein. A subtle pattern appeared that told me we were seeing records from more than the place they raided. When I pointed it out to Hoagie, he didn't see it until I laid it out as a diagram on a sheet of scratch paper. While it could be laid out differently, with different results, I knew we were on the right track. It wasn't enough for a search warrant, but it was a strong lead.

"How do you do that?" Hoagie asked, looking at me like I had just conjured a six-piece brass band from thin air.

"Financial crime is my professional passion," I told him. "That's what I do when I go after dirty multinationals. There is almost always a paper trail. Sometimes it's pretty obscure but it's almost always there. They're too big and that's what sometimes gets them. Too many people are involved and some of them inevitably leave tracks."

He nodded. "Spinks would have never seen that pattern in a million years."

I shrugged. "Yes, but some of his people might. The Bureau has some really good analysts. I've worked with them and they are sharp."

"Yeah, well, I bet it's because you trained them."

"Actually, I did," I told him, earning myself another odd look. "I learned a lot from them, too." I turned back to the papers. "Now the next trick is to figure out exactly where this place is."

CHAPTER TWENTY-ONE

End Game

The house looked deserted. It felt that way, too, like no one had lived there for years. Yet on closer examination it was obvious someone had taken care of it. The tin roof had turned dark but had not rusted and the chimney pipe looked relatively new. All the windows were boarded over and the porch was in good repair, and there was also a power meter still attached to the pole drop.

There were no fresh tire tracks leading from the gate to the front parking area, but we had found a back road in and it had been used since the last rain. Out of habit I'd thought to check on that when we stopped for gas in town. The clerk told me the last good rain had been the week before. "A real turd floater" is how he described it.

"It's going to be hard getting close to the house," Hoagie observed softly. The closest cover was at the main gate fifty yards from the front porch, and where we were at the back, it was close to a hundred.

"I'm not surprised," I replied. "He's kept himself a good field of fire in every direction. On the other hand, that will make it hard for him to get out."

"Not really," Hoagie told me, pointing. There was what looked like a low terrace running from the house into the woods a hundred yards west. "I bet that terrace has another one right behind it. It's not that far to go on your belly."

"His, maybe, but not mine," I answered and Zadovski smiled. My war on gravity is one of attrition and I was obviously losing. "We need someone in the woods at that end and someone at the front."

"Maybe we ought to call for some backup," he suggested.

I agreed. "It would be better if we knew the guy was actually there," I answered. "I hate to cry 'wolf' with him gone. I don't see any sign of a car or a van."

Just then we heard the sound of a vehicle on the dirt drive behind us. I dove to the side, crouching behind a bush as a white van came around the turn. Hoagie had gone the other way and I could see the silhouette of his head clearly even though the was behind a bush. I hoped the driver of the van didn't turn that way and notice.

It looked like we were in luck. The van drove slowly toward the house and circled to the front, and I thought I heard a door open. After a couple of moments I heard it close again but then there was the sudden sound of the engine accelerating to high speed. I realized the driver had only stopped to unlock the gate.

"Shit!" Hoagie swore. "He spotted me. Maybe we can catch him." He started to run in the direction we had parked the car.

"He's long gone," I called after him. "We're almost a mile from the car. Did you get the plate number?"

He stopped. "No, did you?"

I shook my head. "No, it was too dirty."

"Well, come on," he told me, turning toward the house. "At least we can have a look at the place."

"We don't have a warrant," I reminded him. Hoagie gave me an impatient look, but I shook my head. "I think we need a bomb squad. I'd bet he's got the place booby-trapped."

Hoagie looked at me and nodded. It was clear he had not thought of that. "He might. He's slick enough. Are you sure it was him?"

"I couldn't tell for sure. It looked like a Caucasian male but he could have been Hispanic. How about you?"

"Hey!" a voice from behind us shouted. We turned and saw a young man standing about twenty yards behind us, carrying what looked like a pump shotgun. Instinctively I dove to the left and Hoagie, to the right, throwing ourselves flat and pulling out our pistols.

The young man ducked behind a tree. "This here's private property!" he shouted at us. "You better take off before I call the sheriff."

"Call the sheriff!" Zadovski shouted, holding up his reserve officer badge with his left hand. "We're police."

"I can't," the young man shouted back. "I would but my damn phone's dead."

"What's your name?" Hoagie demanded.

"Joe Dan Cozort." The answer came back without hesitation. "Who you?"

"Jazz Phillips," I answered.

"What kind of name is that?"

"That's what I asked my momma," I answered. I signaled Hoagy what I was going to do. He shook his head but I ignored him. "I'm getting up now, Joe Dan. I'm going to come talk to you."

"Put down that pistol, first!" he shouted back.

I walked over to Hoagie and laid my pistol beside him, keeping out of Hoagie's line of fire. "Officer Zadovski has my weapon. Keep the barrel of that shotgun sticking straight up where he can see it."

Joe Dan Cozort turned out to be thirteen years old and once he understood he wasn't in trouble, he opened up. His dad owned the place and one of Joe Dan's chores was keeping an eye on it every day. He carried the shotgun in case he saw a squirrel or a varmint, especially a fox or a skunk.

Joe Dan identified the driver of the van as the man who had rented this place from his dad for years. "He don't come out here much, only once or twice a year, maybe, but he's a nice man. He pays his rent on time and minds his own business. Why do you want to talk to him?"

"Let's make sure it's the right man, first," Hoagie said. He showed the boy a black and white photo, a copy of the one that ran in the Little Rock paper when Victor Quentin Shupe was let out of prison.

"That's him," Joe Dan told us. "What did he do?"

"He killed some people," I told him.

"I thought he got off for that," Cozort said.

"He killed some other people, too," Hoagy answered. "We think it was a whole lot of people."

"Gawd!" the young man declared, making the word into three syllables, as I'm sure he'd heard in church. "He seen you all, you know? That's why he took off like that."

"We need to talk to your dad," I told him, offering him my cell phone. "My phone's working. You can call the sheriff, too." I looked at Hoagie and he nodded. We had enough for a search warrant, too.

❧❧

Victor looked in the rear view mirror. There was no sign of pursuit. He had a good start now and the Oklahoma border was coming up soon. Even if they called it in he would be long gone by the time anyone got organized. There was a place he could hide, a cabin in the woods that wasn't used often. Even if the owners were there now, they were in for an a nasty surprise.

So were the cops who found him. He'd spotted their car parked at the old graveyard a mile from his hideout. The Oklahoma plates had made him suspicious, but this close to the border it could be somebody tending the graves. Yet there was nobody at the graveyard and he saw fresh tracks when he drove by the main gate to the house. So he'd circled around and taken the back road in, keeping a careful watch as he did.

Sure enough, he spotted someone trying to hide behind

a bush and looking back, he spotted someone else. The second one looked like the kid who tended the place, but if the other guy was with the kid, why hide? So he drove on by like he'd seen nothing, and he was sure no one would recognize him. The cab windows of the van were dark and he was wearing a hat pulled low over his eyes.

When he took off, of course, they'd realize it was him and search the place. There was nothing there to incriminate him, except two boxes of dynamite spread around the outside walls in small clusters. Each was set to a trip wire in a carefully selected place, and if one exploded, they all would.

That will teach them, he thought, grinning in anticipation. *That will teach them to mess with me.* He wished he could be there to see it blow up but that was simply too risky. Victor Quentin Shupe liked to watch his victims die, but he hadn't gotten this far by being stupid.

"It was a good thing we ran into Joe Dan," I told Nicole then next morning when I got home. "The whole house was wired with explosives and the boy or his dad could have tripped a trigger just checking the place."

"Not that he gives a damn," she told me. "We need to nail this shit-heel, Jazz."

I was struck by two things when she said this. One was the expression she chose. Nicole does not use earthy expression casually and this told me how angry she was. Yet what distressed me was her saying "we." Call me old-fashioned, but she was the mother of small children and had no business chasing a serial killer.

I knew Nicole would never buy this argument, but I had to run it by her anyway. When I told her how I felt, she gave me a look that would sour milk. "May I remind you, dear husband, that if I had been along one of us would have been watching the main gate. We would at least have had a good chance of catching him. And if it had been me at the gate...."

She left the sentence unfinished but I knew exactly what she was thinking. Had she been at the gate, Victor Shupe would have never made it back into his van. Nor would he have lived to stand trial.

"What if it had been someone else?" I asked. I didn't have to finish the thought, either.

"Give me some credit, husband," she responded. When she calls me that I know I'm in deep caca or have been very obtuse. Yet Nicole never holds grudges, at least, not with me. "I would have made sure who he was. Maybe you're the one who should stay home and watch the kids."

I knew Hoagie would vote with her because she was right. When it came to the skills needed to take down someone like Shupe, I simply wasn't in her class. I suspected she could give Martha McKee a run for the money. Martha is the only one I know who has taken Willie Dill down on his own turf. I know because Willie told me.

"So what do we do with the munchkins?" I asked, though I knew the obvious solution. Zilpha is their second mother and she would gladly help.

Nicole just smiled and raised an eyebrow. She knew I'd thought of Zilpha immediately but she was waiting for me to admit it. "All right," I said. "It's too late to leave tonight but I'll call and let Zilpha know we'll be in Hope tomorrow."

As I said, my bride doesn't hold a grudge once I admit I am wrong. She gave me a smile that raised the temperature of the room five degrees. Once I'd made the call to Zilpha and the kids were down, she proved to me I was forgiven, with gusto.

☙❧

The next break in the case came through identifying

the white van. For some reason, checking with the DMV to see what vehicles were registered to Victor Shupe had been overlooked after the raid on his slaughterhouse. This was quickly corrected after our visit to his hideaway and a seven-state APB was issued.

The break came when an Oklahoma deputy noticed the query we put out about sightings of white trade vans in a fifty-mile radius of the hideaway. He was on the lookout for bootleggers and remembered stopping a white van with muddy plates. Dirty plates was a favorite trick bootleggers used to prevent being identified. Yet, a quick look into the rear of the van showed him it was empty except for a bag of carpenter tools and a duffle bag full of clothes. So he didn't bother asking for a driver's license and let the driver go with a verbal warning to wash his plates.

When the deputy reported for duty late the next day, he recognized the registration number and gave Hoagie a call. Yet there was no knowing where Shupe had gone from where he was stopped. While it was a secondary gravel road, the place where Shupe was pulled over was heavily traveled. From there he could have gone anywhere.

Neither Hoagie nor I thought he had gone that far, so the three of us began to check out different places, staying in touch by cell phone. I didn't like the idea of splitting up, but we could cover more territory that way and it was agreed that none of us would take action without calling in the others. We had to assume Shupe knew what we looked like, so it would be extremely dangerous going in alone.

We searched for three weeks without finding Shupe or his van. I suspected he had probably changed vehicles by now, swapping his van for a truck, but nothing turned up on the hot car list. Nor were any new vehicles registered to him.

Six weeks later we got a lead from a missing person report. A retired widower from Oklahoma City was missing. The last his daughter knew, he was headed for a cabin he used for hunting and fishing, but when his son-in-law drove up to check on him, neither the man nor his pickup was at the cabin. What the son-in-law found was a fairly new white van parked in the barn. He assumed his father-in-law had traded his old truck in, but there were no registration or insurance papers. So the son-in-law copied down the license plate and went to see the sheriff. When the sheriff ran the number, the registered owner was Victor Quentin Shupe. The address on the registration was his place near Oklahoma City.

An all points bulletin was issued for the widower's truck, but there was no response for a long time. Then it looked like we had a hit when the police pulled a truck over down in Muskogee. The elderly lady driving it was outraged at being pulled over by six officers with their weapons trained on her but the VIN on her insurance and registration papers was for the vehicle she was driving. Shupe had simply switched plates with another truck of the same make and color, and we had to assume he had done so since. Sure enough, the elderly lady's plates showed up on another similar truck in McAlester. After that, the trail went cold.

❧❧

Victor Shupe was getting bored. The house where he was staying was more than comfortable and he wondered why the people who owned it never used the place. They kept the power on and there was plenty of propane in the large tank, but it was clear no one expected to be there over the winter. All the windows were boarded up, giving the place the feel of a cave, and the only light came from several well placed skylights.

After breaking in by removing one of the plywood panels covering a window, he discovered the place not only had a small basement, but there was also a tunnel leading from the basement to a detached garage twenty-five yards away. The way it was set up told him this served as a storm shelter, but, more important, it gave him a way to come and go from the place without leaving a trace.

Having discovered this, he quickly replaced the plywood panel and removed any traces of his presence. Then he made himself at home. The place was well stocked with food and a wide variety of videos to watch, and he quickly established a pattern of sleeping during the day and going out only by night when he felt restless.

It was a pleasant existence, but the beast within him began to growl a week after he arrived. Traveling by back roads to Oklahoma City, fifty miles away, he found no end of trusting souls ready for the Reaper, but the problem was how to get rid of the bodies. The last thing he needed was publicity, so he began to look for ways. This did not satiate the beast. Only blood and violence would quiet it completely, and then only for a week or two, but engaging in the hunt did quiet it for a while.

It took him a ten days to figure it out. When he did, he wondered why it had taken him so long. All he had to do was change his methods and his signature, and the cops would think they had another serial killer at work. Then he thought of an even better way, one that would never arouse suspicion.

CHAPTER TWENTY-TWO

Change of Venue

We stayed at Nicole's cabin for a month while the search for Victor Shupe took place. Yet after a while it became apparent he had gone to ground somewhere and we decided to go home. As wonderful as the cabin is, it was simply too small for all four of us, and I missed my study. Or, as Nicole calls it, my retreat.

Zilpha decided to stay on in Hope for a while, which was just as well. McKee had a couple of things he wanted me to research, and that's easier to do in Washington. The Internet is a wonderful resource and could provide much of the information I was after, but it helps to look at the actual documents and to talk to people face to face.

Then, too, the town house McKee provides is spacious and within walking distance of lots of places I liked to go. One is the National Cathedral, run by the Episcopal Church as a ministry to the nation, and another is the mall. I love to go there and walk and Nicole likes to go there with me. No matter how many times I visit it, the Lincoln Memorial always gives me a sense of peace and the Vietnam Memorial across the street never ceases to touch me in a way I find hard to define. Even though I was never outside Saigon and only saw rice paddies from the air, I still find a sense of connection there. Most of these young men and women were part of my generation and had no more idea why we were there than I did. We simply went and tried to do our jobs in a place that made no sense.

Nicole liked the District, too, and after a while she began to do some computer work for McKee. I threatened the man with mayhem and murder if he tried to recruit her to be one of his agents, and he nodded sympathetically. "I know what you mean, Jazz," he told me. "I'm married to one." I also knew his sister-in-law, Martha, had prevailed upon him, too, against his better judgment and was now a special operations team leader. "The point is, that you and I may not have much choice. Angelino tells me she is incredibly good with computer systems, and he's recruiting her very hard."

"I don't mind her doing systems stuff," I told him. "I just don't want her in the line of fire. We have small children."

McKee nodded. "I know. I tried that same argument with Martha and it didn't work. It did with Megan but only because that's what she wanted to do." Then he grinned. "I also blackmailed her. That was the price for my coming back and running this place for her. She's still officially the Head of Agency, you know."

I nodded. Then he looked at me and said, "There's something I've been wanting to ask you, Jazz. Up to now you've had some pretty strong ties to Arkansas. Nicole doesn't seem to be tied there. Am I right?"

"No, there are the grandkids in Ft. Smith, Zilpha's bunch, and a couple of Jeanne's children live around Little Rock, but I actually have closer friends here in the Agency. Dee is the only exception."

"Why don't you move here and continue your work with us? You could stay on as a consultant if you wanted. I think Nicole would fit in well and Michael would be delighted to have her around, even if it was only part time."

The offer was attractive. Nicole had no ties to Ft. Smith but me and Zilpha, and if we moved to Washington, she would have a circle of colleagues as bright, and as competent, as herself. She would also be among people who would understand the life choices she had made, having made some of those same choices themselves. Nor was money an issue. I had been left half of Jeanne's estate and over my objections, her kids insisted that I accept it.

"I'll talk to her, Sam. Our kids could have a lot of opportunities here they wouldn't in Ft. Smith." Then I had a suspicious thought. "You haven't talked to her about this, have you, Sam?"

"Not in so many words," he told me. "I do know she likes the area and she relates well to our people. We have talked about that but not the possibility of her working here."

"Do you think there's any question in her mind that you were not sounding her out?" I asked. "She's pretty sharp."

"I'm sure she knew that's exactly what was going on, but it wasn't me. It was Megan and I know Megan got feedback from our people before she ever broached the subject. She wanted to know the lay of the ground with Nicole before she asked me to talk with you."

I shook my head. "You and I don't have much chance, do we, Sam? The matriarchs are firmly in control."

"They always have been," he nodded, grinning. "They find it convenient to let us think otherwise." Then he became serious. "I know what you're up against with Victor Shupe," he told me. "It's pretty obvious to me that he's after you and Nicole both, for different reasons."

The way he said this told me he was quite aware that she was the original Queen of Spades. He nodded, seeing my comprehension. "We have resources the police don't, Jazz, but we aren't police. I'm not one who endorses vigilante action, but I am a lawyer and I think justice has been served, and served well." Then he added. "I'm not trying to use this for leverage, either. I just wanted you to know I understand the dilemma you live with."

I also noticed how carefully Sam was choosing his

words. No one, recording this conversation, would have more than nuance. "I'm glad you understand our ground rules," I told him and he nodded. "We'll talk about it."

"You also have our resources at your disposal in dealing with Shupe," he assured me. "No strings attached. We owe you more than we could ever repay. You have a team anytime you want it. We're always stretched thin but we'll give you top priority."

"I may take you up on that," I told him. "Oddly enough, I feel much safer here than in Ft. Smith."

Later I would remember these words. When I did I would wonder if it was time for me to be put out to pasture. I'd also wonder how I could have been so naive. I was still thinking the way I'd been trained, like a cop, not like a spook.

⇛⇚

He had watched the house for weeks. Other than the yard man, who came by three or four times a week to check the house, no one was there. Even the black woman who lived in the apartment over the garage was gone. Try as he might, he had not been able to get a line on her. She was a little older than he liked, but she'd do in a pinch.

Nor could he find out much about where the detective and his family were. He knew they had been home, but somehow he'd missed them. It was obvious that someone had been in the house because so many personal items were missing. He knew because he had searched the place thoroughly. The alarm system was no problem and neither were the locks, and he was careful to wear vinyl gloves when he searched. The only place he had not searched was the large fire-proof safe concealed in the study. It required a combination as well as two keys, and search as he might, he couldn't find any of these. Nor could he crack the safe. It was too well made.

He had also found the gun safe, but that was empty and standing open, as was the security safe in the bedroom. It was clear the detective was trying to convince thieves there was nothing of value in the house. Had it not been for the big safe, which he'd only found by accident, he would have been convinced, too. Yet he doubted it could be cracked except by a professional, and he didn't know any of those. At least, he didn't know any except those he'd met in prison, and all of them were still there.

It was the fourth time that he let himself in that he got lucky again. Looking through the top drawer of the desk in the office, he found a small piece of paper jammed into the space between the bottom of the middle drawer and the pencil rack. On it was a phone number, and the area code was 202. Looking in the phone book told him exactly what he wanted to know. This was the area code for Washington, D.C.

He considered dialing the number from the phone in the study, but discarded the idea. Caller ID would identify the location of the call and he didn't want to tip the detective off that someone was in his house. Then he had a better idea and picked up the phone again, but there was no service. At first he wasn't sure what this meant, but it didn't matter. It did tell him that the detective didn't plan on being here for a good while.

Then he realized this wasn't necessarily true. He had probably disabled the line when he disabled the alarm. A lot of them had a radio transmitter for backup, but this one apparently didn't. No cops had arrived after he disabled it and no alarm company trucks, either.

Even so, he had a number and he knew where he could look. Getting there might be a problem. He'd have to drive to bring along any weapons and he'd have to have a valid license in case he got stopped. Yet he knew that wouldn't be a problem, either. All he had to do was to find someone who was the right size and coloration, and who had the same shape head. Nice clothes. a well trimmed beard and a humble attitude, would do the rest.

❧❧

When Nicole and I talked about my conversation with Sam McKee, she told me she'd be happy wherever we both were. We kicked the pros and cons around a while but it became clear neither of us had much attachment to Ft. Smith. All the time I'd lived there, even after I retired, I had simply used it as a base of operations. Nellie was the one with connections to the community, and after she died, I drifted away from the few common friends we had. Then I'd stayed because Jeanne wanted to remain in Arkansas to be close to her children and grandchildren. I had let her take the reins redecorating the house to make it our home, with the exception of my office.

Yet the place reminded me of her and Nellie, too much, I thought. While Nicole had said nothing to me about this and seemed to accept the place as it was, I was aware it was not her nest. As good a place as that house might be to raise children, I thought we needed our own place. I also thought it needed to be much bigger than Nicole's cabin.

The upshot was that we decided to move to the area, and to live in the District until our kids were old enough to begin school. I also wanted to be within walking distance of work, if possible, so we remained in the Agency townhouse while Nicole and Megan scoured the area for a suitable place.

When they found a place, I was astounded how much it cost, even if we could pay cash. Yet both women assured me we would certainly regain our money when we decided to sell it, and buy it we did. Then we remained in the Agency place for a couple of weeks longer while Nicole and Megan furnished the place. When they were done, I was glad I'd stayed out of the process. We had a wonderful, comfortable home, complete with a state of the art security system, and there was even an office for me with a roll top desk and a chair that fit my posterior perfectly.

The only drawback to the place was that we had room for only one car in the garage. There were two stalls but the second was dedicated to storage shelves, now empty, and exercise equipment for Nicole. This was mostly taken up by a huge low-impact running machine that looked more like an industrial metal press, and this was Nicole's retreat.

The other change which bothered me was giving up my old Crown Victoria. There was plenty of room for it in the garage, but eastern city streets tend to be narrow and the big Ford was hard to maneuver in space engineered for smaller cars. Since we only needed one car, we settled for a peppy little Subaru station wagon and I discovered I really liked the sporty feel I got driving it. I wanted to get a white one for safety, though Nicole preferred the red. I suggested we compromise with Mary Kay pink and she just rolled her eyes. So we compromised on a gold one we both liked.

We settled into a wonderful routine with both of us working enough to feel useful and enough time to spend together as a family. One of the innovations the Agency developed when McKee started running the place was day care for its employees, so when we both needed to be at the office, we simply went there as a family. I liked this because I could drop in and visit the kids during the day and Nicole and I could have lunch together.

I also liked the fact that the Agency was near the National Cathedral and I often went there when I felt a need for what I always find there. This is hard to define because I'm not a regular at church, but it has to do with the quiet reverence I find in traditional Anglican churches. Unlike most protestant churches, visiting in the sanctuary is discouraged out of respect for the personal devotions of others. The parish hall is the designated visiting area.

At the National Cathedral, however, on any given day the people in the congregation come from all over the United States. There will also be tourists from every part of the world passing through the outer aisles during worship, but professional ushers keep these folk from intruding. The closest tourists come is about fifty feet from the seating area and the sheer size of the nave seems to absorb the incidental noise the tourists make. The massive silence of the place is also a little overwhelming, too. So visitors tend to speak softly, if at all.

Even when the cathedral is empty, however, there's a palpable presence there that encourages quiet. At least, I find it so and when I am troubled I find it helpful to go and sit there in that wonderful silence. Or, if I have simply pushed too hard without taking time to be restored in body and spirit, that awesome quiet seems to enfold me and give me what I need in a way nothing else can.

Sam McKee often goes there for the same reason. When we run into one another, we normally meet at a local ice cream parlor when we are done. There we mostly hang out, talking about our children and those other things that over the years have built a close friendship. Not least among these are those spiritual interests we seem to have in common.

We were talking about life in the District one day when Sam asked if I knew I was being followed. I started to ask who would be following me, but I stopped and a cold chill ran up my spine. "Shupe?" I asked, being careful not to look around.

"I don't know," McKee told me. "Whoever's doing it is keeping a very low profile and is not getting close. One of my angels spotted someone in the shadows a couple of times but no one was there when she looked." What

McKee calls his angels are highly trained guards responsible for his personal safety. The reason they are necessary is the price that's on McKee's head, and the threat they have to guard against does not come from the lunatic fringe but from professional assassins. Willie Dill tells me their training is even more rigorous than that of the Secret Service, and he should know. One of his jobs is oversight of McKee's personal guard.

The news was very disquieting. I picked up my phone to call home, but McKee stopped me. "Nicole knows. I spoke to her just before I came to find you. Martha and William are keeping an eye out at your place."

"I suppose the bastard knows where I live," I said but McKee shook his head.

"I don't think so," he said. "You've been pretty careful not to go directly home from here."

"Yes, I have," I started to answer. Then I realized he had been keeping me under surveillance. "How long have your angels been watching over me?" I asked.

"Four days," he said. "That was when we first spotted the shadow. We didn't want to alarm you if it wasn't necessary. Today is the second time they spotted him but he got away again. I just found out about it this afternoon myself."

"So that's what the urgent phone call was about as I was leaving the office?" I asked but it was more of a statement than a question.

McKee nodded. "I wasn't able to catch you before you got out of the building." Then he looked at me strangely. "How did you get out, anyway? It wasn't through any of the monitored doors."

I smiled. "Your father-in-law took me out for lunch one day. He didn't realize we were going out an exit I didn't know was there. I didn't know you weren't aware of it."

Nicole was grim when I got home and even the kids

knew something was wrong. "That jerk just won't leave us alone, will he?" she asked me once we got them down. Supper had been one of those challenging times when kids become brats and nothing we did could satisfy them. I knew this was a result of our stress, but knowing this didn't help much. Then at bedtime we couldn't get them to sleep and I had to read and read and read some more before they dropped off. By the time this happened, I was whipped.

Now we were sitting in the living room. At least, I was. Normally we sit together, cuddled on the sofa, but tonight Nicole was too wired. She was pacing the floor like a tiger in its cage, and if Victor Shupe had walked in, she would have torn him limb from limb. It was all I could do to keep her from going out hunting him. "Sam has a team covering us," I told her. "The house is secured and he doesn't know where we live. They would have caught him if he'd tried following me home. The best thing we can do is get some rest."

Nicole nodded but I knew she did not accept what I said. Victor Shupe had evaded us at every turn and I understood her frustration. Her home and her children were threatened and now she was being asked to depend on others for protection. This was neither her nature nor her style and she was ready for combat.

"You get some rest," she told me. "I'm too wound up right now. You can relieve me when you wake up."

Alex Redbone arrived about then and when he saw Nicole, he nodded. "There's no sign of him anywhere within four blocks," he told us. "We have to assume he knows where you are, so I thought I'd wait inside, if you don't mind." Nicole gave him a long, hard look and then nodded.

At some point, I dozed off. Alex and Nicole were talking softly on the other side of the room, so softly their voices were a murmur that seemed to get farther and farther away. Then it was replaced by a series of dreams I did not care to remember, even if I could. When I woke, it was to the smell of fresh coffee, and the kids were already up, ready to rumble. "You look like the wrath of God," my bride told me.

"I feel even worse," I assured her. "Any news? "There was nothing, which was good, and after breakfast I started to feel a little more human. "Where's Alex?" I asked.

Nicole nodded toward our guest bedroom. "I took the last watch," she said. "He said he'd be awake by now." Just then the bedroom door opened and Redbone stepped out, looking as if he didn't have a care in the world.

Over breakfast we talked about plans for the day. Since it would be the safest place we could leave them, Nicole and I decided to take the kids to the Agency day care. I had work to do there and Nicole could catch some sleep in one of the ready team bunks.

Jack was enthusiastic when I told him this and Marie followed his mood, burbling all the way to the office. Yet when we got to day care, Jack was upset at my leaving. So I had to read the whole group two stories before he became bored and fell asleep.

I was feeling pretty punchy myself, so I took the bunk next to Nicole and caught a nap. When I awoke it was late afternoon and she was gone. Nor was she at the office. She had left about a half hour before I woke and had not left word where she was going. This troubled me because I knew what she was doing. She was out hunting, stalking Victor Quentin Shupe. There was no doubt in my mind.

McKee didn't seem too distressed by the news. "I'd hate to be in his shoes," he said. "I don't suppose it would help to point out that she has a lot more experience in this than any of us. She told Redbone she doesn't think he knows what she looks like. I don't think Shupe will recognize her now even if he does," he added. He pushed a few buttons on his computer and the feed from the security cameras showed up on a large screen above his desk. I could see that what we were seeing was taken about forty-five minutes previously.

"Watch closely," he said and I watched the monitor as several people left the building. Three of them were women but none of these was Nicole. I was surprised when McKee stopped the tape. "Didn't spot her, did you?" he asked. "Look more closely." He pressed another button and the video feed started again.

I didn't recognize her this time, either, and it was only on the third time through I saw something. The man who was talking to the ravishing blonde looked vaguely familiar and it took me a minute to realize it was Nicole.

"Don't worry about her, Jazz," McKee told me. "She's with three of the very best we have and none of them is better than her. She went along as a spotter."

"Unarmed?" I asked.

"Nicole is never unarmed," McKee told me. "Even when she's not carrying a weapon. However, I did issue her an Agency ID and our metal detectors told us she was carrying a pistol when she left. The blonde, by the way, is one of our best angels. He takes a lot of guff operating in drag."

"What do you want me to do?" I asked, feeling useless.

"Follow your normal routine," he said. "When you're done here, why don't you join me at the cathedral? There's a sung Compline this evening and we'll have a team covering you all the way."

CHAPTER TWENTY-THREE

Redemption

McKee never made it to Compline. Something broke loose as we were about to leave the office and he had to deal with it right away. He told me he would join me there if he could but it wasn't likely, and I knew he was disappointed. Being able to attend services at the cathedral is one of the perks of the job he enjoys most. He told me once that some days it's the only thing that keeps him from chucking the whole mess of national security.

"It's not the bad guys who wear me down, Jazz," he said. "It's goods guys who get distracted from what we need to do by turf wars. What does it matter who nails the assholes? I know I can get as defensive over turf rights as anyone, but isn't there enough glory to go around?"

I nodded. "I know what you mean. The ones I had the most trouble with were the bad guys in good-guy clothing. Ken Spinks comes to mind."

McKee laughed. "I can name a few of those, too. We weed them out in training camp if they get through screening. What keeps your clock wound, Jazz? You sure don't do this for the money."

"It's the hunt," I told him. He knew I wasn't talking about serial killers, although I do get satisfaction from taking them down. "My payoff comes when we go after Cadre members and put them out of business. I don't even have to be in on the bust, either. What I like most is piecing the puzzle together. Next to that, it's the seminars I do. I like the give and take of teaching."

"Maybe we could use you out at the training camp,"

Sam told me. "Let me give it some thought."

"I'm almost full time now, Sam," I pointed out. "I have a family now, too, and a consulting business. Where would I fit it in?"

He nodded. "I know what you mean." Yet I knew he would come up with something and when he did, I would most likely be interested. He's never a dull man to work for.

Compline that evening was wonderful, and for the three-quarters of an hour the service lasted, I was able to lay aside my concerns. Only when we came to the last part of the rite, when prayers are offered for ourselves and others, did they return. Yet expressing my concern for my bride and our little family made my burden lighter, and when the service was done, I chose to remain, reflecting on the lines from a prayer we had used.

> Keep watch, dear Lord, over those who work or watch or weep this night, and give your angels charge over those who sleep. Tend the sick…give rest to the weary, bless the dying, soothe the suffering, pity the afflicted, shield the joyous, and all for your love's sake.

As I reflected on these lines, I thought about the people in my life, my bride, my children, my friends and colleagues, and even those who wished me harm, and for some reason Jeanne was very present in my thoughts. I thought about Victor Shupe and the harm he had done, taking from me the person whom I loved most in this world, and once again I asked for the grace to forgive the man.

Then out of the blue something struck me. I don't know where such thoughts come from, but I think Forster is right. I think such thoughts, whatever they might be, come from the spiritual realm. Nor does it matter whether these are the voice of God or an expression of a higher self, breaking free. The message is always what I need to hear and it is always right on target.

That night, sitting alone in the cathedral in that awe inspiring space, it struck me that Victor Shupe was no different than the cancer that had taken Nellie, the bride of my youth. There was a reason he turned out the way he did, just like there was a reason for the way Nellie's cells turned against her. Neither made much rational sense in my understanding of the universe. Yet the things that happen are rooted in the choices we make. Nellie smoked for many years, which contributed to her cancer, as did her choice to work in the asbestos plant. I believe that when we become wise enough, there will be a day when we will understand why Victor Shupe began to devour the social body which gave him life, just as the malignant cells devoured Nellie's body.

With this realization came one of the most profound experiences I have ever had. It felt as if all the rancor I held against Victor Quentin Shupe began to slide away, much like a layer of dead tissue sloughing off a healthy body, and I felt a great sense of deliverance and peace descend over me. As it did, the tears began to flow, not with wracking sobs but as gently as a soft rain washing and healing my soul.

I don't know how long I sat there. One of McKee's angels told me it was over an hour before I saw one of the cathedral ushers approaching from behind the altar. The tears were gone by then and I felt whole again, and at peace. So I began to put away the kneeler and replace the prayer book in its rack on the chair in front of me.

The attendant was close by then and I looked up to thank him for his patience. When I did, my eyes caught his and I realized I was looking into the eyes of the man I was after. I also realized he had a knife in his left hand and was thrusting it toward me.

The surprising thing is that I felt no fear, not then nor even later when I had time to reflect. I felt the knife strike, dead center into the prayer book I was holding and lodge there, but I never took my eyes off those of Victor Shupe. Then I said the strangest thing I have ever said to a serial killer, or to anyone else. I said, "You are forgiven, Victor, by me and by God."

Shupe's eyes grew even wider and I saw something I later decided was utter terror lurking there. When he jerked the knife free and raised his arm to stab down I told him, "You don't have to be afraid, Victor. Not any more. You are forgiven."

I have always wondered if he would have tried to strike me then. Strong though he was, I know I could have prevented it striking me, but I don't think this would have happened. My eyes never left his and just for a moment I saw hope born. Then he jerked twice. His eyes grew wide, and I knew he was gone. I grabbed him as he fell and I laid him gently on the stone floor.

When I looked up I saw my bride, her pistol still aimed at what had been Victor Shupe. So I rose and went to her, taking the weapon from her hand, clearing the chamber and laying it on a chair. "It's all right, Nicole," I told her. "It's done." When I said this she began to weep and I held her close as McKee's angels took charge.

❧❦

That was the end of the story for the Queen of Spades. The legal formalities were cleared away quickly, especially once Victor Quentin Shupe was identified and his shooting was ruled a righteous. The only odd note was in the medical examiner's report. Nicole had fired two shots with the .22 but the entry wound was so small that the examiner was surprised when he found two slugs in Victor's skull. He had never seen such accurate shooting from a distance of fifty feet.

Neither had McKee and I am sure he planned to recruit Nicole as an agent. Even so, Nicole laid down her burden, just as I had. She turned in her pistol and told McKee she would be glad to work with his computers or teach unarmed combat at the training camp, but that she would never again carry a gun if she could help it.

Then she and I took a long vacation with our children and spent most of it at the McKee ranch in Wyoming. I suspect that Sam arranged it, but there was always someone there to take care of the children when we wanted to get away for an afternoon by ourselves. Our favorite place to go was a little line shack we could see from the ranch. It was a hard walk up there, but well worth the view, and we spent a lot of time holding each other and making love.

It was there one afternoon when I told her about my personal epiphany and those last intimate moments I spent with Victor. She smiled when I told her this and said, "I knew something was going on. That's the closest I've ever come to hesitating. I'm glad I didn't."

This surprised me and I asked her about it. "I'm not trying to justify it, Jazz. Those shots were righteous, but from what you've told me, I think they were a gift to Victor. He died having hope and I don't begrudge him that, despite the pain and suffering he caused. I think he thought he was beyond redemption, and by human standards he was. Yet, when you told him he was forgiven, I don't think that was just Jazz who was speaking. I'm not sure who it was but I want to find out. Because if there's hope for Victor, that means there is hope for me."

Then Nicole fell apart and I spent the afternoon holding her while she told me what I already knew, from the beginning in New Orleans. When she was done she was exhausted and I phoned the ranch house to let them know we would be spending the night. When I explained that we were just too exhausted to come down, Martha chuckled and I think she thought we were worn out from making love. Come to think of it, that's exactly what we had been doing.

There are some other things I need to set down here before I'm done. One is that Jeanne's sister, Lindy, moved from California to Tulsa and she and Hoagie were married at a quiet ceremony there. We weren't able to attend, much to my regret. One of the kids got sick at the last moment and could not fly.

Another thing was that we decided we liked Wyoming and bought a wonderful place just outside Casper. It's an easy drive from there to the Wind River Training Camp that Alex Redbone set up, just over seventy miles, which is a hop, skip, and a jump by Wyoming standards. This means that Nicole can commute fairly easily when Redbone needs her while I stay home and mind the kids. When McKee needs me to look at something, he can send it by messenger or express service, and with high speed internet service, we never have to travel if we'd rather not.

One of the things I'm doing these days is writing up some of my more interesting case stories, like this one and some others I've already done. These have earned me a small following of fans who pour over each case history and then bombard me with questions. I try to respond to these personally, but lately I've had to resort to an Internet newsletter. The fans seem to like this even more, and one of them even runs the thing. All I have to do is email them the questions and my responses.

I also do a lot more walking these days. With the rigorous climate we have in Wyoming, I've joined the ranks of the gray panthers who prowl the malls of America and I've met some interesting acquaintances this way. After we're done walking, we have a cup of designer coffee and talk about significant things, like grandchildren and the weather.

When they ask me what I did for a living before I retired, I tell them I was a policeman and it's interesting to see the different responses. Nor do they believe that Jack and Marie are my children, particularly when Nicole comes with me. They are convinced I'm helping my daughter raise her kids and Nicole likes to rub it in.

Yet there is another side to walking at the mall. The pace I set is usually too fast for company and I often find myself reflecting back over the cases I write about and all the people I've been privileged to work with. When I think of someone, I send them a note to stay in touch, and more often than not, they respond.

Yet I also think about the strange people I have brought to justice and those moments that have been seared into my memory. One of those was when Nellie saved my life in our home in Ft. Smith, gunning down a professional assassin who was about to shoot me. Another was when Zilpha, the thief I was chasing, pulled me off the railroad track five seconds ahead of a train. Still another is seeing the bomber who almost killed me heave the bomb into the air.

Yet the moment that comes to mind most often these days is that moment when I was face to face with Victor Quentin Shupe. I have no idea why I uttered those words, or why I was not scared out of my wits. The only explanation that makes sense is that I had been deeper in prayer then ever before, and those were the words I was commanded to say. What compels me to believe this is that look of hope I saw in his eyes an instant before he died.

I talked a long time about this with Forster. He agreed with my take on the situation, but he went on from there. "I think you're right about why you said what you did and why you weren't afraid. Yet, I think you're looking at it from the wrong direction. Do you follow?"

"Not really," I told him. "I was completely focused on him when it happened."

"Exactly," he said. "You were looking out through your eyes. But turn it around, my friend. Look at it through the eyes of Victor Shupe and ask what he saw in yours."

"I guess I'll never know," I said. "Not in this world."

"Rubbish!" he declared. "I wasn't there but I know exactly what he saw in your eyes. I've seen it there myself. You may accept it or not, Jazz, but what he saw reflected in your eyes was the joyful image of a loving father, the Father who was anxiously waiting to bring his son home."

A Word from the Author

Gentle Reader, pause a moment before you move on from here. Lay this book aside and think of that last paragraph. Then come back and read what follows, if you wish.

This was the original end to the story. Then something else suggested itself and I added the first seven pages of the epilogue. Even so, this did not seem complete and I added the final section that begins at the bottom of page 255.

Now I believe the best ending is this one. Yet I am not God, not even in my own novels. The stories tell themselves, and as Jazz observes toward the end of the Epilogue "I have to remind myself that each [story] holds its own consequences within its unique burden of loss and grief. Yet each is also full of its own beauty and grace. It is this grace that redeems the burden, leaving me with a sense of profound peace and quiet joy."

So I leave the decision to you, gentle reader, and I do so knowing how unfair this is to you. How can you not read what follows? Yet do so knowing that I believe the high point of this book lies in the last paragraph above, in the last thing Forster tells Jazz. Keep in mind that the Epilogue carries its own burden of heartache and grief. Hopefully, this, too, will find redemption in its own beauty and grace. I simply can't choose. JBR

Twilight Zone

Having said all this, however, there is one thing that happened three years later that really shook us all. We were back in Ft. Smith when it happened, cleaning out the house. The place had sold and there was not a lot left to take but mementoes I couldn't bear to sell or to give away. The kids had been through the house ahead of us, as had Zilpha and her extended family, taking whatever they wanted. The things still left were destined for a charity thrift store. Everything Nicole and I wanted was long gone to Wyoming and I had even prevailed on Forster to move out there so we could continue our cribbage and conversation.

So the place was empty, and cleaner than it had been in decades. The only reason I was there was to go to the closing. We could have done this by express mail, but I wanted to say goodbye to the place, too. It had been my home for more than thirty years.

We were standing in the empty living room, taking a last look around, when an official state patrol car pulled up and a familiar face came to the door. It was the state police captain who had talked to me in the hospital in Little Rock when Jeanne died. When I saw him, I had a bad feeling.

"I don't know an easy way to tell you this, Jazz," he said, looking at Nicole. His face was grave. "We found your wife, Jeanne. She's still alive."

I was so stunned I could not speak. "Then who was that we buried?" Nicole asked. Her face was so white I thought she might faint.

"That was a missing person who was catching a ride with Mrs. Phillips. As far as we have been able to determine, she was driving and Mrs. Phillips was in the passenger seat. When the car crashed, Mrs. Phillips was thrown from the vehicle and the other woman died. People at the Monticello garden club told us someone caught a ride with Mrs. Phillips and that's who we determined died at the wheel." He looked at me, clearly nervous. "When we checked fingerprints from the autopsy, it was pretty conclusive."

"They weren't checked at the time?" I asked, shocked.

The captain shook his head. "Everyone was so sure it was Mrs. Phillips that no one thought to do it. It was an easy mistake to make, Jazz. I'm not making excuses but the woman and Mrs. Phillips looked enough alike to be sisters—almost like twins—and they had on pretty much the same outfits."

"What made you check this out now?" I asked.

"Mrs. Phillips applied for a job in Chattanooga," he told us. "She's apparently hasn't worked in years. Since it was a bank job, they ran a background check, including fingerprints. Mrs. Phillip's card popped up, but indicated she was deceased. So we asked for a second printing and, sure enough, it was her."

"Jesus," I said. It was more a prayer than anything else. My head was reeling.

"This doesn't make sense," Nicole said. "Why didn't she get in touch before?"

"She was suffering pretty severe head injuries," the captain replied. "When the police picked her up in Chattanooga she was wandering around in a daze. They thought she was a street lady at first. A lot of them are mentally ill, and she wasn't able to tell them who she was. She was also pretty beat up and they thought she'd been assaulted."

"Has anyone told her about this?" Nicole asked.

The captain looked acutely embarrassed. "No, we haven't. The thing is, she doesn't remember anything before coming to in Chattanooga. She got out of the hospital about a month later and she married one of the nurses who took care of her a few months after that."

"Jazz!" I heard Nicole cry. I tried to answer but I couldn't. My head felt strangely light and darkness was closing in.

This time I was only out for a couple of minutes and when I came to, Zilpha was there, too. She'd swung by to bring us lunch and walked in just as I fainted. She wanted to know what was going on but I asked her to wait until she had called Jeanne's children. I asked her to tell them I needed to see them the next afternoon in Little Rock. I told her to say it was a family emergency and that I had a block of rooms booked at one of the major hotels. Zilpha gave me a strange look, but did as I asked. When she was done I asked the captain to tell her what was going on.

"Oh, Nicole!" she said, giving the mother of my children a hug. Then Zilpha looked at me like all this was my fault. "So what are *you* going to do?" she demanded.

I was still reeling. "I'm going to do the right thing, Zilpha, like I always do."

"Maybe I'd better leave," Nicole said. Her cheeks were wet with tears. She started to get up but I stopped her.

"No!" I told her. "I don't want you to leave." I was surprised to see Zilpha nodding in agreement. "I don't know how we're going to work this thing out, but I'm not letting you go. "Or you, either, Jack, or Marie" I said, reaching out to my son. He clung to me like a little monkey and his sister looked like she was about to cry. "We'll find a way. It's going to be tough, but we'll find a way."

Nicole also wanted to stay home from the family council but I wouldn't hear of it. "This affects you, too," I said.

"No matter what we decide, I'm not going to abandon you or our children. You're as much a part of this family as anyone and so are Jack and Marie."

The kids took the news much better than I did. At my request the highway patrol captain explained the situation as he had to me. When he was done he answered the questions he could and we all thanked him for his efforts.

The response was pretty much what I had expected. The kids were happy their mother was still alive, sad that she did not remember her former life, and angry about the whole situation. They were careful to let Nicole know they were not angry at her, or even at me. Their anger was directed at the killer who forced her car off the road, and they were glad he was dead.

At some point, one of them asked me where we went from here. I told them that the lawyer was already at work on the legal snarl the situation created and that he would soon be in touch with Miriam, Jeanne's youngest, who was also an attorney. "My primary concern is how we're going to approach Jeanne and her new husband," I said. "I've had quite a shock over this and you have, too. I don't want that to happen to Jeanne, not like it has to all of us."

Miriam pointed out that the man was not really her husband, but I cut that one off at the pass. "That's legally true," I said. "However, that's for you and the lawyer to work out. My concern is for Jeanne and the man she thought good enough to marry, and for Nicole. I wouldn't be standing here talking to you today but for her and our children. She literally saved my life, twice." I gave them chapter and verse how it had taken place both times, except for what followed my thawing out, and I could see they were impressed.

We kicked a number of ideas around and arrived at a

plan. Jeanne's oldest daughter would make the approach, seeing if Jeanne recognized her. She would also let the husband know that Jeanne was still legally married in Arkansas. Then the other two children would pay Jeanne a visit. Depending on Jeanne's response, we would hold another family council and go from there. I thought it best that I stay out of the picture at first and they agreed on this. To work out an acceptable solution, we would need the help of the new husband and he was the biggest unknown factor.

"How do you feel about all this, Jazz?" Belinda, the eldest, asked. "You've told us what you think. I want to know how you feel."

When I started to answer, I almost lost it completely. It took me a while to get my feelings under control. "I feel torn apart," I told them. "I love your mother with all my heart and I loved Nellie like that, too. I also love Nicole the same way. I don't understand how that's possible, but it is. One of those loves does not negate the others. I don't know what else to tell you. You're my children, just as much as little Jack and Marie."

It was Miriam, the youngest whom I've always worried about the most, who resolved the most basic issue that lay unspoken among us. She walked over to Nicole and looked at her gravely. Then she gave her a hug and kissed her on the cheek. "Welcome to our strange family, Nicole."

The only remaining cipher was Lindy, Jeanne's sister. She knew about Nicole and had encouraged me to get on with my life. Yet she had never met Nicole in person. When they arrived I was glad to see Hoagie had come with her. I was also relieved when Lindy greeted Nicole like a long lost sister. "You must be a saint, dear, putting up with this man."

"Oh, he has his redeeming qualities," Nicole responded and the two of them laughed the way women do to remind men of their proper place in the order of things.

Only then did Lindy look at Hoagie and said, "This hunk you sent along for me is working out, Jazz. He'll do." Then she gave the man a kiss that left no doubt about how she felt about her husband.

"Now what's this family emergency?" Lindy asked me. "Our flight was delayed or we'd have been there." I gave it to her straight.

"Oh, dear," she said, turning to Nicole and opening her arms. To my surprise, Nicole responded by returning her hug. "How awful for you," Lindy said and both women burst into tears.

Later on Lindy insisted on going along with Belinda to see Jeanne. Before they left she called to let me know and asked to speak to Nicole. "Don't worry, dear," she told Nicole. "We'll work it out somehow. I promise."

We did work it out, with a minimum of fuss, but there was heartache all around. Nor could it be avoided. Jeanne never recognized any of us, not even Lindy or her children or her grandchildren. Once he knew we were on the same side, her new husband was more than willing to work with us. The legal snarl took a long time and lots of consultation, but there were precedents. So we eventually came up with a settlement that seemed fair to all around.

The only thing I was afraid of was that some day Jeanne might come out of her amnesia and think I had abandoned her. Lindy suggested that I write Jeanne a letter, telling her exactly what had happened and telling her about my new family. Then Lindy added her own letter to this and we left it with her new husband. We also left him pictures of all her grandchildren, at different ages, and all our addresses and phone numbers.

Having done all this, we got in the car and left. It was one of the hardest things I have ever done and I was glad

Nicole agreed to drive. One love does not diminish another, as I told Jeanne in my letter, and my grief was as sharp as the day I was told she died. As we drove out of Chattanooga that afternoon I wept bitterly, knowing that this side of heaven, I would never see Jeanne again.

Even so, life goes on. After a while I felt a small hand tapping my shoulder. "Daddy?" asked little Jack. Somehow he had managed to get out of his car seat and was standing right behind me. Yet I didn't have the heart to scold him.

"Are you done crying now, Daddy?" he asked and I told him I was, at least for now. "Good," he said. "Can we stay in that place that has the water slide?"

I looked at the bride of my autumn years. She was smiling but there were tear marks on her cheeks, too. I unbuckled my seat belt and leaned over the seat, lifting Jack into his car seat. "You know what?" I asked and he shook his head. "I think that's the best idea all week. I think it's time to play! We'll stop and buy some bathing suits." Jack laughed and Marie clapped her hands.

Then I jumped, feeling my bride's hand on my fundament. When I looked her way, her eyes were on the road, but there was this wonderfully wicked smile on her face. "Are you going to make me wear a suit, Dr. Jazz?" she asked.

"Only in the pool," I assured her. "Only in the pool."

≈∞

When I awoke the next morning, I was in my own bed in the bedroom I shared with Jeanne in Ft. Smith. I thought I was dreaming at first, having one of those dreams that seems more real than life itself. So I pulled on my robe and slippers and opened the bedroom door. Nor was I surprised to find myself on the second floor where Jeanne and I had our master suite.

Hearing someone in the kitchen, I walked down the

stairs. Then I stuck my head into the kitchen. It came as no surprise to see Jeanne at the counter, busy making the cinnamon rolls I love best. When I saw this, a bolt of grief flashed through my soul like lightening. It was like a physical blow, almost staggering me, and I had to steady myself on the door frame.

Then the grief passed, as quickly as it had come. This surprised me but I decided to figure it out later. At that moment the dream was too intense, too real, not to embrace completely. So I stood there for a while quietly watching, smelling the yeast and the cinnamon and looking for the fuzziness of small details that accompanies even the most life-like dreams.

The odd thing was that the details were all crisp as a laser print. Oddly enough, details began to lose their clarity as I drew closer and I felt reassured this was a dream. Then I realized I was not wearing reading glasses. I normally carry a pair in my robe pocket for reading the morning paper, and when I put these on, every detail leapt into sharp focus.

I must have made some sound when this happened because out of the corner of my eye I saw Jeanne turn and glance toward me. "Good morning, Jazzboat," she greeted me warmly. "What on earth are you staring at?"

I looked up and smiled at her. When I did I saw the concern in her eyes turn into surprise and something like fear. "Are you back?" she asked, as if she were afraid what I might say.

I answered her with a kiss and a hug. Her response was not as warm as usual and I drew back and looked her in the eye. "Have I been gone?" I asked, knowing the truth even as I asked. "Again?"

She nodded dumbly. Then her face turned white as chalk and the large spoon she was using dropped from her hand. Yet I was able to catch her before she fell. Taking her in my arms, I carried her into my study and gently laid her on the couch. Then I covered her with a favorite lap blanket.

I was still tucking the blanket under her feet when I felt her gaze on the back of my head and turned to look at her. "Are you really back?" she asked, not daring to believe it.

"I don't know," I told her. "I think so, but if I'm not I don't want this dream to end. Ouch!" I cried, rubbing a spot on my waist where she pinched me. "That was mean!"

"I'm sorry," she told me. "I didn't want to hurt you but I had to know." There were deep lines in her face that were new since I'd last seen her. Her eyes were haunted.

"How long have I been gone this time?" I asked.

"Two years," she said. "Just like the last time." Then she began to cry. "I was so scared, Jazz. I didn't know if you would ever come back this time."

"It was the cinnamon rolls," I said lightly, holding her close. "All you have to do is bake your wonderful cinnamon rolls and I'll be back in a flash." Yet rather than laugh, Jeanne began to cry even harder, clinging to me like a frightened child.

That was how it began, my second return. It took a while for things to get back to anything like normal with us, but we got there. Then one day Jeanne asked if I remembered where I'd been and I told her I did, quite clearly. She was surprised and asked me to tell her about it. So I began to tell her of the strange odyssey my soul had taken since I visited the hospital chapel the night she was run off the road.

The telling took a long time and we didn't rush it. There were many times we cried, like when I told her about Jack and little Marie. Yet there were more times we laughed. One of these was when I told about the nurse she married in the other reality.

"Was he good looking?" she wanted to know.

"Ugly as sin," I assured her, ducking when she threw a pillow at me. She missed, but even as I ducked, a pang of loss ripped through my heart as I remembered Nicole doing the same. Yet Nicole never missed.

"What is it?" Jeanne asked. Yet when I couldn't talk about it, she nodded. "It doesn't matter, Jazz. I don't need to know. I can't imagine what it would be like to lose your whole family at once." Then seeing the answer in my eyes, she added, "I know you loved her. That's what you were thinking about, wasn't it?" I nodded. "That's who you are," she told me. "That's the man I fall in love with every day."

"He was a very good man, your Tennessee husband," I told her, answering her first question. "I know it sounds crazy, but I was jealous."

"Good," she laughed. "He must have been a real stud muffin," she added. I knew at that moment that we had just negotiated an important crossing. There would be more difficult crossings to come, but I knew we could be all right.

"That means I can be jealous too," Jeanne added, and the sound of her laughter was the most wonderful music I had ever heard. It was at that moment I came to the decision to retire completely and spend the rest of my days in the company of this incredible woman. At least, I did in this reality. No case is worth giving up two years of life with someone like Jeanne, and we had lost four.

❧

Over the years since then, I have thought about this a lot. I have also bent Forster's ear out of shape with the questions which still haunt me. Which reality do I live in now? Which one is real and which is the dream? Which is waking reality and which one is the lost land of amnesia?

The answer is that I simply don't know. Nor do I ever

expect to know, not for sure. There are days I wake up thinking I am in that other place, that other life. While I never *am* there, I no longer trust my own sense of reality the way I once did. To insist on knowing for sure seems like a sure and certain path to total insanity, and to survive, I have had to find a way to accept whatever reality I find before my eyes each time I wake.

This means I have had to accept the ambiguity of living in both worlds at once at times. For, even though I have never been back to the lost land of amnesia, my mind goes there often. The memories of that time and place are always present and I find myself wondering how life has turned out for Jack and Marie, as well as for Nicole.

When this happens, I have to remind myself that each world holds its own consequences within its unique burden of loss and grief. Yet each is also full of its own beauty and grace. It is this grace that redeems the burden, leaving me with a sense of profound peace and quiet joy.

So I consider myself twice blessed to have been given both. Each day on rising I give thanks for whichever life I am given to live that day. It is this habit of gratitude for whatever life holds that enables me to live within the tension between these separate worlds.

Having said this, I tend to think that my life with Jeanne may be the more real. Since coming back this time, I have never returned to the other life for more than a few moments and I have been present with Jeanne for years now. Oddly enough, it was a conversation with Nicole in this world that led me to believe it is more real than the land of amnesia.

We were sitting alone in a café here in Ft. Smith. It was several months after I returned and not long after the Tulsa copycat had been found dead alongside a country road in Missouri. The cause of death had been a single gunshot to the back of his head from a .22 pistol, and the placement was precise. Yet the body was badly decomposed and there was no way of knowing the exact time of death. Two years had passed since the last slashing and the medical examiner could not tell if the body had been frozen over the winter or preserved by cryonic storage.

There had not been any more Queen of Spade killings in the previous two-and-a-half years, either. So when I called Hoagie, he and I had decided there was little use in pursuing these cases, and I wanted to let Nicole know this without putting her in jeopardy.

To do this I had to stretch the truth a bit. Forster tells me it's not lying when everyone knows some stretching is taking place. He says it may not be the truth but where there is no deception there can be no lie. I'm not convinced.

Anyway, when I called to set up the appointment, I told Nicole I wanted her opinion of a story I was thinking of writing. It was pure fiction, I said, but I thought she might find it interesting. What I needed to know from her was if I had the technical computer details right.

To tell the truth, I expected Nicole to refuse politely and I was surprised when she agreed. So we arranged to meet in person in two weeks and I mailed her a rough draft of this tale. The only change I made was to identify the Queen of Spades as Nicole or Marie rather than use her real name, and to alter a number of details to protect her identity.

I was nervous as a cat the day we met. I had no idea how Nicole would respond to the manuscript, but I was not worried for my physical safety. I had nothing to fear from the woman I knew in the other life, and everything I knew about the Nicole in this life told me they were the same person. I had convinced myself that what I was worried about most was Nicole's state of mind, but as I sat waiting at the table, I realized I was worried about my own, too. My intent was to say goodbye to the other life, but as I sat there I wondered if our meeting in person might not draw me back into it. This fear was so strong I almost left.

Then, all of a sudden, Nicole was there sitting opposite me. Somehow I had been so caught up in my own thoughts and fears I'd missed her arrival.

We sat there looking at one another for several moments. Nicole's eyes were grave and there was no mistaking the uncertainty she felt. "It's good to see you, Dr. Jazz," she told me. "That's some story. Are you here to make an arrest?"

"I'm no longer a policeman, Nicole," I assured her. "Like I wrote in the story, justice has been served. Let's enjoy our food and then we can talk about the story."

When Nicole answered there were tears in her eyes. "I'm not sure I can eat just yet, Jazz. My stomach's been in knots ever since I finished reading the manuscript."

"There's nothing to worry about, Nicole," I assured her. It was all I could do to keep from reaching out to take her hand. "It's only a story."

"Yes, but there's a lot to grieve about, too, isn't there?" She countered. "That other world sounds wonderful, especially with Jack and Marie in it. Jeanne is a very lucky woman." She was quiet a moment. Then she looked at me and I saw something I could not read in her eyes. "Why did you set all this up, Jazz? Why did you want to see me?"

"I thought I made that clear," I answered. "I wanted to reassure you that you have nothing to fear from me."

"Yes, but you could have done that some other way. Why did you set it up like this? Why did you send me the story?"

I sighed. "I thought that if we got together and talked it might help me figure out which life is real. I know I may be imposing, but that's what I thought."

Nicole gave me an ironic smile. It was one I knew well. "Amnesty is never an imposition." The uncertainty was gone from her eyes. "Does there have to be an answer, Jazz? Aren't they both real?" When I didn't answer, she added, "I know this must be driving you crazy. I wish I could help you but I don't see how." She reached out and touched my hand. Gentle warmth spread up my arm, a warmth I remembered quite well.

"I think you just have," I told her, and it was true. With the warmth of her touch I felt a deep sense of peace wrap itself around me. I have no idea how those two things were connected, but I knew they somehow were.

The surprise I felt must have been written all over my face because Nicole smiled. When she did I realized the warmth had moved both ways, as had the sense of peace. Somehow I had the thought that the memory of how that touch felt had been mutual, too.

"Goodness!" Nicole said. She quickly added, "Don't try to explain it, Jazz. Let's just enjoy it while we can." Then she withdrew her hand and picked up the menu. "I'm starved. What's good here?"

I was startled but suggested the ribs, and once we had ordered, Nicole fixed me with a no-nonsense look. "Now," she said. "Tell me about Jack and Marie. I bet you spoiled them rotten."

"Me?" I protested, and Nicole laughed. "I'm not the one who let them have ice cream for breakfast!"

"Maybe not, but I bet you ate some, too."

We were off and running and the next two hours went by far too fast. All too soon it was time to say goodbye. I started to offer Nicole my hand, but she brushed it aside and moved into my arms for a hug. Nor was it a simple hug. Within it was every occasion we ever embraced in the other world. "Thank you for everything, Dr. Jazz," she told me, pulling back reluctantly. "I'm really glad we did this. Let me know how you are from time to time."

I started to answer but something popped into my mind. I tried to shut it away but I was too late. Nicole had seen it. "What?" she demanded.

"Nothing," I evaded. "It was just a random memory. You know, something I saw in the other life."

"Then why are you blushing?" she asked, enjoying my discomfort.

"Very well, woman," I answered. "What I remembered was a tiny birthmark shaped like a spider." I intended to add that the birthmark was not normally visible, but a loud crash from the kitchen interrupted me. I glanced in that direction and when I turned back Nicole was gone. I turned toward the door and saw her opening it, but she paused to look back before she left. When she did I saw her face was flushed. Yet she smiled, and in a way that told me I'd just revealed something I was not supposed to know, not in this world.

"*Obrigado a por tudo*, Jazzbeau" she called softly, blowing me a kiss. "*Você é o homem que o mais maravilhoso eu conheço.*" Then she was gone.

Laughing at myself, and us, and the absurdity of this thing we call life, I paid the bill. Then I left a generous tip for the waiter and headed home to Jeanne. I was halfway there when I realized that as she was leaving, Nicole had used her pet name for me in the other world when she thanked me for everything. She had also spoken in Portuguese and I had understood every word, which stunned me. I cannot remember learning that language in this life. Yet it was the last thing she said which touched me where I live. For she had told me I was the most wonderful man she had ever known.

About The Author

Like his characters, Joel B. Reed has lived many lives. A poet, rancher and lifelong student of the medicine way, he started out as a wrangler and "pearl diver" on a guest ranch in West Texas. Deciding it was more pleasant to ride horses than to clean up after them, he worked at many things getting through school and eventually became a college teacher and then, at mid-life, a parish priest.

After a long sabbatical from parish work, supporting himself as a carpenter and handyman, Reed began writing fiction for the fun of it. What he discovered was a grand passion. Over the last fourteen years he has produced fourteen novels, two volumes of poetry, and a book on spirituality. As this goes to press, he is on an extended tour of the American west and is making his home in Cody, Wyoming.

www.ingramcontent.com/pod-product-compliance
Lightning Source LLC
Chambersburg PA
CBHW07085425062
47159CB00003B/1054